For Johnny O.

CONTENTS

Foreword   i

1   A Long Line   3

2   What I Do   9

3   Hatching The Big One   15

4   Gearing Up   21

5   Here We Go   27

6   Islands in the Pacific   33

7   Cascades   41

8   Grand Coulee   47

9   First Ones Through   53

10   Micro-Pirates   59

11   Hospitality   67

12   Glacier   73

13   Letting Go   79

14   Employment   83

15   The Prairie   89

16   The Routine   93

17   Wild Men   99

18   Center of North America   107

19   Mirrored Shades   115

20   Blood-Sucking Bastards   121

RIDING THE BIG ONE

In the Wake of My Ancestors

IAN OWENS

ISBN-13: 978-1-6986-8611-0

Cover Photos:
Ian and Jane: Ian Justice
Viking Ship: Ian Owens

Cover Design: Rita Toews
Author Photo: Mark Speranza

21 Miss Information   127

22 Deluge   133

23 Beauty Parlor   143

24 Seul Choix   147

25 Two Bridges   151

26 Tea Time   157

27 Transports   161

28 The Only Road   165

29 The Last Resort   171

30 She Ain't Pedalin'   175

31 The Cat's Ass   183

32 The Attitude State   193

33 Lost   203

34 Found   209

35 Atlantic Ocean   213

36 A Parade   217

37 Crappily Ever After   221

 Epilogue   227

 Acknowledgements   229

FOREWORD

On May 1, 1999 I set out on what was for me the ultimate cycling journey; my "Big One": across the USA, west coast to east coast. This story is part travelogue and part memoir. It recounts those 3,811 miles of cycling to the best of my recollection; though I have paraphrased some conversations and changed a few of the names to protect the privacy of individuals still living; and that true story appears in the font you see here. Memories triggered by the events at hand recall true events and also appear in this straight-up, no-nonsense font.

Interwoven with the true stories, however, are musings about my distant and not-so-distant ancestors, based on historical research of the period and the sparse fragments my parents chose to share about their early lives. This part of the book is fictional, and appears in this dream-like italicized font to indicate it's happening only in my head.

So is this book a work of fiction or non-fiction?
It's both, just like life.

BLIZZARD

"The real act of discovery is not in finding new lands,
But in seeing with new eyes."

- Marcel Proust

1 A LONG LINE

I come from a long line of discontented wanderers.

My parents were immigrants. Their parents also didn't settle where they were born. Our family tree has legs instead of roots, with its branches sprouting explorers, exiles, ex-pats, war refugees, migrants, transplants and unsettled settlers. I wonder how far back this goes. With my blue eyes and fair hair, I can easily imagine distant forbearers coming from Viking Age Scandinavia. In the grip of winter's deep freeze, discontent first stirred the blood of my Nordic ancestors...

Norwegian coast, January, 899 AD: A desolate shingle beach nestles in a rocky fjord. Heaven's candle, the pale and shrunken sun, hangs low in the sky and hides behind thick gray clouds. It casts little light and no warmth. On that beach, scattered snowflakes swirl among three men draped in heavy woolen cloaks, huddled about a smoking driftwood campfire. Faces ruddy and weathered, their gnarled and dirty fingers repair fishing nets. One of them swills from an animal skin flask, wipes his dripping blond beard with the back of a calloused hand, and belches loudly.

"By the Gods, Gudrik, your face looks like your arse, but smells worse," says Eyvind. "Point it the other way!"

"Your woman giving you trouble again, little one?" Gudrik leers. He picks a louse from his bushy beard and flicks it at Eyvind. "Heh, I know what she needs!" His chin thrusts outward in petulant challenge.

Eyvind throws down his net and starts to rise.

"Peace, brothers," says Ragnar, eldest. He claps a hand on Eyvind's shoulder. "You do seem unhappy, Eyvind. What troubles you?"

"Why —", Eyvind pulls free of Ragnar and stands. "—in the name of Odin

and Thor—do we live here? We are forever cold, the winter is dark and long, the soil thin and stony. All we do is work and yet we barely survive. Have you not seen our countrymen sail away on long ships and wondered where they go? And why they do not return?"

"They do not return because they die!" Gudrik says. "Beyond the sea is not safe, little brother! The world is filled with barbarians and monsters. There are Danish war-bands, Friesian pirates, wild men painted blue; Saxons with their nailed god and Christian wizards! And beyond that is Jormungand, the huge and hungry serpent, at the edge of the world. You have heard the talk of the merchant crews."

"Those are tales to amuse big children like you," Eyvind scoffs and sits again. "No, I believe there are countries out there beyond our imagining. Rich lands to the south, beyond the sea, where the sun warms your back all the year. Places with endless green fields and thick forests, where the Romans built great cities out of stone. You drink honey mead and fine red wine, feast on spitted meats and sweet fruits and bathe in warm, clear turquoise waters. And the women are all beautiful, dark of hair and skin, and go about unclothed. And that is why no one returns."

Ragnar and Gudrik stare with blank expressions. Into the uncomfortable silence, Gudrik lets off a squeaky fart that sounds like a whimpering dog. "But this is Odin's Land," Ragnar says. "Our people have been here since the Beginning. The bones of all our ancestors lie here, as will ours one day."

"Ragnar, Odin forgot about us ages past. And Gudrik, Valhalla will not admit those who die of boredom. We Norse are explorers. Adventurers. That is our destiny." He stands and walks away.

"Where are you going?" Ragnar says.

"To find a ship," Eyvind says over his shoulder. "And get on board." He walks a few more steps, turns and shouts: "And get away from you two… Kukhoden!"

I imagine Eyvind, with his woman, I'll call her Hild, venturing forth. They cross the sea to the islands we call Britain and Ireland. Yet each succeeding generation finds something lacking in where their parents chose to live, and moves on, mixing with Gaels, Scots, Britons and Saxons. Over centuries of invasions. migrations and conquests, the descendants of Eyvind become MacEwain in Scotland, Owain in Wales, and finally Owens in England. In 1952 my father, John Alfred Owens of Lancashire ("Alf" to his friends), aeronautical engineer and ex-Royal Navy officer, feels the stirring of his Anglo-Saxon-Norse heritage and boards a ship at Liverpool bound for Canada. A few years later he marries fellow immigrant Ida

Elisabeth Tonn, sixth daughter of Gustav and Adoline, German farmers who lived in that part of eastern Europe midway between Hitler and Stalin. She tends to march rather than walk and views most of the world as filthy, inefficient, and in dire need of Ordnung. Together they cross another border into the USA, where my three siblings and I am begotten. In my line, wanderlust is in my DNA; my undeniable inheritance and inescapable destiny.

Detroit Metro Airport, January, 1999 AD: I'm 35 and a seasoned business traveler. Over-seasoned, like iffy meat. Tonight I stand in front of the Departures board as a massive blizzard howls outside. A heavy laptop case hangs from one shoulder, ruining my posture. I look up at the big board as the last of the yellow Delayed statuses turn to red Canceled ones. Over at my airline's service desk I hear enough: "…we'll do our best to get you out tomorrow morning…" to know my immediate future. Faces surround me; I see worry, disappointment, annoyance, but thankfully not rage. They're sensible enough not to try to fight the weather. We in the terminal are the lucky ones, because tonight hundreds of unfortunates would be trapped on board aircraft, grounded on taxi-ways for as long as eleven hours, immobile, food and drinks gone, toilets overflowing. This night would prompt a spate of lawsuits and the creation of the Airline Passenger's Bill of Rights. I don't know I'm becoming part of airline history, but I do know I'm not going home tonight.

In 1999 mobile phones are still rare enough to be status symbols, with smaller devices denoting higher rank. All I have hanging on my belt is a pager: bulky, monochrome, useless. Now the alpha males whip out their tiny, color-screened proxy phalluses to call secretaries and hotels, while the herd forms long ragged lines before the pay phones. "On my way to the Marriott in Ypsilante," one of the alphas booms as he shuts his phone, just so we all know. I've had enough of lines this evening, and six hours in a hotel room is a waste of company funds, so…

First: get a flight home. My German urge to push forward overwhelms my British tendency to queue up. While others contest for phones, taxis and rooms, I shove to the front of the thinning crowd before the service desk. Wordlessly, the man behind it extends a hand. I slap my ticket and gold mileage status card into it and he types ninety words a minute. The printer chatters, spits out some perforated oak tag, and he slides the new ticket into a little paper jacket, scribbles some runes on it and pushes it across the desk. My status pays off. I have a seat on tomorrow's 11:10 am to Boston. Another airline rep is handing things out, so I go there and receive my very own airline blanket, "fun-size" pillow and plastic pouch of miniature toiletries. I take care of business in the men's room and then phone home once the crowds have dispersed.

A lot of us are indoor camping tonight. I prowl the terminal and find my objective: a padded bench without arms between the seats, by a window. I remove shoes, put the pillow on my laptop bag, my head on the pillow, blanket over all and try hard to think happy thoughts. Icy flakes seethe against the window glass and fill in the corners. Outside is a low rumble as plows scrape pavement. Inside, old men snore, toilets flush, zippers shriek, sweepers hum and electric buggies go beep-beep-beep to fracture the late night hours. I drift between various stages of consciousness; dream and reality a hopeless jumble of distorted sounds and images. I'm trying to get home. I'm on a plane that tries to land on Mohawk Road, the street I lived on as a kid. The wings rake rooftops and topple telephone poles. We shoot past my house and can't seem to stop. There is a blinding flash and I'm awake, heart thumping.

Morning sun backlights my eyelids pink. I open them a slit to squint at a pale blue sky and try to remember where I am. It looks like a road warrior battlefield. Bodies sprawl everywhere, some moving, some not. I put feet on the floor and check my belongings. Everything's there. I ache all over, like I partied all night, except it wasn't fun. I'm sweaty and stubbly. "Ypsilanti" and his chums walk in with smug expressions. They look rested, scrubbed and well-fed. They whisper and snicker as they survey us lesser folk, or as Dr. Seuss once put it, those "without stars on thars." My inner German fires up. I gather my stuff and march to the men's room; some cold water and hot coffee is all I need, Gott-dammit.

Rounding a corner, still bleary-eyed, I gasp and nearly head-on collide with a guy from my company. He's in professional services and travels as much as I do, traversing the country each week. His job is to placate our current customers while I help the sales guys reel in new ones. We never travel together, but happenstance brings us face-to-face this snowy morning in Detroit. Red-rimmed eyes blink at me out of a face like putty. Shoulders droop and a capacious belly eclipses his belt. I'm both fascinated and horrified, and my thoughts tumble out uncensored.

"Yikes!" I say. "Do I look as bad as you?"

"Worse," he says with a smirk. "Are you coming or going?"

"I don't even know anymore."

On the flight to Boston, my heavy head wrenches up as I doze in 32B. I'm propped upright between two formidable neighbors who smell, respectively, like meatloaf and a pungent aftershave that makes my eyes water. Their bulk spills over and engulfs the armrests. My armrests. I point my little air nozzle to blow germs at Mr. Aftershave. If only I had two nozzles, but meat smells better to me than vile perfume. I take shallow breaths but it makes me lightheaded. Small creatures with powerful lungs wail ahead and behind. Surround-sound. Surround-smell. In the middle seat on a packed flight, but I'm going home.

This is what I do.
It is not who I am.

2 WHAT I DO

"This job is killing you." Jane, my housemate, future wife, and not one to hide feelings or withhold honest feedback stands in the bathroom doorway with a mixture of pity and anger on her face.

"Look at yourself! You're gray, cold, tired all the time." Back home in Newton, Massachusetts the night after the blizzard, I sit on the bathtub's edge, head in hands, working up energy to brush my teeth. I move like an arthritic octogenarian. In years past I would commute by bicycle, balancing out my sedentary vocation with heart-thumping exertion at each day's beginning and end. It got me through five years at GE still looking svelte despite the ubiquity of sugar-coated pastries and lumpy colleagues in the office. I've gotten lazy. On non-travel days I work from home and merely clump downstairs and flop into my chair, too tired for extra movement. All I can do now is groan.

"Do you know how hard it is to watch someone you love...waste away?" She blinks back tears. We have been dating for eight years, living together for four, but have made no wedding plans since our engagement. I'm in no hurry. We know many couples who have married, produced children and divorced already. And then there's the wedding. In the US, weddings are an industry, Hey-everyone-look-at-me! affairs, on the surface ostentatious and gaudy, while at a deeper level tawdry and desperate. I prefer funerals. It's sad someone is dead, yes, but at least people are authentic, heartfelt, and generally sober.

Jane's moods are like the weather, predictable if I'm paying attention. Usually I see when a storm is brewing, but these words are hailstones out of the clear blue. I'm just being a good corporate soldier, giving my all to the Company.

I am a Software Sales Engineer, a difficult role because engineers love to volunteer information while salespeople know how to dance around touchy subjects and I'm supposed to do both. For example, when asked about our latest release, before I can reply "it blows up if you hold down the Ctl key" the sales rep kicks my shins under the table and says "it's feature-rich and ahead of its time." I give onsite technical demonstrations—we call them "demos"—of our software wherever a sales rep can find an audience. I tailor the demo to illustrate a scenario they might understand, answer lots of questions and attempt to remove any technical barriers to a sale. It's like fishing: the sales rep baits the hooks and drops the lines. If he gets a bite, he calls me over to haul it in.

We have five sales reps covering North America and they have to share one engineer and chaperone me on every fishing trip…that is…sales call. My boss says he can't find anyone else with my skills (also willing to work as cheaply and fly coach). Weeknights find me at a Fairfield Inn or Motel 6, in a manufacturing mecca like Fort Wayne, Wichita, El Paso or Detroit. I might leave on Sunday afternoon and not get home until Friday night, to spend the remains of my weekend shattered with fatigue and bloated from engineered food products fortified with salt, sugar, saturated fat and acronyms. It's not without compensations. I never have to buy soap, shampoo or ballpoint pens, and with frequent flyer miles I can receive similar punishment for free on my own time.

I meet Jane's accusing glare. "I know, I know," I say, standing. She pulls me close. In ancient Sparta, humor was the prized response to severe stress; the mark of a strong mind. My mind is mush. All I can manage is: "My life sucks. I just suck at life."

"No you don't. You just need to look in the mirror and tell me if you see a happy man."

A very sad man gazed back at me in the bathroom mirror.

"Nope, no happy man. Pathetic, downtrodden man. I don't get it. I wanted to travel and this job promised plenty of that."

"It started out all right," Jane said. "You took me along to that sales meeting in England last year. I loved the Cotswolds in February, with daffodils blooming, emerald lawns, sunshine, birds chirping."

"Yeah, and I met all those pleasant English chaps, traded firm handshakes, nodded enthusiastically and injected 'perfect' and 'got it' at appropriate moments during the PowerPoints on our aggressive US sales strategy. We drank pots of hot tea during the day and after work we'd go out for a pint or two of warm ale at the Local. That early spring weather and seven-hour workday seduced me, for sure."

I stared at nothing, lost in thought. Jane's arms around my waist gave a little squeeze. "Then we came home," she prompted.

"Then we came home, and found out I'm the one doing all the aggression depicted on those PowerPoints. So now it's payback time, and this decidedly unglamorous life is the result of eighteen years of formal education and another thirteen as a professional."

"It's a choice. You can quit, you know. You've had a year of this and it's not getting better."

"No, I can't quit, because John Collier hired me away from my last dead end job and I owe him for that. And the US Sales office is just getting established. I can't let everyone down. I have to be a team player; the go-to guy. I'm irreplaceable. I have to be strong and 'suck it up' like a man, although I'll admit I'm getting a bit pear-shaped."

"So why are you doing this? What's it all for?"

"For the money. I want a home. For us."

"We have a home."

"Yeah, but it's not ours. You know what I mean. I've been saving, but every year prices go up."

"It's in-SANE what houses cost around here. We could live other places. You know I'll never make a lot of money, it's just not my thing."

"So it better be my thing. By the time my Dad was 55 he had a wife, a four-bedroom house with an ocean view in Marblehead, a classic Mercedes and four kids headed for college. He left at 7 every morning for his six-by-eight cubicle in Building 40 at the GE plant. He didn't have an office door, so sometimes at lunch he'd go out to the parking lot and nap in his car."

"Really?"

"Lots of guys did it and I can totally understand it now. When I worked there I dozed off one time during the Engineer's Day awards. He must have been bored silly. He'd often work late, come home, eat dinner alone, then move to his chair in front of the TV, where he'd snore, ice puddled in the bottom of his glass of watery scotch as the Ten O'clock News droned on. One night a month he'd be in Boston at the British Officer's Club, where he'd nurse his pint of John Smith's and chat with other grey haired gents named Graham and Terry about the glory days of Churchill and the War and how they kept 'Jerry' out of Britain."

"That was his choice. You're not your father, and I'm not your mother. I can't just stand by and watch you…"

"Well he was my role model. You work hard and sacrifice and…"

"And what? Piddle your life away doing something you don't care about?"

I teared up. "And if he ever dreamt of a different life, no one knew about it."

"Oh, my Love." She rested her head on my chest, her hands rubbed my back.

"So here I am at 35, with no wife, no house or kids and I'm already wasting away? See, I do suck at life."

"You're not and you don't. You're just worn down doing something that takes from you."

"I ran into a guy from work in Detroit, and he looked horrible, and he said I look worse. I used to have fun; wind-surf and ride my bike and ski and play the drums and even fly airplanes. Now all I do is work and recover from work. I've both shortened my lifespan and made it feel interminable and pointless."

"Yeah, this isn't really you," she sighs. "And I feel your struggle. You know I'm not going to be happy in that house if it means you're working all the time. I don't even want a big house. It's just more to take care of. I don't want possessions. I just want you…and experiences."

We're both trapped in lives we don't want. A new job is no answer; I always end up bored and exploited for someone else's profit, my essence picked away like a desert corpse surrounded by buzzards. This is not what I had in mind, back in engineering school. This isn't me. I'm a fraud; a techno-whore.

"But what can I do?" I say, breaking the clutch to grab some toilet paper and blow my nose, which sounds like the warning honk of a cornered goose.

"What is your dream?" Jane asks. "What is your heart's desire?"

Heart's desire? Well, tra-la-la! What am I, a four-year-old? I deal in realities, honey, not fantasies. Life is so hard. And full of compromises. Mein Gott.

I look away, grinding my teeth.

She waits.

Did I ever have a dream?

My childhood flashes past; images of sunshine, wind in my hair, the briny sea. Traveling. Self-contained. Free. An answer bursts through the fog in my head and all is suddenly clear:

"I want to ride the Big One."

She smiles. "Whatever that is, I'm coming with you."

"Seriously?"

"You think I'm in bliss here? I'm exhausted too! You think I want to spend the rest of my life lifting big kids over gym equipment and trying to stop them from head planting? It's not exactly my passion to teach gymnastics, it's just what I thought I could do. If you want to make changes, I'm all for it."

"Give me a week, maybe two, and I'll tell you all about it."

The next morning I have the beginnings of a plan. I'm going to withdraw my savings, give notice at work, and buy a new bicycle.

PREPARATIONS

Norway, April, 899 AD: *Spring arrived in the Northlands, not with flowers and warm sunshine, but with the exchange of one state of misery for another. Cold rain pelted down. Slabs of melting snow tumbled from turf roofs and turned paths into oozing mires. Mountain streams became thundering torrents. Screeching birds flitted to and fro, chasing clouds of bloodthirsty flies. The stink of winter's unburied dead and fresh manure mingled with acrid wood smoke and the sweetness of newly turned earth. Eyvind knew it was time to leave.*

"I'll return for you when I have found the land I seek," Eyvind said.

"We, Eyvind. When we have found it," Hild said. "Am I not left behind enough as it is, while you are out fishing? I too want to see the world. Your dream, husband, is also mine."

Eyvind gazed at his wife a long moment. Then he laughed. "Of course. What a good idea! Women are bad luck on ships, men will stare at you, there is no privacy, and you tend to sea-sickness…"

"And I will not be left behind." Hild stood before him, arms akimbo, jaw set. "Truly, I am as eager as you are to leave here. If you go and I stay…" she bit her lip, "… I might lose you forever."

"And your parents…" Eyvind began.

"They will understand."

"We do not have the silver for your passage."

"I'll sell my goats."

"But when we return…" Eyvind frowned, faltered. He raised his eyes to his wife's; saw the resolution in her face, and the sadness. One cannot fight destiny. He smiled. "So be it."

They packed. In the bottom of his wooden chest he found his most prized possession: his sword, Fotbitr (Leg Biter) in its leather scabbard had been his father's. Apart from Fotbitr, his round willow shield, a comb made from reindeer horn and some oddments wrapped in a spare woolen cloak, he needed little else.

"Do not go. You will die out there and no one will know. Just as your father did."

Eyvind spun to face Hild. "What did you say?"

"I did not speak," Hild said. "You heard a voice? I heard only the wind."

"It sounded like…something Mother might have said."

"A voice from beyond the grave? If she were still alive, husband, I would have left you long ago."

Hild pulled out a fine walrus ivory-handled dagger and felt its keen edge, thinking of Eyvind's mother before she slammed it back into its sheath and strapped it about her slender waist. She made her own tight bundle and brought out her small harp, a gift from her father who had voyaged among the lands of the Gaels in his youth. She plucked the strings and smiled at its tones. She had a fine voice and good singers and storytellers were highly prized at sea. The days lengthened and warmed with the promise of summer.

They would travel light.

3 HATCHING THE BIG ONE

"You really want to do this?" I said. Two weeks after the Blizzard of '99, steaming cups of tea in hand, Jane and I faced one another across the dining room table in the small house we rented. I'd dreamt of owning a home in the Boston area for thirteen years, yet my ideal—the Cape Cod house with a lawn and garage and room for a wife, two kids and a golden retriever—had ever eluded my financial reach. Maybe I'd been chasing the wrong dream.

She nodded. "If it involves travel you can count me in. So what do you have in mind?"

Jane always followed through on commitments and expected no less from others. I'd said I was going to ride the Big One, and she'd said that she was coming with me. Here was a complication. Going alone would be simpler, cheaper and faster. I might not have to blow all my savings. This was my dream, not hers. Maybe I could talk her out of it.

"In the world of long-distance bicycle touring," I began, "the Big One refers to the ultimate ride, the ride of a lifetime. We all have our own Big One in mind as a personal dream to fulfill sometime during our lives. For some it might be to ride to the next state—"

"I could do that," Jane perked up.

"—while others aspire to go around the world." Her eyebrows lowered. "Most never actually ride their Big One; life intervenes and they just keep it a pleasant fantasy, like I do. Some attempt their Big One and fail; but a few succeed and go on to… Bigger Ones. Whatever the outcome, I suppose there's glory in the attempt."

"It's transformative," Jane said "to go for your dream."

"Right," I said. "My Big One has always been to cross North America on bicycle, coast to coast; not as a race, not as a fundraiser, not to break any records or be the first to do it. Dozens, maybe hundreds do it every year, you know. The only prize at the end is knowing I've done it. If there is more…it's…just something I've always wanted to do. Something I have to do." I used to cycle everywhere…

"Keep pedaling, honey, you can do it!" It's 1970, I'm seven years old, astride my first two-wheeler, a heavy steel job, metallic paint with solid rubber tires. The training wheels are off and Mom keeps a steadying hand on the rear fender. I pedal faster and the wind lifts my hair. I feel a strange lightness. Mom's voice sounds far away now, because she is running to catch up. I did it! I'm riding! But now how do I stop?

I cycled to school, then to work, toured for weekends in New England and then for weeks in Europe. Cycling was always my freedom, and I hoped it would free me again.

Now she knew my plan. Trim and well-built, Jane had been a collegiate gymnast and was still a good athlete, although not as avid a cyclist as I. She dreamed of being a singer/songwriter. She loved nature, travel, and lived easily without modern comforts. Her family owned a lakefront cabin way up in Maine, with no electricity or running water, and she reveled in its primitivism. Meanwhile, I'd get antsy after a few days of peace and quiet. She wore no makeup, and tying her long hair back was the extent of her hairdressing. She wore no heels higher than an inch, avoided gadgets and shopped only when in dire need. Capitalism would collapse if all consumers were like her. Except for guitars—a vintage Martin, a Gibson and a modern Ovation—she cared little for possessions and packed light. And she looked fine in spandex.

Suddenly I saw the thing in a new light. It would indeed be simpler, faster and cheaper for me to go off on my own and do the ride my way. I'd done many tours alone, and they'd been fun and physically challenging but hardly life-changing. Now if we went together? I'd have to do the biggest ride of my life while chained to the only viable soulmate I'd met in thirty-five years. That terrified me, which meant it was the better choice because I'd have to face fears. Maybe she'd slow me down and we'd have to quit and I'd resent her forever and we'd break up. Maybe she'd discover I'm terminally dull and dump me in Duluth. Maybe we ought to find these things out before we get married. Maybe I could accomplish several objectives at once, which would be efficient. Maybe everything would change, and that was the whole point. Her brown eyes widened as her tea cooled. "So that's around 3,000 miles?"

"More like 4,000," I muttered. "But it's all...well, mostly back roads and cycling paths. See?" I showed her the set of "Northern Tier" maps I had ordered from *Adventure Cycling*, an outfit that encourages this sort of thing.

"It's all mapped out: Anacortes, Washington to Bar Harbor, Maine. We'll just improvise at the end so we finish in Boston. Supposedly the winds are more favorable going west to east, and I figure psychologically it'll be easier going *towards* home rather than *away* from home; maybe not as tempting to quit? I'm thinking we could take three months; ought to be able to swing that financially, but not much longer than that."

"Three months, ninety days, so that's almost *fifty* miles a day, *average*," Jane said, her brow furrowed in calculation.

"In Scotland we did fifty miles," I said, and then winced at the memory of our first and only cycling tour together, a two-week ordeal four years ago: endless hills, rain and wind; going all day with little or no food; dots on the map that were named like towns but were actually a meagre cluster of lonely cottages; saggy mattresses smelling like ashtrays; lying awake due to the slurred obscenities and tinkling of broken glass outside as the drunks staggered from the pubs at closing time; and holing up in the seaside village of Plockton in the highlands, as we waited for an appointment with the traveling osteopath who would fix Jane's painfully locked knee.

Then I remembered the spectacular scenery: the earthy scent of burning peat, the gentle bleats of contented sheep, the morning birdsong, the seals at play on the rocks, the cheery pubs serving that rich amber ale that fills you like liquid bread, and all the friendly strangers who helped us out, even putting us up for the night when there was no room at the inn or no inn at all. For me, those connections with the place and its people far outweighed all the little difficulties. And those difficulties made it a true adventure. They gave us stories to tell. I longed for that experience again. Jane might have had a different memory of it, however. Her silent stare said as much.

"Some days we'll ride more, some days less." I talked faster, switching into sales mode. "Some days we won't ride at all; we'll be tourists. We'll take it slow at the beginning and work up to the distance. Don't think of it as one big ride, but little rides every day, all in the same direction." Now I tried to convince myself, because I had never done anything like this either and the magnitude of the journey scared me; the distance and time involved, the expense, and if we'd get sick of each other. Would her knees give out again? But as I spoke, her concerned look faded; replaced by the funny little smile she often wore when we set off traveling: a smile of anticipation.

"When are you thinking of going?" she asked.

"Springtime. Late April or early May. It kind of depends on when the western mountain passes are clear."

"Clear?"

"Of snow."

"Oh, right." She looked past me, her thoughts elsewhere.

"Still want to go?" I asked, though I already knew her answer.

She locked eyes again. "You are NOT going by yourself," she said, leaning back with crossed arms. "So I think we better start training."

By March, winter's towering white snow banks had shrunken into dirty gray humps of slush, leaving the roads puddled and sandy but free of ice. With five or six weeks to train before May 1, we wheeled our mountain bikes out every weekend to see how far we could go, to see if we could even do fifty miles. The relentless, aggressive Boston traffic ensured we never made it past twenty. We didn't get up at 5 am; we didn't suck down raw eggs or eat protein powder or do push-ups; nor did we hear Survivor's "Eye of the Tiger" in our heads, except when the Newton North high school kids drove past. Without saying so, we both realized we couldn't realistically train for this. We'd have to train by doing.

Meanwhile I broke the news of my resignation to my boss, John Collier. I'd never met a man named John I didn't like. We'd been through the demise of our previous employer together, and he'd always responded to stress with humor. I told him over dinner while we were on a sales trip, fairly confident there wouldn't be an ugly scene. Instead, he laughed. "I'm not worried," he said. "Go get a life and find yourself or whatever you need to do. I think you'll get sick of looking at cornfields all day and come right back. You can keep your pager so we can check on you." No begging me to reconsider. No offers of more money or a better title. John would never impede my personal development. Instead, he hired Gary, a bright young Canadian who proved both capable and popular, rather sooner than I'd expected. So much for irreplaceable.

In April, as Jane turned in her gym keys and I shipped my company laptop back to the Florida office, we made other preparations. I liquidated my savings for the house I never bought, sighing over all the years of toil that went into that stash...

"One hundred and one dollars and fifty cents. That's a lot of money!"

Eight years old, I gazed at the open page of my first bank passbook.

"You've made a good start," Dad said. "Now whenever you get any money, you put it in the bank and keep it safe. And it'll grow because they pay you interest."

"But can I take some out and buy a ten-speed?"

"You don't want to spend your savings. It's for the future, for college. If you want pocket money, you can work for it. Get yourself a little job. And always live within your means."

My savings. I was pillaging my future. The vision of a cedar-shake Cape with white trim, red front door, brass pineapple knocker, dark green shutters and a little breezeway attaching the garage shimmered and faded. That down payment would now buy cycling equipment, pay the bills that would pile up during our absence, and cover our food and lodgings on the road. I hoped something would be left when we returned, jobless, at the end of it. This made no logical sense. I felt guilty and stupid, quitting my job and spending my savings, but part of me felt liberated and a little turned on. This was expensive and risky and not at all like me. What was I doing?

I could still call it off.

I could admit I was wrong, get a new job and knuckle under. Then I'd have no dream. Apart from dead-end jobs, the Boy Scouts and Air Force ROTC—can't do polyester uniforms or name tags—I never quit anything. And I already told everyone I was doing it.

Emilio Zapata said it's better to die on your feet than live on your knees. To back out now, to not even try for my dreams would be the real failure.

4 GEARING UP

What did we take with us on the Big One? As little as possible, since our puny muscles would have to haul every ounce over nearly four thousand miles of road, and up and over the Cascade, Rocky and Appalachian mountain ranges. Many who do this type of ride go "deluxe," as part of an organized tour. In exchange for a sizable fee these tours typically provide a guide, daily maps, mechanics, meals, shopping, site-seeing, and a van or two to carry baggage and tired riders between prearranged hotels.

We had no support staff. In biker-speak, we were doing an *Un-Tour*, a low-budget, unsupported, DIY tour. We would travel alone and self-contained, pulling everything behind us in a one-wheeled *Beast of Burden* (BOB) trailer. BOB looks like a low-slung sport-utility wheelbarrow made of aluminum tubing and pulled backwards. He comes with a huge removable duffel bag that sits neatly in his bed. With a 60 pound capacity, low center of gravity and single wheel BOB is much more stable and aerodynamic than those panniers that hang off the bike frame. Even though I've got short arms and long pockets, I'll occasionally spend big for a really cool design like BOB.

What did we ride on the Big One? On the Scotland tour of '95, we rented mountain bikes. Being the faster rider, I'd often look back to find Jane nowhere in sight, lagging far behind amongst drum, burn and glen. When Jane overstressed her knees pushing too high a gear, I bungee-corded her frame to mine and towed her along. This time would ride permanently conjoined bikes, also known as a tandem.

Tandems are even more expensive than two separate bikes, which is odd because you get two fewer wheels and only one set of gears and brakes. Since it was the second biggest purchase of our relationship next to the engagement ring, I put it off until ten days before departure. On a sunny April afternoon we walked into *Belmont Wheelworks*, at the busy corner of

Trapelo Road and White Street in Belmont, Massachusetts.

"Can I help you find something?" the sales clerk, a peach-fuzzed college kid, asked.

"We're looking for a tandem," I said. "For a really long tour. Coast to coast."

"Awesome. We have a great selection of Cannondales and Burleys. The main difference…"

"That's fine," I said. "Can we take them for a test ride?"

"Sure, no problem. Were you looking for chrome-moly or aluminum frame? And let me tell you about the gearing ratios…"

"That's OK," I said, waving him off like a mosquito. "We just want to ride them."

"Guess you're not very technical," he said under his breath.

"I'm a mechanical engineer, actually. But if it doesn't feel right then what use are all the specs?"

He humored us. We tried every one he wheeled out, and once around the block was enough. Nothing felt right. They were too stiff or too mushy, too hefty or too spindly.

"That one didn't do it for ya either, huh?" he said as we wheeled the last one back inside. We shook our heads.

"Is that all you have?" I asked.

"There is one more: an *Ibis*. It's a floor model, a couple years old but still brand new. It's in the basement. Give me a minute, I'll bring it up."

Ibis is a small west coast manufacturer of high-end bikes priced competitively with a decent used car. The one our man brought up was an electric-blue *Easy Street*, with artsy little frame details like a tiny molded foot that held the pump in place, and cable guides in the shape of little hands (Ibis calls them "hand jobs"). I already loved the look of it, but the ride sealed the deal. It felt like a living thing burst free of long confinement; a thoroughbred that moved effortlessly and anticipated our desires. It felt like we'd been riding it for years. I grinned over my shoulder at Jane as we pedaled the leafy but narrow streets of suburban Belmont.

"Do you think you could ride this for 4,000 miles?"

"I could ride this forever," she grinned back. "I think it was waiting for us."

Back at the shop, I returned the borrowed helmets. "We'll take it. We like the color," I winked, high on a rush of impulsive consumerism as I watched our man's eyebrows rise. Having made a big sale without talking, he now struggled and failed to find anything to say. What he should have done was sell us accessories.

I pulled out my checkbook and clicked the pen: six figures, if you include cents. I'd write many more. Some items we borrowed, such as our tent, but most of the big ones we had to buy: ultra-light sleeping bags, maps, lightweight compact toolkit, fleece and Gore-Tex outerwear, a miniature propane stove and fuel bottle, new cycling shoes, gloves and extra shorts; sunscreen, bug spray, pepper spray, bungee cords (essential!), and mosquito netting. We allowed ourselves one "non-essential" each: a Martin backpacker guitar (2.5 pounds) for Jane, a handheld computer (15 ounces) for me. To the growing pile of equipment, we added our clothes, books and personal items. Of course it wouldn't all fit in BOB's bag. We discarded half of the clothes and personal items and tried again. Still too much. One more iteration and we had it down to fifty-seven pounds, plus thirteen for the trailer, giving us a load of seventy pounds. Heavier than I'd like, I thought, but figured we could jettison as we went along.

A few last preparations: I cashed in miles for two one-way tickets to Seattle on Southwest (via Las Vegas, Los Angeles and Oakland) and shipped our Ibis with BOB out to a bike shop north of there in Bellingham, Washington, where we knew people and would begin the ride. Pre-social media and pre-smart phone, I coded a website to display journal entries which I would write on my handheld computer. Through a modem, I would email my entries to my friend Kent Holtshouser, who would copy and paste the text on the site's journal page and upload to the site. I anticipated a great following of friends and relatives eager for updates on our progress.

While Jane's mom, Marilyn, an American who wasn't in the War, gave enthusiastic support, our plans did not make much of an impression on my parents, both Europeans who were in the War. Dad was all for having a bit of adventure, but being British, he found cycling arduous and a form of transportation more befitting of Asiatic peasants. "Did you know how the Japs captured Singapore during the War?" Dad said. "The little buggers went round on bicycles! General Percival never imagined infantry could move so fast through jungle and suddenly they were in his rear. They're clever, those. Now when I was your age, I had a motorbike. A Triumph, I think. Or perhaps that was when I had the old BSA. One of the two. No matter. Now that's the way to get round the countryside."

Mom, being German, was even more bewildered. A week before our departure she left Dad at home occupied with the project of buying a newspaper, and met us for lunch at Appetito, our favorite Italian bistro, as a parting gift. Born in a village in what is now Poland, or possibly Ukraine— nobody today is sure of its exact location—but was part of Germany in 1931, forty-plus years in the US had not diminished her accent nor her ability to make snap judgements. She had two ratings for restaurants: filthy, or filthy and overpriced. To her, Italian was ethnic. This was a rare event. Once the bread and water arrived she folded her hands, leaned forward and began the interrogation: "So. Dis big ride. Vut do you hope to accomplish?"

She was serious. German mothering is a weird combination of force feeding and criticism. The food keeps you pinned down while they launch verbal missiles at a stationary target. "Accomplish?" I choked. "Well, it's something I've always dreamed of doing, to ride from one ocean to another, clear across a continent, under my own power. I'm not sure how it'll turn out, but it feels like a calling, like something I have to do."

"Well I would never do such a ding," she said. "It seems silly to ride a bicycle all det way when you haf det nice car now. You could drife it, see the country and be done in a veek or two. Isn't it dangerous? Someone could chust push you over. You're not quitting your chob, are you?"

"No," I said, "it'll be there when I get back." The job would be there all right; it would just belong to someone else. Jane pretended to study the menu.

"Goot," she said. "Because if you don't haf a chob, you can't get a new chob, because no-one will hire you, unless you already haf a chob. You see how it vurks?"

"Have a job to get a job, got it."

She pointed a finger. "Chust don't be wizout a chob, OK? Or you'll end up like det guy."

"That guy…you mean Dad?"

She rolled her eyes. "Can't go to the toilet wizout asking me first."

The week passed quickly as the preparations seemed endless: stopping the mail, arranging for plant care, emptying the fridge, paying bills, unpacking and re-packing. The day before we left, we held a going-away party at the house—not big—just a dozen or so friends who had nothing else scheduled that afternoon. Some dude, a pierced/tattooed cyclist friend-of-a-friend who had ridden long distances laughed and told us we could train all we wanted, but there was no way to prepare our butts for all that time in the saddle. We'd never thought of that. I backed up to a wall and gave my buttocks a discrete probing. They seemed padded enough.

Next morning I hoisted BOB's duffel bag crammed with everything we'd need for the next three months out of the trunk of Marilyn's rusting '81 Volvo and hauled it to the curb outside departures at Providence International, where we'd catch a free flight on Southwest; actually, many free flights as we'd have two or three stops before Seattle. Meanwhile, our Ibis tandem made its own way, boxed up in the back of an eighteen wheeler rolling west on I-90. We were excited to travel, committed to the journey, trusting in each other, and quite naïve.

WASHINGTON

Before it became a state, the territory was called Columbia after the Columbia River, which Robert Gray named after his ship. When it was granted statehood in 1889, they changed the name to Washington so people wouldn't confuse it with The District of Columbia, although the nation's capital city had been called Washington since 1791. So Washingtonians forever have to refer to their home as "Washington State."

Cascadia might have been a better choice.

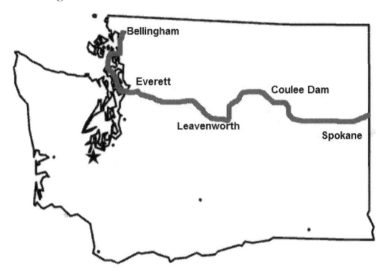

5 HERE WE GO

Bryggen, Norway, 899 AD: *Olaf Thorvaldson, Shipmaster, stood on the jetty to supervise the provisioning and boarding of his knarr, an ocean-going longship named* Wulf Sang *– Wolf Song. He scowled at a ragged group of shambling, worried-looking peasants. Normally the burly, red-bearded Norse skipper had a ready laugh and crinkling eyes, but this morning he surveyed the sorry specimens that would be his human cargo and swore under his breath.*

"It's bad enough that I have a crew of murderers and thieves, but look at these passengers! Outcasts and beggars, every one. In the old days we had a better class of settler. Bold adventurers. Now we're scraping bottom."

Svein, his tall, scarred and grim first mate leaned on a thick ash-shafted spear with a wicked iron point. "Like sheep," he said. "But not as useful, and they don't smell as nice." Suddenly he nudged Olaf with an elbow. "But what have we here?" He chuckled. "Nobility?"

Eyvind and Hild approached. They stood out from the crowd: Eyvind for the sword he carried because swords were expensive, rare and a status symbol; Hild for her golden-haired beauty, silver brooch and regal bearing.

"Let us see what they are made of," Olaf said with a wink to Svein, who returned a twisted smile.

"Shipmaster," Eyvind said. "How much for passage south, for the two of us?"

"More than you have, boy," Olaf teased. "Of course, there are other forms of payment we can arrange, eh, my Lady?" Olaf grinned at Hild. Svein leered, baring his rotten teeth. Hild reddened with fury.

"Insolent bastard," Eyvind hissed. In a blur of motion, Fotbitr flashed in the sun. Olaf's eyes widened as the blade arced on a path that might have split his

skull had he not sidestepped, and Svein's spear shaft, serpent fast, parried and knocked the blade to the ground. Hild gasped. Eyvind lunged for the sword, but Olaf stepped casually on it while Svein's spear point nudged Eyvind's neck.

"More wrist, boy, and less arm, if you want to strike fast," Svein said.

"If I'd really meant to kill, your head would be gone now," Eyvind said.

Olaf inspected the dagger he'd liberated from Hild and laughed. "By Odin, there's hope for this voyage yet! These two have spirit, if not brains." He waved Svein off and handed back the weapons. "Pardon an old sailor's amusements. Keep your silver, Swordsman, my lady, and welcome aboard. Drive those others away, Svein. We have enough."

"I will not be…" Eyvind began, but Hild spun him around.

"He said 'Keep your silver,' husband. Let us get on board, and see where it takes us."

They stepped over the gunwale and boarded the ship. While looking about for a place to stow their belongings, a familiar voice croaked, "There is room over here, young ones."

Eyvind turned and there was Mother, shrunken with age, with that same fierce gaze and toothless grin. He dropped his bundle. His heart raced.

"Mother…" he gasped. "A draugr?"

"Eyvind, what is it?" Hild shook him. He clenched his eyes shut and looked again. An old woman blinked back at him, but he did not know her. She was not his mother's ghost.

Bellingham, WA. May 1, 1999: "Big smiles now!" An eternity later, my face starting to twitch from muscle tension, Kathy Freimund clicked the shutter. You know those before-and-after shots usually connected with diet plans or gym memberships? I looked flabby and pale, but there we grinned, tense and forced like some kind of novice salespeople.

Jane and I stood in front of our loaded tandem bike; the attached trailer mounded high with gear and criss-crossed with bungie cords. All we had to do now was get it home. Was I insane? *A bit late for second thoughts, son. Stop dithering about and get cracking.* Dad was more than 3,000 miles away but nevertheless broke into my thoughts with one of his bucking-up speeches. To be British is to muddle through, and the modern Norman-Anglo-Saxon-Dane seems to be born with the Spirit of the Blitz instilled. Loins stir at the mention of Agincourt, Waterloo or Trafalgar. When under siege they whistle a happy tune and throw about words like *jolly*, *brilliant* and *lovely*. They have a perpetual positive attitude evolved from enduring centuries of continental invaders and millennia of damp, dreary weather. I took a deep breath and squared my shoulders. Right. Get cracking.

We'd spent our last night before Departure Day in Bellingham at the home of our friends, the Freimunds. Kathy had moved there from Boston after a stint with the Peace Corps, met Jeremy, and now applied her experience with tribal primitives to the raising of their three precocious boys, Max, Cole and Nate. All five Freimunds now lined up on the sidewalk to see us off. The boys fidgeted and cuffed each other. Kathy yelled at them to pay attention. Still, we had an audience; I could not disappoint.

"How do you feel?" Jane said.

"I don't know," I said. "How do I look?"

"You look like you feel good."

"Well that's what matters."

I blew out a big breath, stretched a little, trying without success to untie the knot in my stomach. All week long my emotions had swung like hyperactive monkeys on speed, between a kind of overzealous bravado and abject terror. Little things reversed my mood in an instant. In Seattle two days earlier I had seen a bald eagle, my first one ever, soaring beneath the vibrant arches of an afternoon rainbow. "That's a good omen, right?" I'd said to Jane. "We'll fly east like that eagle: strong and true with the wind at our backs." As if the universe cared. Jane, tactful, pointed out that the eagle was actually flying west, but it probably still meant something good. Down came my veneer of confidence; the sourness of doubt crept up from my belly, blazing a trail for dread to follow.

We wheeled our human-powered RV into position, pointed east, and in unison straddled the crossbar. Jane radiated glee, ready at the rear position. She seemed not to think about the months ahead, but focused on today, right now, feeling the warm sun and cool air and letting the future unfold as it would. I slipped on my already well-worn cycling gloves. I settled the helmet on my head and snapped the closure. I gripped the handlebars, squeezed the brakes, and balanced on one leg, slid my left foot into the pedal clip and cinched the strap. I looked back at Jane to see that she was also in position, and nodded.

"Here we go," I said. We shoved off.

A continent lay before us. We would take it one day at a time; one mile at a time; one pedal stroke after another. It was not a race. There was plenty of time…

Pedal, you lug, I told myself. This beast was heavy, and I tried to look cool by waving to our friends. We'd never ridden it loaded before. The bike slewed left, going too slow to balance. I gripped its curved horns in both hands, we gave the pedals three or four good strokes and finally bike, riders and trailer were all going in the same direction. The Freimunds' tinny cheers and ragged claps receded behind us. And in the steady whir of the chain, in the whistle of wind through helmet, and the fresh air filling me, all the fear and stress dropped away. My body relaxed into the familiar rhythm of push-pull on the pedals, in-out through the lungs, and heart thumping to a cadence of 90 per minute. I was seven years old again, white-blond hair flying behind, fast and free, leaving Mom in the dust. I was doing my Big One!

Today's destination was Orcas Island, a place I'd long wanted to visit for its reputation as a cyclist's paradise. This would be a side trip, a shake-out before we turned east for real. Our route took us along Chuckanut Drive, a coastal byway that wound, dipped and rose between colossal red cedars and Douglas fir trees with trunks I couldn't begin to get my arms around. Narrow in places and high on a steep bluff, it offered spectacular views of Bellingham Bay and the many islands of the Salish Sea. After lunch we turned west for Anacortes. We huffed and puffed over the Route 20 bridge joining Fidalgo Island to the mainland, then stopped to rest. Off the bike, Jane gingerly lifted her knee up and down with a worried look.

"Do you hear that crunching sound? I think there's something really wrong with my knee!" Sure enough, there was a faint but unmistakable crunch at every lift.

Suddenly I was back in the Scottish highlands. My mind raced and flailed at an idea. "Hold on," I said. "Do you have anything in your pockets?"

Jane dug into her pockets. "I don't think so....no, wait...." Her voice trailed off, then one hand emerged clutching a crumpled piece of paper and some wadded granola bar wrappers.

"Try it now," I said. No more crunching. The knee was cured.

We finished Big One/Day One in Anacortes, near the ferry terminal and fifty miles from Bellingham. With forethought I'd reserved a room at a bed and breakfast equipped with a hot tub. Jane was too sore to sit in the tub; she crouched. I snickered at this, but the next morning, not so much. We lay in that nice downy bed where we'd collapsed the night before, unwilling to move more than our eyes, knowing every muscle would scream in protest. I tried not to think about our plan for the next three months: to repeat yesterday's torture, fifty miles every day, *on average*. Presently full bladders and empty bellies propelled us up and out.

Soft creaks and groans accompanied our descent to the dining room; not entirely the stairs' fault. We eased ourselves into chairs, proud of defying our pain, cheered at the prospect of a cooked breakfast. Another young couple sat across from us. In stark contrast to our exuberance they barely returned our greetings and were somber and colorless, like they sat under a dark cloud. We got enough conversation out of them to discover that they lived "close to Denver." *What's going on in Denver?* I wondered. Then my blood froze: the Columbine massacre. Ten days before. The news had shocked and sickened us, but we'd put it aside amidst all our preparations. Now the outside world came crashing in. Although unspoken, we sensed that across the table were two souls in torment, hoping to dull their pain with some distance. While I lived my little dream, these two were caught in a nightmare. My heart went out to them, but I had no words. I didn't know death. And sore as I was, I didn't know pain.

6 ISLANDS IN THE PACIFIC

We pedaled off the Orcas Island ferry boat and passed through a time portal into a simpler age: the few cars that shared our road were from the 1960s but appeared new, as if they belonged to collectors and only went out on special occasions, driven at 30 miles per hour along this empty, meandering byway among rolling hills, farms and evergreen forest. I called a halt at the "A-1 Diner," which boasted 25-cent coffee. We seated ourselves. Four minutes went by before a waitress noticed us and ambled over. What was my hurry? We had no appointments that day. This was life in the slow lane.

While waiting, I read to Jane from the brochure I'd picked up on the ferry: "'Orcas Island is the largest of the San Juan Islands, first explored by Spain before being claimed by England. The name Orcas was the nickname of Juan Vicente de Güemes Padilla Horcasitas y Aguayo, 2nd Count of Revillagigedo, Viceroy of Mexico, who ordered the expedition.' That's a mouthful. So Orcas Island has nothing to do with orca whales."

"Interesting," Jane said. "I never knew the Spanish got this far north."

"They were probably happier further south," I said. "This is a real English climate."

"That's what I love out here. Everything lush and alive, the open spaces, the cool fresh air…it makes me happy."

We ordered coffee and a second breakfast and our waitress filled two thick white coffee cups steaming from a big chrome urn behind the counter. This was coffee "light," coppery rather than black, so watery you need six cups to feel any buzz, and then you're up to $1.50 and have to pee very badly. An hour and two trips to the restroom later, we moseyed along.

Jane spotted the sign for *West Beach Resort—Camping* as we coasted down a shaded lane outside of East Sound that afternoon. "Let's check it out," I said, signaling a left turn. Since the camping gear was half our load, I wanted to use it every chance we got. The campground comprised several beachfront acres. We pitched our borrowed tent amid firs and cedars close to the water.

"It's smaller than I remember it," I said, looking down at what appeared to be a nylon house for a dachshund.

"It's a cute little thing," Jane said. "We'll make it work."

Being early in the season we had the place mostly to ourselves. That evening our driftwood campfire glowed, small waves lapped the shore, and gentle breezes sighed through the evergreens. The setting felt familiar, but on a larger scale, like Maine's big brother. Less sore than the previous night, we shoehorned ourselves and our gear into the tiny *tent-ling*, grateful for sleep, cozily sheltered from the rain that pitter-pattered on the fly.

As the morning mist brightened, I crawled out and groped for my sandals, which I'd left outside the door. One missing. A search of the perimeter and under the tent proved fruitless, so I widened my dragnet to include the camp host's cabin. There it lay in the grass, amongst some rubber bones and old tennis balls, slightly slobbered on but otherwise unharmed. The host opened his door. The dog bounded out with him, tail wagging.

"Oh, did he get one of your shoes last night? Sorry about that. He loves shoes and brings them home if he finds them outside." The dog crouched in front of me, hoping for a game of fetch.

"No problem," I said, holding it between finger and thumb. "Nothing a rinse in the lake won't fix."

"Hey, there was some snow last night in the Cascades," he went on. We'd told him of our plans when we checked in the night before. "I checked the passes, and North Cascades Highway is closed, still buried under ten feet in places. I doubt it's going to be open any time soon."

"We'll have to go another way. Are any of the other passes open?"

"Snoqualmie's always open. That's I-90."

"We can't go that way. Bikes aren't allowed on the interstate. Plus, it wouldn't be very scenic."

"And there's Steven's Pass. They plow that for the ski area up there, so it'll be open. That's Route 2, between North Cascades and Snoqualmie. Not a bad road for cycling, and still real pretty through the pass. You could go down Whidbey Island, take the ferry to Mukilteo, and catch Route 2 in Everett."

My careful plans and maps had lasted two days; now I was getting directions. That day we left our baggage at the camp to explore the island unencumbered. We returned for a second night in the tent, shoes safely inside.

The next day was May 2, and we officially began our eastward trek. To make it official we wheeled our bike down to the beach and backed it towards the water until a tiny wave dashed itself against the rear wheel. In cycling tradition, to complete a true coast-to-coast, the rear wheel must touch the originating ocean at the start, while the front wheel must touch the destination ocean at the end. Although Puget Sound is not strictly the Pacific Ocean, it was close enough.

We set off under cloudy coolness and caught the ferry back to Anacortes. After a day without the trailer, faced with the steep terrain of Fidalgo Island, I had to keep looking back to see if the wheel had come off and we were dragging it along.

"I feel like that little dog Max, pulling the Grinch's sleigh up Mt. Crumpet!" Jane said, as we labored up a particularly large hill.

"Yeah, I know what you mean;" I said, "only we don't get to DUMP it when we get to the top!"

From Fidalgo Island we crossed Deception Pass on the high and spindly bridge over to Whidbey Island. I told myself not to look down, but out; out over the emerald waters of the narrow and intricate channel that in 1790 deceived George Vancouver into believing Whidbey Island a peninsula.

It took us a while to pedal the length of Whidbey Island, even allowing that it is the second longest island in the country. I didn't mind; once we got through Oak Harbor the cycling was some of the best we'd ever had: a nice wide road with minimal traffic led us between rolling hills and tilled fields, past small ponds and marshlands, along secluded little coves and windswept bluffs. We arrived in Coupeville at lunchtime, where I thought I'd found nirvana. Coupeville is an idyllic fishing village turned artist enclave nestled on the shores of Penn Cove on Whidbey Island. It faces the Cascade Mountains to the east, which on clear days loom tall, jagged and brilliant with snow beyond the sparkling waters of Puget Sound.

We leaned our rig against a white wooden railing adjacent to the town landing, now carpeted in pink petals from a nearby cherry tree in full bloom. We descended the adjoining stairs to a weathered waterfront café called the *Knead and Feed* and were immersed in a symphony of aromas: brewed coffee, roasted garlic, fresh baked bread, cinnamon, homemade soups; our stomachs growled in audible anticipation. One of the major benefits of cycle touring is that every day is an all-you-can-eat extravaganza. We generally ate six meals a day: breakfast, second breakfast, lunch, tea-time, dinner and supper; with snacks in between; whatever we could carry. With the number of calories we burned by pedaling all those miles, the only way to maintain our body weight was to eat like teenagers. We ate everything and anything; nothing was off-limits. The waitress brought several courses to our table, and knew to keep her hands clear of the whirling knives and forks as we fueled up. After lunch, we took a walk around town and I found myself holding a big ice cream cone. We strolled down a shorefront path lined with fragrant spring flowers: lilac, rosemary and lavender scented the air. A bald eagle zoomed low overhead, silent and magnificent.

"I want to live here," I said to Jane. "It's perfect. Let's just move here." Part of me had come home. Apart from the mountains and eagles, Coupeville reminded me of my hometown of Marblehead, Massachusetts; not the exclusive, gentrified bedroom community of Boston as it is now, but how it was in the 1970s: an eclectic, salty, working seacoast town. The seaweed tang in the air, the giggling gulls, the gentle clang of rigging against mast brought with it the memory of stopping at the town landing on Sundays after church to buy fresh cod off the commercial fishing boats. Our cat gleefully batted the severed fish head around the kitchen floor before he settled down to gnaw on it. That oven-baked flaky white cod, golden buttery bread crumbs on top, with a squirt of lemon was a Sunday dinner tradition.

"Don't you want to see what the rest of the country is like?" Jane said, drawing me back to the present.

"Yeah, I guess," I grumbled. "But I took a picture of the house we're going to buy here." Clouds had moved in; I wondered if we ought to spend the night, but we set off from Coupeville with reluctance. Within a half hour the skies opened up, pelting us with not raindrops but rainballs, that splattered like tiny water balloons. Eventually a roadside café appeared and we pulled in, drenched and shivering.

"Normally we try to avoid the rain," I said to the lady behind the counter, who wore an amused look. "Probably not possible around here, though."

She served up our hot chocolate accompanied by some free wisdom: "You always get what you resist."

Fine. I'm going to resist sunshine and tailwinds and see what happens.

On the advice of one of the other patrons, some lucky kid's jolly old granddad with a full white beard who looked like Santa Claus on the off-season, we stayed in Langley that night, another perfect seaside village of cute clapboarded cottages clustered about a snug little harbor.

The next morning dawned grey and wet. "Might as well get used to this," Jane said. "At least until we get over the Cascades." I agreed: "We'll never get home if we wait for sunny days." We suited up for the damp cool that is springtime in western Washington, pulling on fleece and bright Gore-Tex shells. Finally we slung on our Camelbacks, a hydration system worn on the back that keeps the hands free for important jobs like steering, signaling and pointing out interesting sights. It merely drizzled that day and we arrived at the Clinton ferry dock in good spirits. We rolled onto the nearly empty car deck moments before departure, secured our bike and climbed the stairs to the passenger deck. There, we kept an eye out for porpoises and enjoyed the feel of being at sea, carried along a little closer to our goal.

I stood on the deck of that ship and let the wind snap at my coat sleeves and tousle my hair, and thought of home. I watched the ship's prow plow a furrow of sea foam, and became aware of a deeper yearning, for a different home. New England, for all its charm and familiarity also confined me. *"Everything is right here: the best schools, the best culture, the ocean, and lots of jobs. Why would you ever leave it?"* my parents had often said. But they chose it; I didn't. Here in the Pacific Northwest, the juxtaposition of ocean, islands and snow-capped mountains had an untamed, raw power; a wild freedom that compelled me, beckoned me to come and discover. In the past I had been drawn to similar topography in Scotland and Hawaii. In time I would explore Japan, New Zealand, and Iceland; all mountainous islands. In 1990 I took a job for no other reason than it required travel to Seattle. Now I'd returned, drawn once more to a setting that evoked a feeling of memory, or memory of a feeling; but the image was veiled, indistinct, not of this lifetime. Whether this yearning was passed along through the earthly flesh and bones of my ancestors, or descended from my soul's heavenly lineage, here I was, a wanderer, discontented, searching for the place I truly belonged.

Back on land, we faced a steep mile and a half climb followed by the negotiation of Everett, a small city that was home to a large Boeing plant: the largest building in the world by volume, covering nearly one hundred acres. It's big enough inside that you could build seven Great Pyramids of Khufu within its walls, though not under its roof. I had been there some years before in my old life, on a software project for Boeing. From the high observation deck, looking down, I had felt like an aircraft pharaoh while swarms of ant-like workers assembled at least a dozen 747s and 767s. This time we would keep clear of that plant and push through Everett before rush hour released those swarms onto the roads.

Here my thirteen years of bicycle commuting came to the fore. We barreled down double-lane highways bordered by strip malls, and found Washington drivers less adversarial than their Massachusetts counterparts. The widespread use of turn signals and observance of right-of-way laws made my job up front as driver easy and helped Jane stay relaxed in back. We breezed along until an ominous hiss followed by a steady thump, thump, thump told me that our rear tire had gone flat. We pulled into the parking lot of one of the strip malls, unhitched the trailer, and as I worked the inner tube off the rim, added fully inflated tires to my list of things to resist.

Passing under Interstate 5, we found the entrance to US 2 with the appellation *Stevens Pass Highway* which led us onto a bridge spanning the Snohomish River. Once across the river we were back amongst the fields and flowers as the city of Everett dwindled behind us. Sun sinking west, we swung off US 2 and rolled into Snohomish, a quaint little frontier-era town that looks like it belongs on a model railroad. A mixture of timeless red brick and clapboarded shops with colorful awnings lined the main street. Flowerpots brimming with purple petunias hung from iron lampposts along the main street. We stopped for the night at a farmhouse inn, where a litter of kittens made a furry, purring pile in a cardboard box on the porch. We took an evening stroll by the river along a meandering gravel path bordered by lavender, sage and salal. Towering lilacs added their perfume to the cool dusk.

Muscles now tingled instead of throbbed after a day's ride. We'd clocked over 200 miles, had been rained on and had a flat tire, but the days ended well. Jane and I were not arguing. I had heard it said that whatever direction your relationship is headed in, riding a tandem will accelerate your progress. Two weeks earlier, when we'd purchased the tandem, it was clear from the frame geometry that Jane at 5'-2"and 110 pounds was not tall or heavy enough for the front seat. This meant that I would always sit in front as the "Captain," while Jane would command the rear position as "Stoker." The Captain steered, signaled, watched for hazards, worked the gears and brakes—essentially drove the vehicle—while the Stoker pedaled, read maps, passed food forward and enjoyed the views to each side. Jane could not see directly forward, which precluded backseat driving. I held our lives in my hands and she'd have to trust me; and we had a long way to go.

Trust-wise, we were both a bit jaded, which is why we dated for eight years. We'd had our share of earlier disappointments, so our relationship went in slow motion, both of us treading carefully.

I was twenty-seven the night we met at a mutual friend's birthday party. Jane had made the cake from a recipe with the name of *Decadent Chocolate*. My slice was sweet and richly mysterious, and I projected those qualities on its maker. I already found her extremely attractive in the short skirt she had on, and probably out of my league, but that cake provided an opening. I walked up to her and praised its excellence. Conversation went from cake to food to her cat named Pippin to international travel, and that subject engaged us for hours that passed like minutes. I recounted my solo cycling trip through Scotland the previous year, which seemed to impress her. Encased in a timeless bubble, the party continued around us, far away and unheeded.

I found out we'd both been to Germany and spoke German, though mine was a bit broken. So as I left the party that night with my neglected date, I thought of an ingenious way to send Jane a coded message: *This is not goodbye. I want to see you again.* Instead of good night I said "Grüss Gott," which is a friendly Austrian greeting, basically "Howdy." Later on I would learn that this missed the target completely, as Jane's reaction was: *Wow, his German is really bad. He doesn't know hello from goodbye!*

A month like a year went by before I could arrange a first date, dinner at the *Chart House* in Boston. I picked Jane up at her mom's house, where she lived at that time. I stood at the front door holding a dozen long-stemmed red roses and as soon as I rang the bell, panic hit me: the roses are too much. They'll embarrass her. I looked in vain for a place to ditch them. She opened the door. I smiled and held out the bouquet: "These are for your mom." Problem solved, and her mom instantly won over.

Over dinner the conversation turned philosophical: does magic exist? Not magician's stage tricks, but spirits and angels, past lives, the Otherworld, myths and legends? My parents' Catholicism left me cold, but I didn't have an alternative. I had my own ideas about past lives, other worlds, universal oneness. I had theories that needed proof.

"I'm a scientist, so I believe it when I see it," I declared.

"But without belief," she countered, "you might never see it. Sometimes believing is seeing."

I chuckled. She had a point there. You can't invent something new unless you see it in your mind first.

Our embrace at evening's end told me everything. Our bodies fit together, peaks and valleys matching like mortise and tenon, soft meeting firm in all the right places. My nose, resting on the top of her head, took in a scent of pine needles and winter wind. My insides danced. She held me long enough that I figured a second date was in the bag. I drove home, unaware of the small paper bag left under the passenger seat; the bite-sized piece of fish from her dinner which would never make it to Pippin's dish, but would lie undiscovered for many days. When a guest leaves something behind it usually means they want to see you again; even if that something is a bit of spoilt fish.

Now, while riding the tandem, I needed to let her know my intentions. For a turn, she needed to lean; to accelerate, she needed to pedal; for stops, she needed to quit pedaling. If we couldn't communicate immediately and pull together, we would be pulled apart. Our next challenge loomed nearer: the Cascades, the volcanic mountain range that separated cool verdant western Washington from sun-browned, arid eastern Washington.

7 CASCADES

We spent two days surmounting the Cascades, going the 92 miles from Snohomish to Leavenworth. Traffic diminished to a trickle as we followed Route 2 East. The road barely rose at first, but gradually steepened as we entered the foothills. Abundant sunshine out of cloudless skies warmed our shoulders. We paralleled the rushing Skykomish River, a sparkling ribbon of liquid ice. Flanked by towering Douglas Fir and Western Red Cedar, we breathed hard, climbing. Every half mile we stopped for photos or simply to catch our breath only to have it taken away by the unspoiled majesty before us. Each town we passed through was smaller than the previous one, with an optimistic name reminiscent of prospecting days: Sultan, Startup, Goldbar, and Index. I wondered if there was any gold in them thar hills. We established base camp in Skykomish, reasoning that the remaining 3,000 feet of elevation in the eight miles to Steven's Pass was best attempted with morning legs.

The next day I experienced the wonderful effects of endorphins, those natural pain-killers that also make us forget physically torturous experiences so we can do them again and again. Although the road was nicely graded, never too steep, we climbed all morning: one foot up for every fourteen forward. To give you a sense of it, fill a backpack with six or seven five-pound sacks of sand, put it on and then spend four hours on a Stairmaster. I welcomed the mindless physical labor after years of sedentary brain work. The day dawned warm in Skykomish, but increased altitude brought a drop in temperature; starting out in tee shirts and shorts, we added layers as the miles, then tenths of miles, clicked by with agonizing slowness. Fortunately traffic was light and we had a nice wide shoulder to wobble in while we gawked at the tiny waterfalls trickling among the lush mossy greenery around every bend. When we started seeing snow on the ground we knew the pass was near. Strong headwinds blew through altitude-stunted trees to slow us to a crawl.

We had a respite from the winds as the road wound around the southern face of the mountain in a hairpin turn to the west about four miles from the pass. But soon the road turned north again, exposing us to the full force of the alpine wind tunnel. We rounded the final bend to the east with the top of the pass in sight as the now howling gusts tore at our clothing, as if trying to push us off the mountain. Only our heavy load kept us from being blown over. Endorphins muffled the screams of outraged muscles, tricked us into believing our bodies had more to give. Backs bent, heads down, we gritted our teeth and pushed. "Sixty more seconds and we're there!" I played coach to the former coach sitting behind me. "C'mon, fifty more seconds! Push! Forty-five—"

"PLEASE!" hollered Jane. "THAT'S NOT HELPFUL!"

Coach didn't need a coach, so I just yelled in my head.

The road leveled off, the winds seemed to give up their sport with us and blew elsewhere, and we arrived at the Steven's Pass Ski area, much to the surprise and delight of a dozen construction workers who were making off-season improvements. The facility was shut down for the summer, and not a tree or bush in sight. The workers had a couple of porta-lets set up for their use, however.

"Hi guys," I said cheerfully, feeling no pain, but a definite urgency. "We're... sanitation safety inspectors. We need to confirm that your porta-lets are to code. I'm just going to have a quick spot-check." They got the joke and waved us on; but we really had to go.

"All downhill from here," I stated the obvious after we spent some time chatting with the workers and basking in our achievement: the conquest of a major mountain range. I was still high on nature's painkillers and greatly relieved in a couple of ways.

Going down the back side, the headwinds worked in our favor to keep speed just below white knuckles and tearing eyes. We mostly coasted for thirty-five miles, following the meanderings of the Icicle River as it grew from brook to stream to river whose banks nearly burst with dangerous leaping whitewater. On this side of the Cascades, wiry long-needled Ponderosa Pines and birches with bright new leaves replaced the impenetrable shade of Douglas fir. We spotted a black bear in the distance as it frolicked among the wild pink rhododendrons on our descent into Washington's Old Bavaria, a town called Leavenworth.

Leavenworth was a logging and sawmill town in rapid decline by the early 1960s, when someone had the idea to give it a makeover as an Old Bavaria themed town. The residents, drawing on their German heritage, with great industry and the determination inherent in that race, transformed the town into a tourist attraction. The motif fit well with its alpine backdrop of the snow-peaked Cascades, rushing Wenatchee River, and evergreen forest. We felt as if we had ridden onto a huge movie set, ready to film the "Munich Oktoberfest" scene. Tyrolian architecture, stucco walls, window boxes of red geraniums, oom-pah music and a great big blue and white striped May pole in the market square ignited a strong craving within me for sausages, sauerkraut, a liter stein of beer and a giant soft pretzel with mustard.

The scene took me back nine years to September 1990, just before I'd met Jane. I visited my sister Wendy, aka Gwendolyn, who lived in Munich back then, and we attended the real Oktoberfest. She had always been more of a discontented wanderer than I, moving from Boston to New York to London, Brussels and now Munich. She is a city girl who loves business and people and in those ways we were opposites. Her free spirit and social ease had always made her a lightning rod for our mother's hostility, which took the heat off me, and for that I am ever grateful. Wendy and I sat at one of the long oak tables in a beer hall the size of an airplane hangar, flanked by chummy drunken strangers while we swayed to the oom-pah music and hoisted our one-liter steins.

"Good to take a vacation from Natasha[1], isn't it?" Wendy shouted in my ear to be heard over the noise.

I nearly choked on my beer at the mere mention of my borderline-stalker girlfriend. "Is it that obvious? Yes, I'm thrilled she has no way to call me here."

"She's a smotherer. I could see that when I visited you."

"I know. I like her, she's smart and usually a lot of fun, but so needy. I have to end it…"

"I could set you up with some hot euro-babes. You ought to work in Europe. You can get a British passport like I did. It's a great lifestyle here. You work thirty, thirty-five hours a week, take two-hour lunches, and get six weeks paid holiday a year, minimum. They're such workaholics in the US. It's not healthy." Wendy always had far grander visions for me than I ever did.

"Maybe I could." That would be one way to avoid a break up. I was young, arrogant, making money, without responsibilities, on top of the world—and lonely. After a long succession of short and forgettable relationships I was certain I would never meet someone who didn't: (a) need continual reassurance, (b) consider shopping a worthwhile use of time, (c) act like she owned me, or (d) appear to be a half-wit. It had to be more than physical. She needed to have a love of travel and the outdoors, to be athletic, and to have a good sense of humor. She needed to be intelligent. But there was something else…was it passion? A sexy mind…but then, what would a woman with all that want with me? And if she did, there had

---

[1] Not her real name. She's still out there somewhere.

to be something else wrong with her. This was the conundrum that kept me single. It was a bit like house-hunting. If they were available, they couldn't be any good.

Feeling like celebrating our conquest of the Cascades, we stopped at the Tourist Bureau and selected "Autumn Pond" B&B which offered gourmet breakfasts, a private pond and panoramic views of the surrounding mountain-scape. They had us at "gourmet breakfasts." We pedaled over, checked in, cleaned up, and contemplated dinner.

Our hosts, John and Jennifer, one could imagine ten or so years earlier as the big handsome football hero and head cheerleader, respectively: wholesome and all-American. But looks were deceiving, because big hunky John donned an apron and turned out those gourmet creations in the kitchen while petite and pretty Jennifer drove the tractor and tended the horses.

I was in the lounge helping myself to tea and trying to calculate how many of John's freshly-baked cookies I could remove from the platter and not deprive any of the other guests when I felt eyes on my back. I turned to see a smiling, open-faced young woman watching me.

"Are you the ones who cycled here?" she said. "Because we saw you on the road."

Canadians Linda Dom and her mom Rita had passed us in their car hours earlier near Steven's Pass, not quite believing what they saw. Rita had a Germanic accent that reminded me of my mother, while Linda had the bubbly geniality and incessant curiosity of my sister. Like their respective family counterparts, Rita mostly observed and made silent judgments while Linda cheerfully grilled us like a seasoned reporter: Where did you start from? Is it a race? Why are you doing this? Are you teachers with the whole summer off? They decided we were a pair of benign curiosities and offered us a lift into town for dinner. We followed the oom-pahs to Gustav's, because it was my German grandfather's name and also because I stopped counting beer taps at thirty— my kind of place. Jane kept up our end of the conversation while I focused on my beer, würst, pretzel and sauerkraut. Rita, originally from the Netherlands, invited us to stay at her house if we happened to pass through Kingston, Ontario on our way east. I'd been invited to stay in the homes of total strangers during my travels in Europe, but had never experienced it on this side of the Atlantic. But then Rita was European. I wondered if Americans would do the same. I'd lived most of my life in upscale Boston suburbs. We locked doors and armed alarms. We rarely spoke to strangers, never mind invite them into our homes, but maybe out here in the west, in the small towns, America still practiced the old ways. I hoped they did.

We spent a day off in Leavenworth, resting our legs while rosy-cheeked youths in lederhosen and dirndls danced theirs around the May pole. Jane is not fond of huge crowds. She tunes in to the emotions of others, and in a big crowd can become engulfed in the swirling turmoil and tenses up. Today I didn't notice her discomfort. Like some kind of privileged lord, I surveyed the sea of ordinary tourists. How many of them, I mused, had cycled over those mountains to get here? We were more than halfway across Washington in only five days. I chuckled at my earlier fears. This was easier than I'd imagined. All that worry for nothing. Maybe I could ride around the world. I shouldn't underestimate myself.

The next morning, after a gourmet frittata and with freshly baked baguettes in our pockets we set off towards Lake Chelan, taking Route 97 north. I had never seen eastern Washington before. The clouds, low, gray and plump with moisture, in numbers uncountable filled the sky on the Seattle side. Over here only scattered wisps drifted over the Cascades, the skeletal remains of clouds, sun-bleached and picked clean of their watery flesh. Gone were the huge conifers, ferns and mossy flora. This was an open, sunny landscape of hills and valleys covered in coppery grasses, tough, wiry little shrubs and field after field of pink-blossomed orchards. We pedaled through Washington's Avalon, the land of apples.

Outside of Brewster a car passed us, pulled over and stopped a little ways ahead. The driver got out and waved us down. My city-trained mind got suspicious, my body tensed for action. Then a woman also got out and as we drew closer, the man bore a striking likeness to my junior high school shop teacher so I braked to a halt. Al and Meg Hymer had recently relocated from Colorado and also had a tandem bicycle. They wanted to know what we thought of the trailer, all about our ride, and where we planned to spend the night. We gave them a full report of our adventure so far, and they were duly impressed.

"My folks have a place just up ahead," Al said. "You could camp in the yard, but they'll insist you stay in one of the rooms." Apparently I hadn't seen much of America, because the custom of inviting travelers into one's home was indeed being practiced here just like everywhere else. This idea comforted me.

"That's very kind of you, Al," I said, "but we're planning on camping at Bridgeport tonight." I didn't feel that we needed that sort of help just yet, and I was sure that Jane wasn't ready to stop for the day either. She made no protest. Al wouldn't let us go away empty-handed, however.

"I understand. Say, would you like some oysters with your dinner tonight? They'll broil up great. My sister raises them for gourmet restaurants so I've got a whole load of 'em here." We took a bagful, with gratitude. Food was always welcome. We exchanged cards, shook hands and parted.

Lake Pateros brought us to a crossroads. Studying maps, we noted three major mountain passes—all of them higher than Steven's Pass—ahead of us if we followed 97 to link up with the North Cascades Highway, and no knowledge of whether they were free of snow. A wrong choice could mean 100 miles or more of backtracking, so we decided on the more direct, if less scenic route to the south along 174 to US 2. The road, winding its way up from the Columbia River's edge to the plateau of Bridgeport State Park was all the climbing I could manage at that point.

"Well, where in tarnation [2] is this place?" I shouted back at Jane as we labored up the hill. We were tired and the hour was late. But a little while later, we had pitched our tent in the lee of the huge hemlock, home to a pair of barn owls, judging from the furry pellets we found underneath. With the clouds reflected in the mirror of Rufus Woods Lake, the oysters boiling on our little stove, I'd quite forgotten my tiny tantrum over that tiny hill.

---

[2] OK, this is not the exact word I used, but I want to keep this family-friendly.

8 GRAND COULEE

Augvaldsnes, Norway, 899 AD: *Wulf Sang sailed south, keeping Norway's jagged coast just visible to port. The wind blew steady and the sun's rays slanted in from steerboard, sparkling the sea beneath a clear blue sky. At the stern, Eyvind played out a fishing line. Hild looked at the bucket placed in the small "privy" space beneath the stern decking, turned to see all the men staring at her, and looked at Eyvind imploringly.*

"I told you they would stare," Eyvind said. He secured his line and strode toward the watching men. He parted his cloak to reveal his sword.

"This is Serpent's Fang. She has taken many men's eyes and hungers today." The men just stared. Behind him, Svein turned over the steering oar to a crewman and motioned Hild aft into the privy. He stood at its entrance, faced forward and spread his cloak wide to shield Hild from view, then smiled his grotesque smile at the watching men, who suddenly lost interest in the spectacle and averted their gazes.

"Ha!" Eyvind scoffed, relieved that his bluff seemed to work, then started when he turned to face Svein. The next boast died on his lips. Instead, he laughed and hauled in a salmon on his fishing line. "Voyaging is so easy. Why did we not do this long ago?"

Hild emerged from the privy, nodded thanks to Svein, who returned the nod and reclaimed the steering oar. "Oh, do not say this is easy," she said. "Never say that."

"We only hug the coast," Svein said, hauling on the steering oar. "We are not at sea yet, boy."

"That is when the fun begins, eh?" Olaf said, who had come aft to check the lines. The ship now entered a fjord with low green hills and scattered woodland on

either side. "Before that happens, we stop here to take on cargo."

"What is this place?" Eyvind said.

"Augvaldsnes."

"And who is Augvald?"

Olaf leaned on the gunnel and pushed his unruly red hair from his face. "Augvald was king here in centuries past. Tales tell of great sea battles where Augvald won his kingdom, aided by his two daughters who were renowned warriors: shield-maidens." Hild was rapt. "Augvald also had a sacred cow that he always kept with him, believing he owed his victories to the cow and the power of its milk."

"Tits and milk!" Eyvind laughed. "Of course, that is how to win battles!"

"Eyvind!" Hild remonstrated. "Master Olaf, what happened to Augvald?"

"Killed in battle with a rival, King Ferking. The best way to die, in battle. But Augvald's daughters were so distraught at their father's death that they threw themselves in a river and drowned. They were buried over there," he pointed to a distant hill, "in Stavasletta. Two great stones stand there. I have seen them; both taller than a man. They are called the Skjoldmøyene: The Shield-Maidens.

Bridgeport, WA May, 1999: "What is a 'coulee,' anyway?" Jane asked the next day, studying our Washington road map. We were headed for Grand Coulee that day.

"Darned if I know," I replied. Neither of us were desert people. "I thought coulees were little guys who carry your luggage on safaris. Whatever it is, it's got to be better than climbing a 5,500-foot pass."

"It sounds like a French dessert," Jane said. "I could go for some crème coulee."

It turned out that coulees do not carry your luggage; nor are they cool, sweet or creamy. Our landscape for that day was once a granite-bedded inland sea until around 15 million years ago, when a series of volcanic eruptions from the Grand Ronde Rift began filling it with basalt lava, over a mile thick in places. Horses, camels and rhinoceros grazed and frolicked in the balmy, eternal summer of the Pliocene era. All that changed with massive global cooling and glaciations during the Pleistocene. Ice sheets 10,000 feet thick advanced and retreated, forming a titanic lake that stretched to the Montana Rockies. About 18,000 years ago, the ice in retreat again, Lake Missoula deepened due to a glacial blockage at what is now Lake Pend Oreille. The lake ice began to float and grind against its ice dam, which eventually burst and sent 500 cubic miles of water roaring across the Columbia Basin. The deluge carved out 50 cubic miles of earth and basalt, washing it out to sea. The coulees, deep, unhealed scars in the earth, remain a dry, bare, inhospitable testament to the ancient floods, their shadows plainly visible to orbiting astronauts.

We felt like ants, a thousand feet down in the bottom of one those scars, struggling to climb out of what was for us a steep shadowy canyon comprised of jagged rock, crumbly dirt and dried weeds. Several hours of hard labor brought us to the surface and out of the shadows. Our day consisted of riding twenty-five miles uphill, another sixteen of flat and very empty desert, and the last five miles all screaming downhill into the next coulee, while we prayed that the brakes didn't ignite.

Along the way we passed no towns, no food or water sources, and not a single drive-thru espresso stand. Grand Coulee, a tourist destination, sat at the bottom of a big crack in the earth where it sported a concrete dam more than 500 feet tall and nearly a mile long with a lot of wires running from it. We'd loaded up on water in the morning and had none left by day's end; the most grueling ride so far. We skipped the grand laser light show that every dam person in town attended that night. I felt strange there, off-balance somehow, like the strong magnetic fields from all those power lines were pulling at the iron in my blood, disrupting my inner compass. I was restless and wanted to leave but there was nowhere to go.

We chose a nameless lodging by chance, in an ordinary residential home owned by a single, middle-aged man who was fond of hunting. Dead glassy eyes stared down at us from the trophy heads of elk, deer and sheep that graced the living room walls. Otherwise the house looked sterile and quiet as a morgue.

"I hope he doesn't have a hidden gallery featuring heads of the inn's previous guests," I said as we bedded down.

"Let's just get some rest, okay?" Jane said, making the best of it. Mournful coyote howls punctuated the night as we lay, tense and alert, waiting for the dawn and its promise of the open road.

Next morning Jane raised her head from the pillow and brightened at the electric whirring sound coming from the kitchen. A juicer? "Fresh-squeezed juice," she said. "Maybe we'll get a decent breakfast at least." Alas, the exciting sound accompanied the opening of a can of peaches, embalmed long ago in thick sugary goo, bearing as much resemblance to the fresh fruit as those silent disembodied wall decorations bore to the wild animal spirits that once animated them. The ham came out of a can as well, and if eggs came in cans we would have been served those too.

Eager to move on and assisted by tailwinds, we notched a pair of fifty milers in the next two days to arrive in Spokane, our last overnight in Washington. Once we left Grand Coulee the land rolling under us gradually came back to life. Fifty miles replaced the barren wastes with clusters of black cottonwood, western paper birch and Oregon white oak; pasture fields and farms appeared, dotted with small marshes alive with water fowl. Along the way we crossed the 500 mile mark. Now that we'd navigated cities, climbed mountains and crossed a desert I felt like we had seen it all and that the rest would be easy. The wind at our backs, sun shining, we rolled effortless, unstoppable, like a bowling ball along the smooth and level pavement. I turned to Jane and said, "I wonder when this is supposed to get difficult?"

"Oh, don't say that," she replied with a smile. "Never say that."

Spokane is where US 2 briefly meets I-90, which ends at Logan Airport in Boston. Since Spokane passed for a sizable city in these parts, we did our best to avoid it, trying to find the "Centennial Trail" cycling path which promised safe passage through the urban areas. Somehow we missed the trail and ended up breathing tailpipe fumes and jockeying for position with frazzled commuters on a major thoroughfare. We reached Millwood, a sprawling suburban outgrowth east of Spokane, a town of 1,700 souls densely packed into the narrow space between the Spokane River and I-90. Here we called it a day. Camping wasn't an option due to the deficiency of natural terrain. We pulled over at a busy corner while I scanned the motel signage on the horizon for a cheap place to crash.

"It looks like Super 8 is $41," I said. "And I see a Motel 6 for $33. Do you see any Motel 2's? They ought to be around $11, right?" Engineers are trained to look for patterns. To find them is a source of inexpressible joy.

"They're all pretty cheap," Jane said. "Let's just get a clean place."

I forget which number motel we ended up at, but that evening the sky was aflame with shades of crimson, salmon and ripe peaches. We had broken 500 miles that day, and were fifteen miles from the Idaho line. We felt strong. I was ready for anything.

Almost anything.

IDAHO

Idaho law forbids a citizen to give another citizen a box of candy that weighs more than fifty pounds.

9 FIRST ONES THROUGH

We craned our necks to take in the hand-painted purple and yellow sign that loomed over us and marked the end of Washington State Route 290. "Welcome to Idaho." I could now appreciate the size of these western states. Back east, I had cycled across Massachusetts in two days during the annual *Pan-Mass Challenge* fundraiser; we had just spent twelve traversing Washington.

Being mid-morning and time for our second breakfast, we pulled into the first roadside diner to appear. This one had Marion berry pie. I told our waitress we were cycling across the country and that this was my first time in Idaho. She paused for a second to register what I'd said, refilled my coffee cup, and snatched up our empty plates.

"Well I've never been out of Idaho," she said. "You two be careful. We got narrow roads and crazy drivers." She slapped a bill on the table and tended to her other customers.

Crazy drivers. I wondered if they could be any crazier than the ones who routinely rolled down their windows and yelled "Get a car!" or "Get the hell off the road!" or "Nice legs!" back in the eighties when I cycled to work at the GE plant in Lynn, Massachusetts. I'd get up at 5:30, shave, pack my bags and eat my cereal in dark silence, then set off into the pale dawn, lights flashing, to arrive at the plant twelve miles later with enough time to shower, dress and be at my desk by 7:30. One wintery morning, Rose, the matronly subsection secretary eyed my panniers and flushed cheeks with concern as I breezed into my cubicle.

"You DO have a car, don't you?" Rose demanded.

"Sure I do. I just choose not to drive it. By riding to work, I get a free workout, there is one less car on the road, less pollution, and I save money on gas and maintenance. And I'm healthier. I've never had a sick day. It's very efficient, don't you think?"

Rose's eyes narrowed. "It's also very dangerous," she said, "and I think you're nuts."

She had a valid point. During December and January, I'd ride home in darkness as well. Down to 10°F I could stay warm enough in cotton/wool/nylon layers, with a face mask, ski gloves and plastic bags (bread bags worked well) lining my shoes. There were no bike paths or special lanes in those days; the roadsides contained only potholes, broken glass and parked Chrysler Cordobas with massive barn doors that swung open without warning, the drivers oblivious to my approach. Today I marvel at the dumb luck of it; dumb to have done it, lucky to have survived. I can only conclude that my destiny lay on a different road, or else I would have lain on that one. If I ever have a kid, I hope he has more sense than I did.

The waitress' comment about crazy drivers didn't surprise me. During my commutes enough of them had cut me off, given me the finger, blasted their horns at close range, and thrown trash at me. Fast, heavy vehicles have a way of making bullies out of victims.

What did surprise me was that we were in the skinny part of Idaho and this young woman had never left it. At that time I couldn't conceive of a life lived in one place any more than she could comprehend our journey. I had many friends back east who returned to their home towns after school, got local jobs and bought houses, raised families with parents, relatives and former schoolmates as neighbors. While I envied the old-fashioned simplicity of that, I couldn't do it. My immediate family had already scattered, and being the son of immigrants, all my other relatives lived overseas and I'd never met most of them. They were family, but foreign to me.

By the time I'd finished college in 1985, houses had gotten expensive [3] in Massachusetts, and my family had all moved away by then. Discontented wanderers have no homeland. We're nomads. To stay in one place equates to stagnation; to going nowhere in life. I had to prove I'd moved up in the world. My goal was to do exciting work in an exotic place. As it turned out I took an engineering job at GE, my Dad's old workplace, and shared a tiny apartment in Marblehead with "Bud," my former high school classmate. Maybe we do get what we resist.

After pie we pedaled along Idaho Route 53, turned north onto State 95 which would take us up to Sandpoint where we would rejoin US 2. Our waitress was right about the narrow roads: only a foot or so of shoulder

---

[3] Even adjusted for inflation, median home prices in Massachusetts more than doubled between 1980 and 1990, by far the highest increase in the US, and the largest increase during any decade in the recorded history of Massachusetts (Source: US Census). Just my luck.

separated the travel lane from the ditch.

We had friends of friends in Idaho whom we'd never met, but lived near our route and through our friends had invited us to stop by. Though narrow and flanked by precarious ditches, State 95 was the only paved road between Spokane and Sandpoint and carried a steady stream of speeding commuters. Cars whipped past us with barely a foot to spare, creating an air wake that shoved us towards the ditch. I was used to near-death experiences due to my long acquaintance with Massachusetts drivers (sometimes referred to as Mass-holes), but poor Jane was not having fun at all, nearly coming to tears at a pull-over when half of the granola bar in her shaking hands snapped off and fell to the road. I would have eaten it if I was alone [4]. She wasn't just hungry; she was scared. I was up front and had a rear-view mirror, so I knew what was coming from behind, but Jane in back would be startled each time. Her yelps of surprise were turning into howls of injustice.

Soon after the sacrifice of the granola bar, our road appeared and we gratefully turned off. The black and white world of commuting traffic dissolved into color: a kaleidoscope of red and orange flowers, happy swaying yellow willow trees, and a little brown dirt road leading us up a green hill to Ira and Suzy's place in the wonderful land of Cocolalla.

Cocolalla is not a remote South Seas island, but a remote rural oasis in northern Idaho, where our hosts, Ira and Suzy, had set up a small farm to grow and sell herbs such as echinacea, peppermint and lemon balm. They also sold nutritional supplements and in their spare time prepared themselves for Y2K. We can laugh about it now, but in 1999 many people thought that chaos and anarchy would ensue when 2000 arrived and all the computers crashed, so they invested in personal fortresses, stockpiled them with food and water, and armed themselves against their potentially marauding neighbors.

Past forty, bearded and occupied with three different tasks at any given time, Ira had been a Wall Street trader, in the pits, shouting and waving his arms in a way that made him lots of money. The suit was gone but he still wore his cordless headset everywhere. He made deals outside while he tended the gardens. Suzy, his petite, perky and perpetually sunny partner, prepared delicious meals that we eagerly devoured. In the kitchen, while watching her tip cutting boards loaded with chopped vegetables and fresh herbs into a meaty, bubbling stew, we asked about her former career.

"I used to be a nutritionist at a hospital back east," she began. "Some joke, right? But hospitals really do employ us. The food was awful there, all processed stuff, and I'm telling management 'Hello? How do you expect

---

[4] I can be lax about sanitation, believing that what doesn't kill strengthens, while Jane is rather strict, and keeps me under adult supervision.

patients to get well if you're feeding them crap?' So they let me make changes. I bought local organic ingredients and worked with the cooks, letting them be creative. And I encouraged them to personally serve their creations to the patients, who loved the meals. The cooks felt appreciated. It was going great. Then I found out that some of the heavier nurses were raiding the food lockers at night. Sometimes they would leave the refrigerator doors open and all this food would spoil and we'd have to throw it out; hundreds of dollars' worth."

"So what happened then?" Jane asked, munching a carrot slice. "Did you get them fired?"

"I wish," Suzy said. She dipped a spoon into the pot, tasted and then got busy with the pepper grinder. "It was really political. Apparently the nurses didn't want some 'little city girl' coming in and changing things, and they wouldn't give up control of the food pantry. It got kind of unpleasant and I had to leave. But I'm much happier now." She glanced out the window at Ira, who was gesturing wildly at the elderberry to make a point with an unseen caller. "We both are."

"I bet that hospital went back to serving crap, the food that big nurses like," I said.

"Poor patients," Jane said. "It seems so ironic now I think of it: you are what you eat, so to get well you have to eat well, but hospital food is notoriously bad."

"They make their money on sick people, not healthy ones," Suzy said. "Try that." She scooped a steaming sample from the pot and held it out to me. I took it, blew on it, and then experienced a symphony of beef, tomato, onion, fennel, cilantro, and other delights beyond my ability to name.

At Suzy and Ira's we felt like travelers of old, exchanging our news and tales of the road for food and lodgings. We had a vacation day to eat gourmet meals, wander the gardens, launder our stinky clothes, and catch up on news of the outside world—in that order. The outside world hadn't changed much in two weeks. It offered up the usual stories: war, crime, celebrity gossip, the economy and sports. This week's news included the war in Kosovo, investigation of the Columbine massacre, the fears over Y2K, a bus crash that killed twenty-three people on their way to a casino in New Orleans, the Dow climbing above 11,000 and Buffalo tying the playoff series with the Bruins. I had always prided myself on staying current by reading newspapers and journals. I followed the stock market and kept up with politics and technology; interesting information then but just noise to me now. Ignoring it all freed up my attention span for what was happening in front of me.

On our final evening at Ira and Suzy's we played them in a game called Taboo, where your partner draws a card with a word or phrase on it, and a list of "taboo" words. The object is to get your partner to say the word or phrase by giving clues that do not include the taboo words. Jane and I were one point behind Suzy and Ira, and down to our last play: Jane gave me the clues.

"Oh, this is easy. McDonald's, Burger King, Subway," Jane prompted.

"Fast food? Hamburgers? Crappy food, junk food?" I guessed.

"No, no. McDonald's, Denny's…there's a lot of them. C'mon this is so easy!"

"Places we go to the bathroom? Breakfast places? Places with urinals? Urinal cake buyers?"

"No! Come on! McDonald's, Breugger's Bagels…you know?!"

"Drive through windows? Cheap food? It's not 'fast food'….?"

"Time's up!" Ira said, "Yeah! We win!" He did a little victory dance and high-fived with Suzy.

"What the heck was it?" I asked.

"FOOD CHAIN! What else?" Jane said, clutching two handfuls of her hair at my uncharacteristic dimness.

We bid farewell to Ira and Suzy the next morning, restored by our mini-vacation. Soon we approached the causeway that bisected Lake Pend Oreille (pronounced Pond-a-ray) on our way to Sandpoint, an oasis of artistic expression on the lake's northern shore.

"What did I tell you, Jane, a bike path!" The causeway included a separate paved lane for bicycles, roller blades, skateboards, jogging strollers and other non-motorized vehicles.

"First one in 600 miles," Jane said. "I seem to remember something about *all back roads and bike paths.*"

"I'm sure I said *mostly*. And we only just joined up with the mapped route. There'll be more of this from now on. Probably." Where is the adventure in complete safety?

In high spirits we pulled into Sandpoint and found out why most of the cars passing us were heavily chromed and highly polished Bel-Airs and T-Birds driven by old men with Elvis-like pompadours. Today was Annual 1950s Day. Being children of the sixties, this theme didn't resonate with us. We had other business to attend to: the skinny road tires supplied with our Ibis were worn thin and needed replacing, and after 600 miles we were due for a tune-up. No sooner had we pulled into a sizable bike shop than a pair of fresh-faced, pony-tailed young dudes popped out and instead of the usual questions, the one named Toby simply asked, "You headed east or west?"

"East," I said. "To Boston."

"Cool!" said his brother Andy, offering high fives all around. "You're the first ones through this year!"

We didn't have to explain ourselves. They were fellow bikers. Then I thought, *No way, really? We're first?* It wasn't a competition, but my ego loved being first at something. Toby and Andy, brothers and co-owners of Alpine Designs, became our personal pit crew, changing tires and completing a nineteen point inspection almost before we could dismount. We felt like celebrities.

For the afternoon we spun a leisurely twenty-five miles along the shore of Lake Pend Orielle, then coasted into Sam Owen Campground, within a forest of Ponderosa pines, red cedars and poplars that stood alongside the lake. Tom and Lorraine, the elderly camp hosts, were like a pair of garden gnomes come to life: squat, rosy-cheeked and terminally merry. They had just opened the camp that weekend, May 15. Lucky us. We pitched our tent on a grassy spot near the shore.

10 MICRO-PIRATES

North Sea, 899 AD: "Look at them run!" Olaf roared with glee, pointing at the receding pirate ship with his two-handed battle-axe, its blade stained red. "I am a son of Njord! Olaf rules the sea!"

"Come back and die like men, you whore's turds!" Svein yelled, his scarred face twisted into a taut and frightening grin. Both men crouched, facing the enemy ship, shields held ready.

The Frisian pirates had glided their ship out of the dawn fog, attempting to board what appeared to be a defenseless merchant ship. Instead, the first three raiders were cut down by Olaf, Svein, and Eyvind, who had hidden themselves and lain in wait. The fight was quick, savage and decisive. The pirate ship's oarsmen now backed water frantically, turning their ship to escape. Eyvind, emboldened by the easy victory, sprang up, grabbed a spear and made to hurl it after them. "Feast on this, cowards!"

"Stay down, you fool," Olaf barked, too late. An arrow hissed past Eyvind's ear. Then he doubled over with a groan and sank to the deck. A second arrow found its mark and now protruded from his leather jerkin. Time slowed down as he fell. He heard a piercing shriek rent the dawn. He saw his mother spring up and rush at Olaf.

"You killed my son, you reckless bastard!" Mother wailed, pounding her feeble fists on Olaf's belly. "Now what will I do?"

Olaf swore and swatted the air. The old lady vanished. Hild rushed forward to examine her husband's wound. "We must get him ashore. I need fire. Now!" Nobody moved. All looked at Olaf.

"I give the orders here, woman," Olaf said, his eyes fixed on Eyvind, considering. "He fights well; I can use him." He turned to Hild. "If we go ashore, *you can save him?"*

"He has already saved you," Hild said, her bright blue gaze intense and unwavering. Olaf looked away, shifting his feet. This woman commands too readily, he thought, yet what she says is sensible. Good fighters are valuable.

"Make ready," Olaf said to Svein. "We go ashore. Keep watch for that ship!" Svein and his spearmen quickly stripped the dead pirates of their weapons and valuables and dumped them overboard before returning to their benches. The fog dissolved in the morning sun as the oarsmen pulled the ship toward land.

Lake Pend Oreille, ID, May 1999: Our camp dinner was rather awful after Suzy's homemade chili the night before. We should have thought to pick up something for dinner in Sandpoint, because grocery stores were nonexistent in this part of Idaho. We scraped together our meager supplies. Typically we carried only snack items like power bars, bananas, crackers, peanut butter, and usually some rice or pasta, keeping our load light while relying on bakeries, grocery stores and the occasional diner or cafe for the main meals. Jane liked beets and so tonight we had a can of them from the local general store serving as the main course. I brushed my teeth to get rid of the taste only to replace it with something worse: the bitter, metallic camp tap water. I'd forgotten to ask Tom and Lorraine if it was safe to drink, but didn't think I'd swallowed much. While I fell asleep to the distant laughter of loons, a tiny evil presence awakened within me and gleefully went to work.

The first wave struck predawn. Jane awakened to my cries of "OOOW! CRAP! AAAAAH!" as I struggled to free myself of sleeping bag and tent in one quick motion, but only succeeded in causing muscle spasms in both legs.

"What's wrong?" she asked, as she poked an arm out of her sleeping bag and groped for the penlight.

"Leg cramps," I gasped, jamming the zipper part way, flat on my back, legs in the air.

"Leg cramps?" She sat up and wedged herself into a corner, trying to keep clear of my flailing limbs.

"Stomach cramps," I rasped. One leg was free.

"Well, which is it, legs or stomach?"

"IT'S EVERYTHING!!" No time to explain. I shot out of the tent like someone who really wants to avoid crapping in his pants and spent the next half hour hoping nobody else would need the toilet, because this one had no door on the stall, and I can never think of what to say in those situations.

I spent the day in and out of that campground toilet—cycling was out of the question—while Jane went in search of some decent food, challenging in its own way. If we wanted organic, or even fresh, we'd have to hunt and gather it ourselves, as the only other options were small trading posts and general stores stocking dusty cans and boxes with cunningly smudged expiration dates. Food was of no interest to me anyway, in my condition. A shower would have been welcome, though, as the lake was newly thawed. The nearest lodgings with hot water, beds and flush toilets lay fifteen miles east, just short of Montana.

The next day I still felt rotten—aching, tired and nauseous—but I didn't need the bathroom quite so often. Tom and Lorraine had been wonderful to us: they brought firewood, gave us fresh fruit and pure water and took Jane into town to get saltines and ginger-ale for me, although I ate nothing. Now they saw us off as ominous black clouds gathered in the east.

"You kids take good care," said Lorraine.

"It looks like rain," added Tom. "You can always stay here another day or two."

I forced up a weak smile and a languid wave. I was determined to spend what little energy I had to get us to a better place for recovery. Within the first mile the abdominal pains started anew, along with the rain. Both increased in intensity with each succeeding mile. Those unfamiliar with the tandem riding configuration should know that most of the time the Stoker's face is inches from the small of the Captain's back, which poses a problem when the Captain is suffering like I was. Honor dictates that a gentleman should never audibly pass gas in the presence of a lady, never mind straight into her face. But with my insides a bubbling and seething cauldron, holding it in was not possible. We worked out a system: when a discharge was imminent I would shout "Gas!" and Jane would take cover as best she could.

As for the ride that day: it might have kept on raining; we might have met people; I don't know. Through the tunnel vision of my torment I perceived a row of small log cabins facing a still pond, a shrieking peacock, some unfamiliar but concerned faces. There was a moment of relief upon entering a clean and modern bathroom, more pain as my insides erupted convulsively, then blackness as I collapsed onto the bed, pale, weak and shivering.

"One hundred and one," Jane said, holding the thermometer we'd packed in our first aid kit up to the light the next morning. Although a hot shower and a deep sleep renewed my will to live, I wasn't about to get on that bike again.

"You've picked up something, that's for sure," she continued. "Maybe we just need to stay put for a while. Do you have any appetite?"

"I think it was those canned beets," I said. "I never want to see beets again. I could eat maybe saltines, or steamed rice. Anything else is nauseating."

"Must be serious, if you have no appetite," Jane said. "You're probably just purging the toxins you picked up from all that business travel."

"I think I lost some of my insides," I said. "Hopefully nothing important."

No longer feeling like a celebrity, or maybe like one in rehab, I laid low for two more days, subsisting on water, saltines and ginger-ale. Mostly I sat in an Adirondack chair by the pond and stared at the Northern Bitterroot Mountains, the shorter Idaho cousins of the Montana Rockies, blue with distance but still sharp-peaked and white-capped. I watched the peacock strut about and fan his electric blue finery. All my finery had fallen out. I had nothing to strut about.

You see what happens when you quit your chob? You should be working. You should be independent. You should never need help [5]. My mother, even 3,000 miles away, always brimmed with useful advice, and she broke into my thoughts with impeccable timing.

What's all this mucking about the countryside? You ought to find a nice hotel, get some decent meals in you. Sod the expense, enjoy yourself while you can. Now Dad chimed in. It astounds me they ever got together. They never laughed at the same time. A typical conversation went something like this:

Mom: Now Mein Gott, Johnny! Haven't you finished hanging that bloody picture yet?

Dad: Do you want it done fast, or do you want it done well?

Mom: I want it done fast AND well.

I ended up with a strange philosophical mix. I'd feel guilty taking vacation, then regret having felt guilty and not having enjoyed it more when back at work, since now I had to work extra hard to make up for "lost" time. That was no way to live. Jane walked over to my chair, squatted down to my level and placed a glass of ginger ale on the armrest. "How do you feel?" she asked.

"How do I look?" I replied, trying and failing to force up a smile.

"You look like you feel terrible."

"I feel like I look terrible."

"Honestly, you look worse than when you came home from Detroit. We could take you to a doctor…"

"No, really, it's not that bad. I just need to rest for a bit."

"You're going to tough it out?"

"That's right," I said, my lips a tight, thin line.

"Yep, that's what we always did in my family. We'd never go to the doctor, no matter what. I think our medicine cabinet had nothing but aspirin and cotton balls in it."

---

[5] This voice had a German accent. Germans love to say "should"; it's their favorite English word.

"With the cotton balls saved from old aspirin bottles," I added.

"Right!" she grinned. "Of course you never buy them!"

She looked at my face and became serious again. "You know, this is all part of the journey. I think whatever darkness you're dealing with, inside, you have to go down into it before you can come back to the light."

"Maybe..." I said. "Maybe. But I just can't sit around and be sick, be dependent. I'm letting you down, letting me down."

"You're not letting anyone down. It's nice here. I'm having the best time on this ride with you. But it takes more strength to face those feelings you're having now than to keep on riding," she said. "So if you can do that by staying put then I really believe this will make you stronger in the end."

"I'm supposed to have my shit together, and it's all over the place. Literally."

"I'm happy to look after you, but you need to tell me if it gets worse. And I'm here to talk if you need to talk."

"Yes, thank you, but I'm fine, so no thank you," I said, and looked at the mountains again. I needed to be tougher. I always was a soft, overly sensitive little twerp....

Marblehead, Massachusetts, 1967 AD: "This is your little sista Ann?" our new neighbor grinned down at me. I was four and we had just moved to Marblehead. I turned red. Wendy's eyes went wide.

"Oh, no, that's my little brother! His name is Ian, not Ann."

"It's Scottish for John," Mom added helpfully.

"Yan? Eon? Eye-yan? I'll get it eventually. Sorry about that. You're very cute, though."

"My husband is English, and he chose det name," Mom said. "I would haf picked something German, like Helmut, ha, ha."

Jeez. Nobody could get my name right. I wished we lived in Scotland.

One time I asked Mom if I could go by my middle name instead.

"Ja, sure, we could call you Patrick. Little Patty, eh?"

"Never mind," I said.

I sulked for two days, eating little and reflecting on a lifetime of feeling different from everyone else, of not fitting in anywhere, and on wasting my time being sick and not accomplishing anything. The critical voices in my head seemed to have a German accent.

And like a fool, I listened to them. Each night I thrashed and sweated as the sickness wormed its way into my core. In dreams I drove a car without brakes too fast on a treacherous mountain road, at night. I was in school with no pants on and everyone stared and laughed. I stood in a muddy World War I trench, with rats nibbling my toes while steel grey horrors with red eyes rose from the ground and spewed poison gas and my lungs dissolved. My hair and teeth all fell out, my skin peeled away in clumps, my insides poured onto the ground. I fell into bottomless holes, couldn't move, couldn't breathe, was buried alive.

By the third day I felt stronger, my insides had quit seething, and I was eager to get to Montana, the state that I always considered the Wild West; in so many ways the opposite of Massachusetts: big, pristine, untamed, and uncrowded. Montana had soaring mountains and sweeping prairies where Massachusetts had lumpish hills and stagnant bogs. Montana had a two-lane road with one car per hour on it where Massachusetts had jammed eight-lane central arteries with traffic moving at one mile per hour. Montana had thundering herds of wild mustangs while Massachusetts had jacked up Mustangs with thundering exhaust systems. I wanted out of Idaho; we'd spent a week trying to cross fifty miles of panhandle.

Convinced I was good as new, we chanced a thirty-five-miler that took us into Big Sky country. Emboldened by this success, at lunchtime I downed a colossus of a sandwich, huge slices of fresh-baked bread piled high with roast beef, cheese and oily grilled onions at a little Amish place. Bad mistake. That sandwich just sat there in an indigestible lump, claiming for itself what little life force I had recovered. My energy fled, squandered on self-gratification. It left us at a place called "Bull Lake Lodge" which turned out to be filled with Montana hospitality—fortunate for me—since that's what I needed the next day: a hospital.

MONTANA

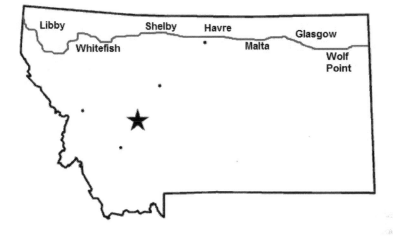

An average square mile in Montana contains 1.4 elk, 1.4 pronghorn antelope, 3.3 deer, and six people.

11 HOSPITALITY

Scotland, 899 AD: *In the dream, a boat carried Eyvind across a misty river. Ancestors' faces looked down at him and whispered voices in a strange language. Then he was outside of the great hall of Asgard, pounding on the doors to Valhalla. But they would not open. Weary, he lay down and slept…*

His eyes opened to a bright light. He lay on a rough bed, a mat with straw ticking. The roof was low, thatched; the walls of mud and wattle. He smelled farm animals and wood smoke. Sunlight poured through the smoke-hole. This was not Valhalla. "Hild? Olaf? The Frisians are attacking!" Trying to rise, a stab of pain forced him down. The draugr, his mother's ghost, peered down through the smoke-hole.

"You see what happens when you leave me? That girl turned you against me!" it screeched.

"That girl is my wife, and you are dead," Eyvind rasped.

"She is no wife. I was not at any ceremony, so you are not married. Leave her here, give up this foolishness, and come home." A large puff of smoke billowed up through the hole, and then Eyvind could see only sky.

"No, no, no! Be gone! I won't give her up!"

Now a golden head appeared over him: Hild, her eyes glistening sapphires. She smiled. "Nor will I give you up."

"By the sound of it, our wee Northman is back among the living." It was a man's voice, strangely accented. A silvery head now glided into view. "It seems the good Lord has other plans for ye, heathen though ye be. Och, ye'll be rapin' and pillagin' agin in nae time." The man strode to the door flap. "Bloody Vikings."

Now they were alone. "Eyvind, that was Hamish. His Christian magic helped to heal you. Olaf's men brought you here, paid him silver, and told him if that if you died Olaf would return and use his skull for a piss-pot!" She laughed at the memory. "But Hamish is really an old dear. He has been kind to us."

"What happened to the ship? Where are we?"

"The ship has gone ahead, but we can go over land and meet it where it comes ashore. Hamish calls this place Caithness, in the kingdom of Alba. He says we can ride across the country to the western shore where you can see an island called Skið. Olaf's ship will be there at midsummer. All we need is a horse, when you are well enough to ride."

"I'm no horseman, I'm a fisherman."

"But we are Norse. We really ought to learn to ride, my Love."

Troy, Montana, 1999 AD: "All right, all right, I'll go. I'll get us there," I said. In our room the next morning Jane and I were coming the nearest to an argument yet on this journey. Since my life force missed roll call again, Jane felt it was time to seek medical assistance. She was 105 pounds of solid obstinacy. Enough was enough. I reluctantly agreed, but felt we needed to get there under our own power.

"Let's go talk to Alex and find out where the nearest doctor is," Jane said. We dressed and went to see our hosts, Alex and Eileen.

"There's a clinic in Libby," said Alex, a real cowboy who could have played the part of the Marlboro man, minus the cigarettes. "That's about forty miles away. I'm not sure what their hours are."

"I'll call them," said his cowgirl wife Eileen. "They might not be open all day on Saturdays."

A moment later she returned. "Good news. The clinic is open until noon today. Closed tomorrow, though."

"Noon?" I checked my watch: 9:25. Forty miles. "We'll never make it there by noon."

"Sure you will," Alex said. "I'll take you in the truck."

"Well, actually..." I began, but never finished.

"Thank you so much!" Jane said. *No way*, I wanted to say, *are we going to ride in a truck!* This was my Big One and that would be cheating, like Rosie Ruiz riding the subway to victory in the Boston Marathon. But I had no fight left in me.

"We'll get packed up right away," Jane said, and off she went. Libby was along our route, and taking a truck there meant we would not technically be riding my entire Big One. Maybe we could circle back and ride those miles afterward. It made us frauds, not doing it on our own.

A couple hours later we waited for test results at the clinic. They had taken some blood, but ironically I could not produce a stool sample. I sat thinking about cowboys and why aren't they called "bullmen," since "cow" is feminine and most cowboys are male and grown up? And why don't we have a word for a male ballet dancer, like "ballerina" for the females? Would "ballerino" be the correct term? Or maybe "baller?"

A lady doctor emerged from the lab and sat across from us. She wore horn-rimmed glasses, a stethoscope, a white lab coat, and a reassuring smile. Good news, I hoped.

"Without a stool sample, we can't be sure," she began in that low soft silky tone meant to put us at ease. "But I think you picked up a protozoan, possibly giardia. It's easily dealt with; you're going to feel better real soon. I have a prescription for you, and you'll need to keep away from certain foods while you're on it: fats, meats, dairy and sweets are all off limits, I'm afraid. I made a list so you can remember."

"In other words, everything that tastes good," I said and she flashed her smile again. Fortunately, I had no appetite, and could probably live several more weeks on the midriff fat remaining from all those business trips.

We found a pharmacy in Rosauer's Supermarket in Libby and got my prescription filled, then sat down on the curb in front, mulling over what to do next. It was early afternoon, but we didn't feel like riding. We'd never been to Libby Montana before, and knew no one. For the first time on this journey, we wanted *Home*.

A shopping cart trundled past, pushed by an elderly lady with a kind face. Jane made eye contact and then hopped up. "Hello," she began. "We're touring the country on bicycle and just arrived here. My husband needed to go to the clinic; he's been feeling a little sick; probably a stomach bug. Do you know of any nice places to stay in town? Someplace … homey?"

"Husband" was not technically correct. Jane was thinking fast. Her grandmother would not approve of an unmarried couple sharing a room, and this lady, being her grandmother's contemporary probably held similar views and Jane didn't want to alienate a potential ally.

Dee Youso, steel grey hair pulled sensibly back into a bun, wore age-appropriate navy slacks and a hot pink blazer. She seemed comfortable in her seniority, a respectable elder without pretense of youth. She took one look at me and said: "The only ones I know of are motels; not very nice when you're feeling sick." She paused then, looking us both over, but you could almost see the wheels turn as maternal instincts engaged.

"Listen, honey, I've got a spare room upstairs nobody's using. You're more than welcome to it."

And it was arranged. Relief and gratitude washed over me at this invitation to stay at a total stranger's home. But I also had a pang of trepidation: what was the hidden catch? What would be asked of us in return? Would we be safe? Didn't the Unabomber come from Montana? I would stay alert. *You never get something for nothing*, a voice said.

A few minutes later we rode at ten miles per hour, following Dee's enormous powder-blue Lincoln with the Montana license plate MA&POPS into the huge carport attached to a neat little ranch house. Her husband Al, retired, welcomed us with a big smile, as if we were his visiting grandkids. He stood tall and dignified, big hands strong and roughened from a lifetime of working with them. When his warm hand enveloped mine, I didn't want to let go. I never had a grandpa. "Want to see where I do my wood work?" he asked.

Somewhere during the workshop tour, Al's gentle manner and warm enthusiasm penetrated my armor of suspicion. I forgot about being on alert and my shoulders retreated from up around my ears. Al and Dee had no hidden agenda. They lived by the Golden Rule. They took us into their simple and tidy home only because we were fellow humans, far from home, in need of a friend.

Al possessed exceptional woodworking skills; mostly nature scenes of local flora and fauna. I particularly admired a snarling cougar cribbage board carved from a single piece of Douglas Fir. Part Two of the tour took place in the Lincoln as Al drove us around town, pointing out the sites where his larger works were on display. Intricately carved bears reared up; eagles took flight, totem poles thrust skyward, and a colorful mural covering an entire wall inside of a church. It depicted their town with the image of Jesus, ever watchful, rising over the distant Rocky Mountains.

"I painted this a few years back after a medical episode. I almost died from internal bleeding. I saw all my ancestors gathered around the hospital bed, and in that moment, I knew there was a world beyond this one; a life everlasting."

"That's amazing," Jane said. "My stepfather had the same experience just before he passed over. He saw people around him that we couldn't see."

"I don't fear death anymore," Al said. "I know that Jesus watches over all of us."

Al *knew* death, not as an ending, but as a natural transformation from matter to spirit; from seen to unseen. First-hand knowledge had confirmed his Christian beliefs. Al spent his elder years adding beauty to this world, which countless others would enjoy long after he'd passed into the next one.

I have always admired artists: their passion and creative drive, their ability to say something wise or poignant in an original, beautiful way, and their ability to be fed by their art. Most artists I knew were far from wealthy, and I admired that sacrifice as well. Growing up, I was not aware that people could make it their life's work and even study art in school. Art was a luxury, a hobby; not a career. I had to make a living and support myself. Later on I would make time for art.

We got home as Dee put the finishing touches on a simple steak-and-potatoes dinner. Jane and I switched roles temporarily; she devoured the steak while I picked at a dry potato. I leaned close and whispered, "I thought you didn't eat red meat."

"Today I do," Jane said.

After dinner Al stepped outside to light his pipe. He would not smoke it indoors during our visit.

We tucked into the twin beds in the spare room that night. "Are you amazed?" I asked Jane.

"It feels like we're at Perk's [6] house," she said. "It has the same smell, like family and memories; and the same peacefulness. I feel very safe here."

"That they would take us in at face value amazes me," I said. "We could be anybody."

"But we're not, and they knew it. They live in a different place than we do."

"And come from a less crazy time. A more innocent time? But the Depression and the War, was that less crazy or more innocent? Maybe it was, because we knew who the bad guys were."

Silence followed. Like a little child worn out from a busy day; warm, safe and protected at Ma 'n Pop's, I fell fast asleep.

Despite my paltry dinner, the next morning I felt like Clark Kent bursting out of the phone booth as Superman, full of energy, due to the combination of antibiotics and surrogate-grandparenting. Al presented us with a parting gift: the cougar cribbage board, which he offered to ship home to us, knowing it was way too heavy to carry. And after persistent efforts by us, they finally, laughingly told us what we could give in return: a pair of Maine lobsters. I wondered if it was possible to ship them and vowed to get lobsters to them, somehow.

We pedaled away, waving big and riding steady, while I thought about the grandparents I'd never known. Dad's English father, Frederick Owens, died when Dad was three; his Irish mother, Ethel Burroughs, died a few months before I was born. Mom's German father, Gustav Tonn, survived the war but also died before my time. My remaining grandmother, Adoline Jesse, whom we called Oma, I met twice. When I was three we made our first family trip to Germany with Mom, while Dad took in the 1966 World Cup soccer tournament in England. I don't remember much about that trip. I had fun climbing the big stairs into the airplane, but in the middle of the night everything shook terribly and I wailed for my Daddy. And then Germany seemed filled with strange giants who spoke loud gibberish and force-fed me. We made another trip five years later when I was eight. Oma

---

[6] Perk is Jane's grandmother. Her real name was Hilda. She lived her whole life in Pittsburgh, drank copious amounts of coffee, had hundreds of friends, traveled all over the world and lived to 99.

lived with my Uncle Paul and his family in a stucco house adjacent to the elevated rail line. Milk came in plastic bags, and there was a market square nearby where we amazed my cousins with a Frisbee. Uncle Paul kept pigeons for racing, and ate them if they lost too many races. Oma spoke no English, had spent time in Soviet labor camps after World War II, and sometimes took her teeth out at the table. In her mid-seventies, she seemed ancient. I was fifteen when Mom got one of those blue airmail letters from Germany. She was crying and I asked my sister what happened.

"It's Oma," she said. "She died."

"Really? Oh, well, she was pretty old, right?" I said.

12 GLACIER

From 2,000 feet of elevation in Libby, we would eventually ascend the Rockies to cross the Continental Divide at over 6,000 feet. Our second major mountain range loomed into view. This one would be longer, higher, more desolate than the Cascades, but we were stronger now, and the weather warmer. Late May and far inland, we now enjoyed mornings mild enough to dispense with outerwear. From Libby, we rode north along Lake Koocanusa, so named because it straddles Canada and the USA (Koo-Can-USA). The land rose before us, gradual but steady.

Even compared to Washington, Montana is big, covering 147,000 square miles [7], its 900,000 residents spread thin. Like islands, towns can be fifty or more miles apart; not a big concern when driving, but on a bicycle, no food or water supplies for fifty miles calls for a bit of planning, which I'd dispensed with back in Washington, when Cascadian snowpack had relegated my detailed maps to excess baggage. Consequently, our camp breakfast one morning featured steamed rice and dry granola, with twenty miles between us and lunch at a roadside diner. Still on the joyless prescribed diet, my hungry eyes followed every bite of Jane's BLT and fries while I chewed dry pancakes. After lunch we only managed another ten miles in the afternoon heat before a flat tire in Eureka finished me. I was not up to full strength yet. The good news: I lost seven pounds of ugly fat in as many days, and discovered a simple formula for dramatic weight loss:

Step 1: Acquire parasites. Giardia intestinalis works nicely.
Step 2: Stop eating (easy once you do #1).
Step 3: Get moderate exercise.

---

[7] Montana has 14 times the area of Massachusetts and approximately one seventh the population.

By the time we got to Whitefish, in the foothills of the Rockies, 800 miles had rolled beneath our wheels and I could ride fifty-plus miles in a day without much trouble. It seemed Jane's strength had increased to compensate. Western Montana's back roads took us over rushing streams and railroad crossings, past miles-long cattle and horse ranches, and through grassy fields spangled bright yellow with dandelions. To celebrate my true recovery we checked into the appropriately-named "Good Medicine Lodge," a luxurious B&B that featured a huge jetted tub, bathrobes, a king bed and of course, a gourmet breakfast. It broke our budget and I didn't care. Whitefish is an upscale resort town, like a miniature Aspen, with two busy seasons: winter and summer. Our timing on the cusp of summer was perfect: sunny warmth without summer crowds. For many years I'd pored over photos in cycling magazines of Glacier National Park's soaring peaks and pristine turquoise lakes. I longed to put myself into those pictures. Now Glacier, called "The Park" by locals, lay only forty-five miles away.

The next day we pedaled through its gates and gasped at its majesty. Sunlight streamed through gaps between giant evergreens in misted beams that formed golden light-pools on the road. Red, yellow and white wildflowers accented the lush open meadows. Sparkling columns of melt water plunged from precipices to shatter on the rocks below, making rainbow arches we rode beneath.

Encompassing over one million acres, The Park offers easy solitude; unless one stays in the campgrounds. Even with most of the facilities still closed, more than a few vehicles passed us on the way in, headed for the same destination. We had been enjoying the extra breathing space that Montana offers and now felt hemmed in by the smattering of RVs and popup trailers parked at the campground we chose. Fortunately a one-acre area had been set aside for hikers and bikers, and this enclosure appeared to be ours alone. We parked the bike and dismounted.

"I think bears are a problem here," I said, as we scouted out the perfect site for our little tenting. "Look at this bear-proof locker. You could climb in and survive a nuclear blast." It was made of thick steel and set in concrete.

"Did you see this sign?" Jane said, trepidation in her voice. She pointed up at a signpost filled with a list of helpful tips:

Do not store any food in your tent.
Do not leave food outside.
Dispose of trash in approved bear-proof receptacles.
Always wash and brush teeth after eating.
Do not wear any clothes to bed that might contain food odors.

Do not dispose of dishwater anywhere.

We cannot guarantee your safety while hiking or camping in bear country.

"Wow, that's pretty uptight," I said. "What about: *Never dress up like a female bear*, and *Don't roam the woods at night smeared in honey*? They must think we're idiots." I turned around in time to see a couple of girls camped nearby get into their car and drive off, leaving behind their blazing campfire, beer and snacks laid out on the table. I'm sure they were only going down the road for cigarettes, but I contemplated raiding their camp and making it look like a bear did it. That would teach them.

"At least if a bear does come around in the night, it'll leave us alone and go for them," Jane said. "We have no food." She was right. We had little more than a handful each of uncooked pasta and rice, a golf ball-sized glob of peanut butter, a column of crackers, half a packet of cream cheese, and a good supply of tea bags, with the nearest provisions a twenty mile round-trip we didn't want to make.

The next morning, cloudless and bright, we took a ride up the "Going to the Sun" Highway, leaving BOB the Trailer with all our baggage in camp. We anticipated even more stunning views from its heights and maybe spotting some big wildlife; shaggy white mountain goats or even a grizzly. We put our meager provisions in a day pack, zipped up the tent, and set off on our naked bike, feeling feather-light and hot-rod fast. We cruised along a level road that ran beside Lake MacDonald, not too far from camp, gawking up at the towering peaks and waterfalls, when suddenly I braced myself to keep from vaulting over the handlebars, jammed on the brakes, and yelped "Bear!" We went from 22 to 0 in a second or two.

Jane peeled her face from the small of my back and craned her neck to look forward over my shoulder. Directly in our path, not thirty feet away, an enormous grizzly bear, an *Ursus arctos horribilis*, stepped onto the road from our left. We froze in amazement. It lumbered along, and like a 600-lb squirrel, stopped halfway. The enormous head turned and locked eyes with us for a few eternal seconds, nostrils flaring as it seemed to consider our fate. Being from New England, Jane and I had only ever met up with black bears, far smaller and not especially aggressive. Next to this thing a black bear was as menacing as a black lab. It filled my field of vision. The shock of being so close to this much primal energy without intervening glass or bars rendered us unable to move or make a sound. What do we do? Options flashed through my mind: play dead, make noise, make myself big, or back away? None of them seemed right. Where was that pepper spray? Would that just make him mad?

In the space of five heartbeats the bear decided things. He bounded across the road with surprising speed for his size, four-inch claws rasping on the pavement. I'll never forget that sound, or the deep gouges left behind in the heat-softened asphalt. It appeared we were of no immediate interest, so I thought it best to move along. We started on our way again, hearts and minds both racing, hoping to sneak past unnoticed where the bear had crossed the road. He was still close, but heading away from us into the bush. Suddenly he detected our movement and swung his massive head around and let out a growl, the memory of which still quickens my pulse and dampens my palms. I swear I felt his hot breath as I stared into a gaping pink maw lined with jagged yellow teeth. Then he turned away and lurched into the forest. The message was clear: *This is my territory, punks. Do not cross my path again.*

We pedaled on as the bear was lost to sight and sound. A mile down the road we stopped again. Our bodies crashed together in a clumsy, wobbly-legged embrace, and I mumbled something about it not being our time yet. The color had drained from Jane's face and probably my own as well. Dazed, we rode on to a ranger station down the road a ways, our mouths still hanging open. I had to find out how fast a grizzly could run.

Our bear encounter surprised the park ranger.

"You're really lucky to see one up close like that and survive it. None of the other rangers have seen any yet this spring. The bears are just waking up, still kind of groggy from hibernation."

"How fast can they run?" I asked. "We could have outrun him on our bike, right?"

"Not likely. They can do thirty, thirty-five miles per hour at a clip. You don't want to run from a grizzly. Better to stand your ground. Good thing he wasn't too hungry. Although, they sometimes kill even when they're not hungry and bury it for later. They're unpredictable. He probably had never seen a tandem bike before; couldn't figure out what you were."

We were a ferocious, blue, two-headed, four-legged dragon, lucky to be alive.

Trusting in that luck, we continued going to the Sun. Without the ball and chain of our loaded trailer we flew up the switchbacks, climbing easily to a lunch spot that overlooked the whole valley. Since the road beyond here was closed due to snow, we were in no danger from oversized RVs. The adrenaline rush of meeting the bear had drained from our bodies, replaced with a gnawing hunger. We carefully meted out rations, seated on the crumbling stone retaining wall by the road. I savored everything: the tang of the cream cheese and saltiness of the crackers, the warm sun on my back, the freshness of the snow-chilled breeze ruffling my hair, the view of the verdant forested valley surmounted by the majestic snowy peaks of the Rockies. No more than a hundred feet from us, four white mountain goats grazed casually on the steep slopes. I wanted to yodel.

"Are you happy?" Jane said.

"Yes, I'm happy to be alive, to see all this, and be here with the one I love."

"Every day is a gift, isn't it?"

"You know, in Idaho I felt like I was dying and wanted to go home, when all I had was a little stomach bug."

"That was a major parasite infestation, but yes, you felt like you were dying."

"All along I was worried that *you* would need help; that *you* would get tired, blow out your knees and get sick of the ride, but..." The words caught.

"But?"

"But you've been solid. No complaints. I'm the one who needed help."

She smiled and leaned her head on my shoulder. "That doesn't happen very often. I'm just doing my part. I love you, but sorry to say, this is not all about you."

My Big One was no longer solely mine; it was ours, and I realized I didn't mind that; it comforted me. This journey had grown beyond me and developed its own life force that would drive us onward.

Today we could have died, and did not. Had that bear wanted to make a meal of us, nothing smaller than a bazooka could have stopped it. The terror and bravado from back in Washington were gone with the realization that our lives could end at any moment, and that I couldn't control what happened to us. I was alive, yet parts of me were dying: my arrogance, my self-importance, and hopefully my isolation.

13 LETTING GO

On a cycling tour you usually have something to let go of every day. If the day was lousy, you let it go and trust that the next day will bring better weather, friendlier people, smoother roads, less traffic, more abundant meals, and more spectacular sights. And if the day was outstanding, you have to let that go too and move on, knowing that the next day may not be as good. Sometimes it's better. It's always different.

Despite our fondness for Glacier, we had to make up for the time lost in Idaho. We had been on the road nearly a month, one-third of our allotted time, yet still 3,000 miles from home. Our next challenge: the Rockies. Like a general, I studied the maps to plan our assault. They directed us along the *Going to the Sun Highway*, which we had just found blocked by snow. Once again we would divert south, this time through West Glacier, along US 2 that paralleled the rail line. Our day's objective: a mountain village halfway to Maria's Pass; a place called Essex.

The ride up to Essex underwhelmed us compared to the Cascades. We found a well-maintained road and minimal traffic, but especially after the splendor of Glacier, the scenery accompanying these smaller peaks to the south did not inspire: any interesting features such as lakes, waterfalls or scenic vistas were marred by the aging motels, kitschy general stores and quickie marts that sprang up to claim any loose tourist dollars that happened by. It seemed a place for passing through, on the way to someplace else.

In Essex we had one option for lodging: The Izaak Walton Inn. In the 16th century, sometime after Henry VIII created the Church of England so he could upgrade wives and still go to heaven, Sir Izaak wrote "The Compleat Angler," a sort of bible for the religion of fishing. The inn, however, served as a kind of temple dedicated to the railroad gods of Steam and Diesel. At seventeen miles from the summit, Essex is where helper engines latch onto the mile-long freight trains heading east and boost them over the top. In the 1930s, the Great Northern Railroad established a station and switching yard here and built the inn to house the railway crews. Now, with between fifteen and thirty trains passing through every day, the inn hosts railroad enthusiasts of all ages. Well-preserved in its original style of a cross between Craftsman and Tudor, the inn is a museum of railroad memorabilia and a historic landmark with no TVs or telephones in the rooms, which suited us well.

After dinner we strolled onto the big wooden porch, where several hummingbird feeders hung from iron hooks above the railings. From a distance, in the dim evening light, they seemed to be vibrating of their own accord. When we got closer we saw that a swarm of hummingbirds, flashing iridescence, surrounded each feeder, creating a resonant low hum, like super-sized bees around a hive. I'd never seen more than one hummingbird at a time.

"The hummingbird is a messenger of joy; perhaps a symbol of starting anew," Jane said.

"That's me," I said, "back from the brink. What's the grizzly bear a symbol of?" Jane had books at home on animal symbols, and had studied ancient spiritual practices with teachers who had trained under native shamans of the Pacific Northwest. She studied ancient magic, while I studied the modern magic. I could explain to her how semiconductors work, while she could explain a fire ceremony.

"I'd have to look that up. Strength, maybe. Or awakening?"

"It sure woke me up. 'Just waking up,' that ranger said. Seems appropriate."

"We all have animal guardians, often more than one animal. They'll usually appear at important times in our lives, to teach us something, protect us, or bring us a message. We've had bears come to us a number of times now and never been attacked, so the bear may be a guardian for one of us, or both of us."

We stood there for a long time, arm in arm, watching the complex and colorful aerial ballet, while the rosy glow fringing the western sky faded to indigo, then to black.

Maria's Pass is just under a mile above sea level; it is among the lowest of the passes through the Rockies. The Blackfeet Indians used it until they deemed it haunted, bewitched by evil spirits. Judging by the touristy development along its course, I had to agree with the Blackfeet. In the morning we labored up our second major mountain pass, in many ways a replay of going over the Cascades. We knew the drill by now: hunker down and get it done.

We'd gotten about halfway to the top when Jane yelled "Café!" and I yelled "Lunch!" and we pulled over to fuel up. I had resumed my teenager diet and now anything was fair game. Late for breakfast and early for lunch, we had our choice of tables, so we chose the one next to a vibrant young couple wearing Gore-Tex like us and huge smiles. Scott Smith and Alyce Moore turned out be fellow discontented wanderers. Between courses we filled one another in on where we'd been and where we were headed. We planned to spend that night in East Glacier once we got over Maria's Pass.

Scott and Alyce had just quit their corporate jobs in Arkansas, fashioned a trailer out of mostly scrap lumber and chicken wire, hitched it up, tossed in their few belongings and driven out here to work in Glacier for the summer. After that they would head for St. Thomas and then spend the next summer in Denali. An hour passed in what seemed a few minutes, but we had a Continental Divide to cross. I rose to leave. Scott, however, had important news.

"So which way are you headed from East Glacier tomorrow?" he asked.

"We're going to stay east on Route 2, all the way across Montana," I said.

"You should know they've got that road torn up for about sixteen miles between East Glacier and Cut Bank. It's basically unpaved, and mostly mud now with all the rain."

"I'm so glad you told us," Jane said. "Is there any other road?"

"Not unless you want to head north and climb over another pass." He glanced at Alyce, who smiled wider. "Tell you what, we can borrow a pickup tomorrow and give you a lift through the construction."

I laughed inwardly. Here again was someone offering us a ride, helping me "cheat" on my Big One. But now it struck me that my Big One did not command me to ride all the miles; that would have been too easy. Instead, it insisted that I share it with others. And for me this was much harder. I steeled myself and replied.

"That would be awesome, Scott. Thank you." We left the cafe with their phone number.

Back in the saddles, we neared the crest, into howling headwinds like three weeks before, when some more help arrived. I mentioned that the road paralleled the rail line. A silver and orange BNSF engine, pulling a long line of freight cars, drew level with us. The window opened and the engineer gave us an enthusiastic wave and sounded his horn. Somehow that engine threw an invisible lasso around us and pulled us right up to the crest with the train.

If North America was a roof, the Continental Divide would be the peak; the ridge marking our highest elevation on the journey. Like a roof, water that fell from the heavens east of the Divide ended up either in the Atlantic or the Gulf of Mexico rather than the Pacific. As we crossed that peak, marked by a stone obelisk like a miniature Washington Monument, we were over North America's hump. We began to flow "downhill" with the currents of the waters instead of "uphill" and against them. If all went well, we would end up in the Atlantic too. On average, we would descend from this point onwards. I dismissed the thought that it would be easy from here. I knew better.

Now descending the eastern face of the Rockies, we coasted to the bottom, entering the town of East Glacier within the Blackfeet reservation. For dinner we inhaled a Montana-sized meal at an Indian restaurant (the Native American kind, not the kind that serves curry), and for dessert I found the ultimate source of highly concentrated calories: Indian frybread, which is like extra-greasy fried dough, topped with butter and powdered sugar. Compared with Indian frybread, Dunkin' Donuts are rice cakes. I walked over to the restrooms and studied the signs. Tonight my choice was between "Standin' Bears" and "Squattin' Bears." The previous day's options had been "Bucks" or "Does." Too easy. If I had a place, I'd make it less obvious. How about "Drones" and "Workers," or "Cobs" and "Pens"? That would keep things lively.

The next morning brought a new coating of snow on the mountains, but for us down below only a chill rain. Our day brightened, however, when Scott and Alyce pulled up in a huge red pickup truck. We hoisted our dream machine and trailer into the truck bed and jammed ourselves into the cab. We spent the next hour bouncing happily along the muddy road, rain pinging on the roof, sharing adventure stories with our new friends. For the first time ever, I appreciated the utility of a big-engined, jacked-up truck.

If people felt good by helping us, who was I to deny them that pleasure? *Just pipe down and be grateful; they want to give this*, I told myself.

I would let go of some of my control and let the Big One go where it may.

14 EMPLOYMENT

Scottish Highlands, 899 AD: Eyvind and Hild, who now wore deerskin breeches, rode the sturdy grey mare Hamish had sold them across the grassy moors of the Scottish highlands. Small crofts dotted the landscape. Tiny white lambs scampered about; wobbly-legged calves nursed. The world was fresh-washed, bright with color and teeming with new life. A sizable lodge, protected by a log palisade, lay beyond the open meadow. "I need to stop before I burst," Hild said. They dismounted. Hild squatted behind a nearby bush, but peeked over it to gaze at the lodge. Eyvind turned his back to Hild and the meadow to relieve himself while the mare nibbled the grass.

"A worthy home," Hild said. "It must have fine feather beds and a blazing hearth. One day, my love, you will have such a lodge as that. And I will be its queen." A sudden movement caught her eye. On the road leading past the lodge were four figures on horseback: three seemed to encircle one. A glint of reflected sun was followed by the distant clang of steel on steel. Hild stood, staring. "Three against one," she breathed. Eyvind turned to look in time to see the mare's hindquarters receding toward the meadow, Hild on top, blonde hair flying. "Hild! No! It is not our quarrel!"

She kicked her heels back and the horse pounded across the field. Her knife blade flashed. She charged the group, screaming an unearthly war cry that even she had never heard before, because she'd never ridden a galloping horse before and it terrified her. It terrified everyone.

"Riders! It's a trap!" shouted one of the mounted men. "Go!" They gave up their quarry and spurred their mounts in the opposite direction. Hild reined in; the mare danced, blew and snorted as Hild squealed, tumbled backwards and landed with a thud.

"Much obliged t'yer, laddie," said the man. He sheathed his blade, dismounted and extended a hand. As Hild rose he could not hide his astonishment. "Lassie," he gasped. Then he grinned. "Brunhilde, I presume? The Earl MacDonal, at your service." A gold chain glittered about his neck and his long and colorful woolen brat was held in place by an intricate jeweled silver brooch.

Hild understood enough of the foreign tongue to hear gratitude in this speech, and wondered if 'Earl' meant the same as 'Jarl'; a Lord. "Not Brunhilde, just Hild, Jarl," she said. Eyvind, breathless, sword drawn, ran up to them. He scowled at Hild, who smiled sweetly. He sheathed Fotbitr and breathed hard.

The Earl clasped Eyvind's hand. "You must be Siggurd."

"Eyvind," he puffed, "Mac Haakon."

"Never heard of no Mac Haakons. No matter. I'm grateful you two came along just now. Those Shaws caught me out here alone. We will feast good and proper tonight at my hall," he said, nodding toward the lodge. "May we have the honor of your company?"

Havre, Montana, 1999 AD: On the last day of May we crossed the 1,000 mile mark and finished our day with ninety-six more, just four miles short of a century, which is one hundred miles ridden in one day. We didn't ride those last four miles because I became employed, as a result of Jane having to pee very badly.

Scott and Alyce had deposited us in Shelby, a little town east of the Rocky Mountain foothills and at the western edge of the vast grassy flatland known as the Prairie. This looked like a whole new country: flat as a billiard table and nearly devoid of trees. A single ruler-straight road pointed east.

We set off that morning with the goal of making Havre by evening, 102 miles distant. The conditions seemed ideal to attempt a century: partly cloudy skies, cool temperatures, tailwinds, and flat terrain ahead. As we got going, the winds picked up out of the west and pushed us along. The ground became a blur as we hit thirty miles per hour. We sprouted wings. Never had cycling been so effortless. The ground whipped past our feet while the air, matching our speed and direction didn't stir a hair or make a sound but gathered us up with it. We literally rode with the wind.

Mid-morning we stopped for snacks in Devon, America's fastest growing town: the population had increased 67 percent last year, growing from three to five. Dave and Jeanie, who comprised forty percent of that population and ran the general store by the road, told us how the prairie is so dry they have their water trucked in. I suspected their population boom would not sustain. They also told us about the young man from Whitefish who had cycled through Devon on his way to Providence, Rhode Island. He made it there in twenty-eight days. Although my male competition reflex stirred briefly and my left brain began calculating our progress in relation to his [8], with an effort I derailed that train of thought and didn't comment; just ordered another thirty-five-cent ice cream cone, because I'd probably never get another chance in my lifetime to buy an ice cream cone for thirty-five cents.

By the time we reached Hingham, forty miles from Havre, the skies darkened as ominous black clouds overhauled us and big drops beat a staccato on our helmets. We ducked into a roadhouse bar that offered a large overhang where we parked our rig next to half a dozen Harleys. A biker bar! *We're bikers too*, I thought, and smiled at the memory of one of the lathe operators at the GE plant I used to work at. He had lit up when I mentioned that I rode my bike to work, although he seemed thicker-set and more tattooed than any cyclist I knew.

"You ride your bike to work? That's great," he said, "so do I." He was easily double my weight, kept his head shaved, and had forearms as big around as my thighs. "What kind of bike you got?"

"A Raleigh," I said, thinking that cyclists come in all shapes and sizes, and I never would have guessed it from the look of this guy. One should never prejudge.

"A what? A Harley? Really?" Now he was excited, and I had some backpedaling to do.

At this biker bar we were a novelty. Curious about our journey, the pool table fell silent while we entertained a roomful of leather and denim-clad, bearded, bandana-topped bikers with answers to questions like: *How do you know if she's pedaling? How come you don't have Boston accents?* and *Have you been to 'Cheers'?* Underneath the piercings, the ink, the hair, the big muscles and beer-bellies, these "bad boys" had families, jobs, struggles and triumphs, hopes and fears just as we did. I saw the storm had passed and as we got up to leave, a guy with a gold tooth and matching earring offered to tow us to Havre if we needed it. That would have been great fun, but this time we declined the help. The winds were still in our favor, and we had plenty of time left to complete our century.

Late afternoon, the town of Havre shimmered in the distance. Occasional farmhouses interrupted the grassland. Almost there. The trip odometer clicked to ninety-six miles. "Wait! Stop! Pull over!" Jane commanded a halt. I hit the brakes and we squealed to a standstill.

"What's the problem? Bug in the eye?" No large animals occupied the road ahead.

"That's a B&B!" Jane pointed. "We need to stay there!" Jane was

---

[8] He did about 2,600 miles in 28 days, averaging 93 miles per day, while we had done 940 miles in 30 days, averaging 31 miles per day. He certainly outstripped our mileage, but I wonder how much of the ride he remembers.

possessed. One of her unique traits is that when traveling she will never disclose when she needs a bathroom. She prefers to keep that information private unless a dire emergency. I should have paid attention to the signals, like when she went silent an hour ago, but I was too fixated on my century. I suddenly realized she had to go and couldn't last any longer. The prairie, treeless, offered no cover and traffic near town was now heavy, with at least one car per minute. We had stopped in front of "West Prairie Bed and Breakfast," a whitewashed farmhouse fronted by well-tended flower beds. I owned it had some charm, but hoped it was closed so we could move on. I wanted that century, although it looked like Jane had different priorities.

"We're only a few miles from town, and we've done ninety-six miles. Can't you wait four more miles? Jane?" But she wasn't hearing me. Jane trotted up to the door and rang the bell, while I parked the vehicle. After about ten seconds she rang it again. I stood next to her now, hoping nobody would answer. Presently, Ed Hencz opened the door halfway, looked us up and down with a frown and said, "Sorry, we're full tonight."

Jane didn't move. It was 6:30 in the evening and we saw no cars out front. The door hadn't closed. She called Ed's bluff. "Full? Are you SURE you have nothing available?" She was being awfully persistent. Over the years I had learned to trust Jane's intuition, especially around lodgings. Something about this place had drawn her to it, something more important than a century, or even a clean bathroom. She determined that we would stay the night, so I stayed neutral and let the scene unfold.

Ed looked at the floor a moment, resolution wavering. "Well, I can maybe fix up a room for you, but it'll be a patch up job. And I can't offer you breakfast." He looked down again, hoping we'd take the hint and leave.

That settles that, I thought, *no dinner and no breakfast!* I turned to go, but Jane sensed weakness and closed in on her prey. He hadn't said no. "Oh, that's perfectly all right. We have sleeping bags and food with us." We didn't have any food that I knew about. I wondered where this would go, but kept silent.

Suddenly Ed chuckled and opened the door wide. "All right, all right, you can stay. Come on in."

It turned out that Ed was looking forward to a night off, and didn't normally take people "off the street." But he couldn't turn away two "yuppies in spandex" who reminded him of his own kids. The place was empty. After we'd gotten settled in and Jane's eyes stopped spiraling, I understood why she wanted to stay; the inn was spotless, tastefully furnished with antiques, and comfortable. I suggested we talk to Ed about dinner options. Maybe we could ride into town. Back in the lounge, Ed looked up from his laptop. "Say, is either one of you a computer genius?"

"Maybe," I said. "What's the situation?"

Ed was having a website done for his antiques business and had a few technical questions to which I supplied the answers with ease. When I'd finished talking it was like I'd sprouted a crown and scepter, for Ed's attitude toward us changed from polite tolerance to open worship. He moved us to his best room, and then held out a set of car keys. "You guys must be hungry. Take my truck into town. There're a couple of good places; I can draw you a map. What would you like for breakfast?" Ed was eager to please.

The next day we stayed put and I went to work with his laptop. Ed needed some software upgrades and a few changes to his website. My left brain hummed to life again after a month of near-idleness. I enjoyed getting back into problem-solving mode in the familiar world of bits and bytes, where everything added up neatly and followed the rules. It felt like a vacation. I was in nerd-vana, thrilled that my skills had a practical use on this journey, and within an hour or so completed all he'd asked. Ed looked at me in awe, as if I'd parted the Red Sea. "You guys are not paying for this stay. You saved me at least $400 in consulting fees the guys out here would charge." I did a double-take at this. "I want to offer you another night on the house."

Our eyebrows shot up in tandem. "Really?" Jane said. "Fantastic," I said.

"My wife Margaret is fishing up at our cabin in the Bearpaw Mountains today. I'm going up there this afternoon. Do you want to come along? You can go canoeing on the lake." We'd grown to like Ed during our fifteen-hour acquaintance, and it seemed to be mutual. He kidded us, saying that we must be some kind of royalty, traveling incognito, with hidden secret service agents following us which he always pretended to look out for.

"We would love that," Jane, breathless, a hint of a tear in her eye, answered for us. Canoeing up in Maine was a favorite pastime of hers, and she had been wondering how to get in some canoeing this summer. A few hours later we paddled along placid lake water that glittered in the summer sun, immersed in the music of the red-wing blackbirds' conk-a-ree call, the cicadas' drone, the dragonflies' whirr. As on the bicycle, I rode in front and Jane in back. But she now steered the canoe while I only had to paddle and enjoy the ride. We watched a beaver snort past as he pushed a freshly-hewn log toward his new lodge.

"The beaver is the builder," Jane said. "The builder of the home."

In the evening back at the cabin Ed grilled up hot dogs and hamburgers while Margaret lit a campfire and poured wine, and we talked and laughed together into the night, easily, like old friends catching up.

Jane didn't care about making a century. Instead, she led us to this experience. Left up to me, that night we would have been holed up in some generic motel in Havre, eating out of cardboard take-out boxes as we celebrated our century alone, unaware of what might have been. How many other good times, how many friendships had I missed over the years? Riding that century only fed my craving for nice round numbers, for little accomplishments to make me feel good about myself. I had security in one hundred miles because I lived in the world of numbers, neat structures and correct answers. Jane saw the world differently and I was drawn to her because she possessed something I lacked. Where I had information, she had insight. Where I calculated, she intuited. Where I analyzed, she felt. In her mind, ninety-six miles was good enough, and having a clean bathroom and a nice place to stay mattered more than those extra four miles. Only after she got us in the door could my skills enhance the experience. We complemented each other, filled in the gaps we had as individuals to form a whole stronger than its parts, just as we rode stronger in tandem than separately.

15 THE PRAIRIE

The next morning there was talk of staying all week, Jane working the antique store while Ed lined up other consulting gigs for me. Appealing as this was, we realized it was time to let go and follow that road. That road, however, had other ideas. The winds had shifted to due west at twenty miles per hour, straight into our faces. In a car, wind is negligible. You gain or lose a couple of mpg depending on its direction but otherwise don't notice it much. When cycling, however, wind direction can mean the difference between a day of gut-wrenching hard labor to eke out twenty miles, or an easy afternoon's jaunt to breeze over eighty. Wind is your staunchest ally or your most intractable foe. Hills are neutral. They don't change on you. If they go up, they come down again. But the wind has no such obligation to ever blow in your favor. You're at its mercy.

We strained an hour at the pedals, thighs and lungs burning, to go six miles. We stopped at the bike shop in Havre for a new chain and cogs, having worn out the original parts after a thousand miles. The shop, empty all morning, suddenly got extremely busy and was staffed by the world's slowest mechanic. Two hours later found us back in the howling gale that bent the prairie grasses horizontal. We decided to stop fighting the elements in Chinook, after a mere twenty-nine miles. Chinook is also where Nez Perce Chief Joseph decided to stop fighting the US government, an unstoppable force of another kind, declaring: "From where the sun now stands, I will fight no more, forever."

That evening, our motel phone rang. We looked at each other with question marks over our heads. "Who can that be?" I wondered. "Nobody knows we're here." I picked it up. "Hello?"

"This is the Chinook Police Department," a man's voice said. "We have a report that you have an unmarried woman staying in the room with you." I was dumbfounded for a moment. Did Montana have some weird Puritan laws we didn't know about? Then the light went on.

"Ha, ha, that's a good one, Ed. You had me going for a minute, there." Ed Hencz laughed at the other end. During our stay he had pretended to be shocked that Jane and I were not married and shared a room. His real reason for calling was to tell us that a four-day storm was moving in, and that we could come back to Havre and work for food and lodging if we wanted. We were sorely tempted once again, but Jane and I agreed that it would not do to go backwards, to try to recapture a moment in time that was unique and sublime and also complete. The unknown still had a strong pull on us. And we had to be home by August 1.

The storm moved in the next day as we moved out. Rain soon joined the headwinds and in no time worked its way through every layer of clothing, then seemed to penetrate skin and muscle to chill the bones. Maybe the gods were flicking us back to Havre, but we didn't give in. We pushed, ground and slogged east. Visibility diminished to nothing and on the narrow road a semi-truck rumbled past, close enough to reach out and touch, and its wheels launched a puddle that crashed over and soaked our lower halves. We eked out two dozen or so miles and came to ground in Harlem, hard by the Fort Belknap Indian Reservation, all that remains of the vast ancestral territory of the Blackfeet and Nakoda. I had always wanted to see real cowboys and Indians. After checking into the motel, we wandered down South Main Street on foot. We followed a powerful aroma, a mixture of roasted garlic, bubbling cheeses and pungent oregano to "The Hitching Post," a pizza place with a rough-hewn log façade. And here they were: Indian cowboys, complete with braids, ten-gallon hats, kerchiefs and boots. Back home in Massachusetts those outfits would work for Halloween only. Out here, our Gore-Tex and Spandex were the outlandish get-ups.

Fortunately the four-day storm only lasted two days, but it felt like most of the rain landed on us, especially while we fixed three flat tires on the second day. We spent two evenings decorating motel rooms with every piece of our clothing, sleeping bags and maps. We even spread out dollar bills to dry overnight. Over time, the waterproof trash bags in which we had packed our clothes became perforated with innumerable tiny holes and were now both breathable and leaky.

Being east-coasters, we had never seen the prairie before this journey. On the prairie there is earth and sky and precious little else. Cycling through the Montana prairie is a sailing voyage across a grass sea. Here and there are little islands with a few trees huddled next to a building, and every fifty miles or so lie larger islands; towns where you can come ashore, tie up, and re-provision.

The world has many overpopulated places; Montana is not one of them. Montana is like a very spread out small town. Everyone we met seemed to know everyone else we met. Our road, US 2, was locally known as the *Hi-Line*, and the only road connecting the northern towns. We could not get lost. After our lunch stop one day, a familiar vehicle approached from the east. Ed Hencz from Havre was returning from an antique auction. We had met the wife of the auctioneer for that auction the previous evening. From our progress Ed could see that we were serious about heading east, so we said our farewells again. We made plans for me to do some more work for him remotely after I got home.

My former job had sent me on this journey; now I had my first freelancing client.

Later that day, we stopped for our afternoon refueling and met Gary, a long-haul trucker from California. In his late fifties, Gary was thin and wiry, taut like a coiled spring, but with soulful brown eyes that often gazed off into the distance. His radio handle was *Moonshadow*. He'd been driving since 1960 and logged 3,600 miles in a typical week; miles that would take us three months to cover. He invited us to sit in his '95 Kenworth cab, four years old and painted cherry-red, which already had 700,000 miles on it. He told us many stories from the road, but one in particular stayed with us.

"A few years back, I was on the freeway, driving in the right lane just behind another rig. We were going to pull off at the exit." Gary swallowed hard. "Well, we got up to the on-ramp for the exit, and this little Honda, a woman driving with kids in the back…it's moving fast; and just swerves out onto the freeway! No signals, no looking. It went right underneath that rig in front of me, just ahead of the rear wheels. Christ, what a god-awful mess. The car was crushed, no survivors. At least it was quick for them. But that trucker? I just remember him kneeling in the road, screaming, pounding his fists into the pavement. He never drove again."

We were all silent. Being a problem-solver, my mind raced, trying to come up with an appropriate response. I wanted to fix it somehow, or give it some meaning, but I found nothing to say. Gary sighed, his features relaxing. Sharing this story seemed to unburden him somehow. All we had to do was listen. Gary never mentioned a family or a home, and with him on the road something like ten hours a day for six days a week, I didn't see how that was possible. I found Jane's hand next to mine on the cab's passenger seat and gave a little squeeze, which she returned.

Back in Idaho Tom Youtsey said to me, "Everyone you meet can teach you something." At home we see truckers all the time on the freeway, but we'd never met one before, never heard stories from the road, or even thought about the lives they lead.

16 THE ROUTINE

We pedaled 400 miles of ruler-straight and railroad-level strip of Montana asphalt known as the Hi-Line, making no turns, seeing not much more than tall grass and big, endless blue sky sometimes clear and pristine, other times banded with high feathery cirrus or crowded with low puffy cumulus clouds. The towns, outposts really, seemed to differ only in name. Each one was made in similar pattern: motel, bar, bank branch, diner, post office, traffic light, church, general store, gas station, and grocery huddled close to the Hi-Line like wagons circled against attack. In the distance off to the left or right stood a couple of grain silos; the only tall structures, and the odd ranch house on its own lonely road.

"Imagine those early settlers, driving across this prairie in wagons, making ten or fifteen miles a day, hostile Indians around," I said. "Where would they get water?" Jane and I leaned on the wooden railing in front of *OB's Bar*, a watering hole in the truest sense, sipping Gatorade.

"I can't imagine," Jane said. "This terrain hasn't changed for a week. I feel like we were here yesterday, and the day before."

"We're in the Twilight Zone, doomed to live the same day forever" I said, more to myself, since Jane didn't watch television.

"And we have it easy," she continued. "We have a road, towns every so often, and nobody coming after us. I love the wide open spaces, the fresh air and so much sky to look at."

"Big Sky is right. The space. Nobody crowding you. Like the Scottish Highlands."

"A lot flatter, but yeah, that kind of freedom. I know I grumble sometimes about getting up in the morning? But once I get on the bike, it's freedom."

"And meditative," I said. "We don't need maps, there's no traffic, no way to get lost. Nothing to do but keep going forward. I can shut my brain off, think about nothing. But those settlers must have wondered if this land would ever end. Each day, seeming no further along than the day before. They must have felt like Sisyphus or Tantalus or one of those guys who don't get anywhere."

"Well we're definitely getting somewhere," Jane said. "You can't see the Rockies anymore."

Not every day on the road was filled with adventure, drama or enlightenment. Some days were routine: we woke up, washed, dressed, got some breakfast and went to work, which was riding the bike. The morning's activities depended on where we had spent the night.

At motels we simply packed up and left. They were impersonal places, usually clean and inexpensive. We'd go for a motel to get out of the weather, if no other option presented itself, or if we wanted some privacy.

At a bed and breakfast we felt obliged to socialize with the host or other guests over breakfast before leaving. We (Jane, really) always chose the best ones; the cleanest and most elegant. Due to the expense and our guilty feelings of indulgence, we limited ourselves to no more than one per week, unless I could work for the owner and we stayed for free.

We camped whenever dry weather and a decent campsite coincided. We weren't brave or cheap enough to simply pitch our tent in the wilderness. We loved being under the stars, out in nature, and feeling really self-sufficient, but it meant more work. We'd have to find and prepare our own breakfast, in addition to taking down the tent and packing up the camping gear. And its appeal wore thin in a chilling downpour.

If we stayed at a total stranger's house, we socialized a bit longer with our hosts; for instead of exchanging money we would exchange stories and information, like in olden days. This was the rarest and therefore the favorite option, and always took us by surprise.

After seating ourselves in our "office chairs," we'd do about twenty miles before second breakfast, then perhaps another thirty before lunch. We'd get the bulk of the day's ride done in the morning. Over lunch we'd study maps and agree on a destination for the day. If we were headed somewhere historic with a museum, or with natural beauty like a national park, we'd want to get there early enough to take in some sights; otherwise we'd plan to arrive in time for dinner. About once a week we'd plan a rest day in an area of interest, like we did in Glacier, and again at Ed and Margaret's.

We each had jobs to do. In addition to driving, I was chief mechanic, navigator and scribe. I kept the maps in order and journaled the day's events in my tiny computer. In addition to stoking, Jane was in charge of packing and parking. We kept most of our gear in the large duffel bag that sat on the B.O.B. trailer. When arriving at our destination, the bag exploded, disgorging its contents in every direction. Jane, with the organizational genius of a stone-mason, would fit it all back in every day. Since our tandem bike with trailer was about twelve feet long, articulated and weighed over one hundred pounds, no kickstand made could hold it upright. But Jane would always find the perfect solid object to lean it against every time we stopped.

It was a simple life. We washed clothes in the sink, bought groceries, mailed home packets of souvenirs, gifts, rolls of film or gear we no longer needed. We became attuned to the weather and the terrain. We traveled slowly enough to notice the colors and scents of wildflowers by the road, the running speeds of various dog breeds, the dress and demeanor of each place's inhabitants, and the aromas of their dinners cooking. We rode silently enough to hear the twittering chickadees, the robins' chirrup, the hawks' screech, the whoosh of wind in the trees and the rumblings of distant thunder.

Our lives were free of the usual complications and distractions, like jobs, money, news, mail, the internet, vacuuming rugs and cleaning toilets. We seemed to age backwards. Our bodies tanned and became trim and corded with new muscle. We ate constantly but got thinner, enjoyed abundant energy during the day and at night, most nights, fell at once into deep, restorative sleep. We became more trusting and more of one mind. We had little or no conflict, and talked less while on the bike because our thoughts seemed to exchange without words. We often had long periods of silence while riding, lost in private thoughts, or no thoughts at all.

When I was very young and we'd moved into a new house, Mom had named each of the rooms: "Here is the kitchen, in there is the playroom, this is the living room, and that is the dining room." But I'd heard *dying* room. We had a living room and a dying room. My brother and I would play a little game, pushing each other into the dying room, where we'd pretend to sicken and collapse and have to crawl back to the living room so we could keep on living. Now Montana had become my living room.

Sometimes Jane would write songs in her mind and play them in the evening. My mind tried to process all that I experienced, tried to square the new information with my old beliefs, struggled, gave up and finally threw out those old beliefs: the German-accented voices that said I was foolish to quit my job, that I was wasting my time and money, that I should not need help from anyone, and that I should be happy with what I had. Out here on the prairie those lies, those verbal turds, dried up, crumbled to dust and scattered in the wind.

I loved my time in Montana. In the eighteen days it took to cross the state, nearly 700 miles, I'd discovered some strengths, and weakness. I craved outside approval and feared my own vulnerability because I believed others would think less of me. I got what I resisted. My worst fears were realized when the parasites laid me low. I had to purge those toxic old beliefs, turn myself outward so Montana could show me a new way; a way that didn't isolate.

I have to admit Jane was teaching me how to do this ride differently. I saw how she used her intuition, connected with others and found experiences that would have eluded me. She had the confidence to ask for help instead of being afraid of what others might think. This is the difference between arrogance and confidence: confidence is not afraid.

All my life I'd been proud of what I could do on my own. I'd never allowed others in, accepted their help and offered my own, and this had kept my world small, my connections few, and my achievements modest. No man is an island, they say. I would build some bridges; or at least start a regular ferry service with my fellow humans.

On June 8 we rode into the morning sun one last time in Big Sky country. That afternoon we crossed the state line into North Dakota, where as usual, everything changed.

NORTH DAKOTA

North Dakota passed a bill in 1987 making English the official state language.

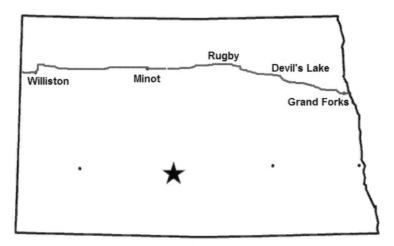

17 WILD MEN

Scotland, 899 AD: *Midsummer approached. The Kingdom of Alba, already heavily settled by Norse, was a land of rich soil and verdant fields, peaceful villages, sheep pastures, and orchards of trees laden with swelling fruits. They could have made a home there, but Eyvind was determined to go farther south, to see for himself the lands of endless summer. Between Alba and Skíð lay Dal Riata, a remnant of unexplored land that still held pockets of Pictish people; dark-skinned natives who hated the Danes, with whom they had fought bitterly a generation ago. The Earl Mac Donel had warned them to avoid these dangerous, "godless" savages.*

They had stopped on a path that ran through a birch wood. Eyvind tended the horse. A twig snapped, followed by a wild flapping of wings. They whirled around in time to see the grouse tumble to the ground. And from the trees they came, a dozen of them, arrows on strings: wild men, painted blue. They stared at the travelers for a long minute.

"Danes. Or, friends of Danes." Their leader, an old man past forty, spoke Danish. "You trespass with weapons. Give me a reason not to kill you now."

"Kill him! Kill the leader! The rest will flee. Use your sword, coward! Those savages will kill you and your whore!" Eyvind looked up. There was Mother's ghost, in a tree, berating him.

"Be gone!" Eyvind shouted at it. The hunters bent their bows, arrows aimed at the pair.

"Wait," Hild said. "We are no Danes. We're Norse travelers. On our way to Skíð." No response. Eyvind tried. "I am Eyvind, son of Haakon. We…" At this the hunters jabbered to one another, repeating the name Haakon. Their leader raised a hand for silence. He strode forward and looked hard into Eyvind's

face, then gazed down to Eyvind's sword hilt.

"Haakon...White-Beard? Can it be?" He barked an order. His hunters lowered their bows. "I am Broichan, Chief." He pointed at Eyvind. "You have the look of Haakon White-Beard, and the sword you carry is known to me. If you are his kin, you can live." He grinned, clapping Eyvind on the shoulder, then frowned, "Are you lost?"

Eyvind and Hild nodded, too stunned for speech. The hunters shouldered their bows and advanced to examine the strange foreigners, their horse and equipment.

"We have luck to find you, son of Haakon," Broichan continued. "Your father was friend of my people. Danes, we kill. Slowly." The hunters growled their approval at this.

Broichan glanced up at the trees. "You see spirits?"

"Only one," Hild said.

"My dead mother," Eyvind said. "She haunts me."

"Your father spoke of that one. I am sorry. This mother-spirit clings to you. You must cut her from you."

Buford, North Dakota, June 1999: Although state lines are arbitrary boundaries, drawn on maps by humans, we always felt a subtle shift when crossing them: the road surface, the topography, even the weather seemed to change. Soon after we passed the huge painted sign that read *North Dakota – Welcome to the West Region*, the flat sea of prairie grass vanished, along with the tumbleweeds. Now the ground undulated gently. Lines of cottonwood and hackberry trees formed windbreaks around corn, soybean and sunflower fields, and in the distance lay grassy hills crested by jagged grey rock. Our last three days in Montana had been sunny, and that morning had promised another dry day, but not in North Dakota. We crossed the state line and tripped a dimmer switch on the sun. Black clouds swept down from the north as if eager to greet us.

"Do you smell that rain?" called Jane

"I can feel it," I said. "We'd better get indoors." A low, cedar-sided bar and casino appeared to be the only structure in sight. We pulled over, parked under the roof's eave and ducked inside. Well-lit but quiet as a church, a brassy square island of bar dominated the single large room. Within the bar, a young blond woman looked up from a paperback. A couple of empty card tables topped with green baize stood on one side, along with an unlit pool table, while mutely flashing slot machines winked at me from the opposite wall. We had the place to ourselves.

Minutes later, rain crashed down, boiling in the road while I fed quarters into a promising slot. They had the old heavy mechanical kind, not the new computerized ones. The handle made a smooth descent, sending the wheels spinning audibly on their greased bearings. One by one they clicked into place: orange, cherry, bar. Zilch. But that sound and anticipation was worth 25 cents. I was mad with desire to open up the machine and take it apart; see how it worked, and see where it kept its payload.

Jane engaged the barmaid, Sharon, in conversation, finding out about road construction ahead. Sharon advised us to divert south towards the Missouri Breaks.

"Missouri?" I feigned ignorance. "How'd we end up in Missouri? I thought this was North Dakota." The Missouri River meanders through six states before joining the Mississippi in St. Louis.

"Do you need more quarters?" Sharon said, well-accustomed to ignorance, whether real or pretend.

I let go of the handle, which sprang to attention, wiped my palms and turned away from the machine. "No thanks, I'm cool."

The Missouri Breaks is a series of badland areas characterized by rock outcroppings, steep bluffs and grassy plains adjacent to the upper Missouri River. Heading down one of those steep bluffs we hit forty-six mph, a new top speed. I smiled as we hurtled downwards, wind tugging at my cheeks, heart quickened at the thought of breaking the posted speed limit of 40. I doubted that Jane was enjoying the same rush, but didn't dare turn around to see. Back on the level, the shadow of Thor's hammer blotted out the sun. The Thunder God saw us and drove his stallion forward. The rain we didn't worry about, we'd gotten drenched enough times to take that in stride. But being out in the open, the tallest object around, riding a large hunk of metal in a thunderstorm worried us plenty. A pale line of sickly yellow swallowed up the sky behind us. "Pedal fast!" Jane screamed. "Lightning! We need cover!"

"I've got the pedal to the floor!" I yelled back, then checked the map I had stuck into the clear pouch of my handlebar bag. "Five miles to Trenton." We were heads-down, flat out at twenty-two mph, but the storm continued to close the gap. Big drops spattered us and the first electric whips lashed the air and shook the sky. Four miles to go. Twelve minutes. We'll never make it. Another lightning bolt sizzled the air, and a heartbeat later the thunderclap hit us like a hammer blow. Just pedal. And look for shelter: a barn, a deep ditch, anything. Keep breathing. Three miles to go. Another flash-boom in quick succession made me jump. The storm was on us. We should leave the bike and find a ditch. Eject! But what's that up ahead? A building! With one last flurry of desperate pedaling, we swooped off the road, skidded to a stop and hauled our bike onto the porch of the Trenton General Store, conveniently located two miles west of Trenton. As we sucked wind and thanked our lucky stars, a weather radio sat on a small table blaring its tinny warnings: *Severe weather alert for the Williston area: A fast-moving front from the west will bring high winds, rain showers with periods of heavy downpours and possible thunderstorms...*

"A narrow escape," said a voice from the doorway. We turned, and there stood a miniature squaw.

"My name is Mutch. In our language it means mischievous." Barely five feet tall and rail-thin, Mutch was a grandmother in the Hidatsa tribe, and also ran the store. Twin steel-grey braids framed cheeks that bulged under the force of her wide grin.

"Too bad," she continued, glancing at the sky. "Another guy on a bike just left for Williston. Thought he'd outrun the storm. He's gonna get wet."

"Or worse. That was terrifying," I said. We went inside.

"What can I get for you today?" said Mutch.

"Hot chocolate, please," Jane said. "Me too," I added.

"Sure thing," said Mutch, starting on the hot chocolates as we climbed onto the stools at the counter. "You don't want to mess with the storms around here. You get hit by lightning, that's it. Although, I know of one person who got hit and didn't get killed. One time there were three guys just out there by the road where you were, using pitchforks to clear the drains. A big storm rolled in fast, just like this one, and BANG – lightning knocked them all over. Well one guy, he's got a pitchfork driven right into his middle. Right here," she indicated just below her ribcage.

"Skewered?" I said. "No way!"

"Yah, it's true. The other two, they know enough not to try to pull it out. They laid him in their truck and took him to the hospital." She placed the two steaming mugs in front of us.

"What happened to him? He lived through that?" Jane asked, warming her hands on her mug.

"Oh, he survived all right," said Mutch. "He was a lucky one, though."

"Thanks, Mutch," we said together, sipping our chocolate and wondering if our luck would hold today. The storm passed and we continued on to Williston, finding no signs of the other cyclist.

Back in Montana, Ed Hencz warned us. "Under no circumstances," he said, "should you ever spend the night within a reservation. There's a lot of poverty and drug use. You would not be safe." We had grown to trust Ed, and kept his advice in mind as we traveled in eastern Montana and now North Dakota. I had scant knowledge of Native Americans: a grade school field trip to Plimouth Plantation where knowledgeable Wampanoag natives cheerfully helped re-enacted European settlers; the stereotyped painted and grunting savages from Hollywood westerns; the required American history unit on westward expansion that didn't go into detail about who already lived on the land the US government parceled off. More recently, the exhibits in the Blaine County Museum in Montana told us of the pursuit by the US Army of 800 Nez Perce who refused to resettle to their designated reservation in 1877. I guess we invaded them, destroyed their culture and pushed them off their land. That was all a long time ago. How did the red man feel about the white man today? I had no idea.

The day we made it to Minot, a sizable city in the northwestern part of the state, the wind howled and the rain spat on and off. The road meandered among undulating hills covered with waist-high grass, spasmodically bending low in the gusting crosswinds. As we struggled to keep from being blown over, a metallic *thunk* resounded from the rear wheel as an overstressed spoke snapped in two. We stopped and I did what I could with a spoke wrench, using it to even out the extra load on the decapitated spoke's neighbors. The wheel wobbled but was still rideable.

We hadn't gone far when the rear tire played a different note: *hisssssss*. This was going to be one of those days. I unhitched the trailer and dug around for the spare inner tube as a well-used pickup truck pulled over ahead of us. Two huge Native American men got out; a good five hundred pounds' worth. They looked like brothers: long black tresses bound into ponytails, faces brown and round, thick necks and heavy limbs. They were built like wrestlers far beyond my weight-class.

Jane didn't seem worried; just stood there smiling. She loved Native American culture, was fond of silver and turquoise jewelry and hung a dream-catcher over her bed. She had learned the spiritual practices of the Pacific Northwest Salish and other ancient tribal cultures from her spiritual teachers. But I had no information. Indians were scarce in Boston. Reservations were what Jane made for dinner when I was tired of cooking. We were at the mercy of two very large specimens of the most unpredictable and destructive life form on the planet: *homo sapiens*. Chivalry commanded me to edge in front of Jane. They were young, perhaps in their early twenties. As they approached I observed their open and guileless faces, bet on Jane's intuition and finally relaxed as well. They were boys. Very big boys. They stopped at a respectful distance, twenty feet from us.

"You need a ride?" one of them asked in a voice surprisingly soft given his size. "We're going to Minot for some building supplies."

"Minot? Oh. Yeah! Sure, Minot," I said, louder than necessary. "That's where we're going, too. Minot! Why not? Thanks!" They advanced and reached for the bike as my reflexes made me jump back. "It's been one of those days," I said, with an awkward and unnecessary attempt to help them load our gear into the truck bed. One of them picked up the seventy-pound trailer with one hand like it was a lunchbox. We squeezed into the middle of the cab, firmly wedged between the two big, warm bodies. Far from feeling threatened, I felt comforted, a child engulfed in a protective fleshy embrace.

Jane looked from one to the other. "Are you brothers?"

The driver—we never did get their names—grinned, teeth dazzling white against ochre skin. "White way, we're cousins, but Indian way, all cousins and mother's side uncles are brothers."

"And all father's side uncles are fathers, and all mother's side aunts are mothers," added his cousin.

"So you ARE brothers," Jane said.

"Indian way, yes," said our driver. "We're Hidatsa. From the rez."

I tried to imagine having that many mothers and fathers and I was envious. I'd never met half of my real aunts, uncles and cousins, mostly scattered across Germany, since Mom was one of ten and Dad was an only child. I had a brother in New Hampshire, another in Maryland, and a sister in London. My parents were in Massachusetts, but they'd moved from there once already, when I was still in college, and were liable to move again at any time. Moving was their solution to difficult problems.

Marblehead, MA 1984: "You're moving... to a beach?" I said.

"Virginia Beach," Mom said. "It's where Pat Robertson is. We got to see them do the 'Seven Hundred Club'. It's so nice and warm there. Ja, we've had enough of these cold winters."

"And wait until you see that beach!" Dad added. "White sand, warm ocean, lots of pretty girls. Golfing year-round, too. I'm fed up with Taxachusetts."

"Uh, okay," I said. "What about our house?"

"Sell it, of course," Mom said. "We can make a lot of money on it, and houses are cheap down there. Why do you think we built it, eh? To make money. That's how you get rich."

"I still have one more year of school, though," I said. "All my stuff..."

"We'll move in the summer, so you can help us," Mom said. "You can drive the big truck; that'll be fun for you. And we'll have a big yard sale, ja? You can get rid of all that junk and make some money."

"I have to get away from GE," Dad said. He looked downtrodden. At 62 he retired early, looking like he wouldn't last another year.

Such is the lot of the discontented wanderer. We're nomads. We don't put down roots. We detach and roll with the wind like human tumbleweeds. We have no tribe.

Although the brothers had a tribe, they had done some wandering of their own, riding the rails. "Safety is the most important thing," said our driver. "Those freight cars can crush you and nobody would notice. You never walk on the rails, or cross under cars."

"You wear dark clothes so the Bull don't see you," said his cousin. "The Bull, that's the railroad cop. Pack light, and dress in layers. You never know if you're gonna be stuck out in an open gondola all night. You talk to the yard crews. They know which trains are leaving when, and can help you get a catch-out."

"A catch out? Like, literally catch a freight train?" I said.

"Yep," said his cousin. "And it ain't easy. Those cars are high off the ground. You gotta pull yourself up. But I was a rail back then. Had me a six-pack." He patted his capacious belly as I tried to imagine the washboard abs buried underneath.

"Now he drinks them six packs," our driver laughed.

They admitted that life on "the Rez" had its challenges. Poverty, gambling and alcoholism were rampant. Generations of government dependency had taken its toll. The young didn't honor the ways of the ancestors, didn't keep the language alive; they wanted the better life that seemed to be everywhere else. I could relate.

They knew the best bike shop in Minot and got us there fifteen minutes before closing. They were gone almost before we could thank them, expecting nothing more from us.

On a bicycle, out in the elements, we were vulnerable. And approachable. I would never think to walk up to a car, tap the window and start a conversation, yet people everywhere we went seemed comfortable walking up to us to ask questions, offer assistance, or invite us into their homes. It is a paradox of technology: our low-tech method of transportation invited connection because people would think we were poor, lost or hungry. And quite often they were right.

18 CENTER OF NORTH AMERICA

The fifteen foot obelisk was made of rounded river rock masonry and topped with a shiny steel pinhead the size of a basketball. Jane read the bronze plaque set into it: "Geographical Center of North America - Rugby, ND." In 1931 a Department of the Interior geological survey determined that if the continent of North America were an enormous piece of cardboard, you could poke a hole in this spot, tie a string onto it, pick it up, and it would balance: the geometric center-of-gravity of a planar shape described by the continent. It's an utterly useless piece of information that nonetheless makes Rugby unique. No other place on earth can make the same claim...unless you include Central America as part of the continent, as most atlases do. Then somebody in South Dakota could raise their own phallic symbol. Useless or not, the obelisk shook me.

"Holey shirt, we're at the halfway point!" I said. We had covered a bit over 1,500 miles by then and were not quite to the middle of June. Still, the startling realization that our journey was nearly half-over struck like Big Ben: *we might actually finish this ride.* I thought of being home again. What would happen then? I had gotten used to this life; no, I had come to love it. I didn't want to stop, even if we ran out of land. What if we kept going? From Boston, to Europe, Asia, around the world...a bigger Big One! I didn't want to go back to that small world I'd been living in. I'd have to trust that by the end of the ride we'd have clarity around what happened next. Today, I had no clue.

At the bike shop in Minot, we'd seen a shipping box filled with the gear of a touring cyclist. When I asked about it the mechanic said it belonged to a guy who was doing the same ride we were, but had given up and was going home. I felt bad for him and wondered why he had quit. Had he gotten sick? Lonely? Tired of the headwinds and rain? Had he run out of money? Maybe it was the guy who had gotten drenched in Williston. We never found out. Had I done this ride alone, it could have been me.

Still following the Hi-Line, we passed into eastern North Dakota, an area dominated by Devil's Lake. The land was exceptionally wet and swampy, with marshlands enclosed by low wire fences. Who fences in marshland? Then we discovered these were fields, now underwater after weeks of drenching rains. A local told us that eight tornadoes had touched down the week before. Had we not been behind schedule, we might have gotten sucked up and blown into Oz. Those parasites did us another favor.

Devil's Lake is the largest body of water in North Dakota and getting larger all the time. The lake has no natural outlet and has quadrupled in size since the early 1990s, swallowing up nearby homes and land. The Sioux originally called it by a name that means "Bad Spirit Lake" due to the high salinity (bad to drink) and the frequent mirages (spirits) seen across the lake. The white settlers interpreted this name as *Devil's* Lake, which now seemed to be living up to White Man's label: expanding, consuming and ever-hungry. The world is what you think it is. We quickened pace with an unspoken, mutual desire to get to higher ground.

Those last few days in North Dakota we pushed hard, making good use of favorable tailwinds, partly to make up for lost time, partly because I wanted my birthday to be a special day at the midpoint of our journey. We figured Grand Forks, being the third largest city in North Dakota (although still smaller than Newton, MA), would give us the greatest number of options. The day before my birthday we needed to cover 90-plus miles to make it to Grand Forks. Of course, now that I was attached to getting there, obstacles appeared left and right. As we churned along the rain slicked road, my eyes squinting into the wind-driven spray, an invisible hand shoved us sideways, towards the ditch. I fought for control as a behemoth RV passed by, giving not an inch, as if we didn't exist.

"Mother-freaking dingleberry [9]!" My mouth won the race with my brain this time. In answer, the sickening thunk of another broken spoke followed by the rear end of our machine gyrating like an overloaded washer. I braked to a halt and met Jane's cold stare of disapproval at my potty-mouth and middle finger I had flipped at the RV driver.

"Sorry. I couldn't help it. That creep could've moved over." I looked at the wheel. "Jeez, karma works fast here."

Discovering I had no more spare spokes, I got the oblong wheel somewhat round again with my spoke wrench and we limped along, hoping no more spokes would let go. After sixty miles another storm caught up with us. Storms in North Dakota are intense, but seldom last long. We found a roadside picnic shelter and waited under it, digging out the last of our provisions, peanut butter and crackers.

---

[9] The actual language used was a bit stronger, but you get the idea.

Here we met Robert, a real live drifter, who would have been called a *hobo* in the old days. He seemed to materialize out of the background scrub and trees. Tattered, faded clothes hung on him like he'd lost a lot of weight since they were new. His weathered face and hands matched the dull earthy tones of browns and grays he wore. Every part of him blended with the surroundings like camouflage, except for his eyes. Robert had supremely piercing sky-blue eyes; eyes that had seen a lot of hard living; eyes that seemed to miss nothing. He had a feral quality about him; he approached us warily, a hungry cat, padding silent as he gauged our body language. Would we send him away, or offer a handout? Robert saw we had food. And we were approachable.

Back home, I would have told Robert to get lost. I disliked beggars. I thought them weak, irresponsible, lazy, without dignity; parasites who lived off the labor of others. I'd earned my own money from age six and always had some kind of job ever since. Allowance was something the soft, pampered kids got. If I wanted something, I worked for it and saved up. But now, after being helped by so many strangers I could not repay, and after looking into his eyes, like a reformed Scrooge, my heart swelled with the spirit of generosity.

Robert told us he was walking to Idaho. He had been on the road long enough for his body to become highly resilient. He could drink any water, eat anything he found on the ground and not get sick [10]. Although we hadn't eaten much that day, we gave all our food to Robert. He wolfed it down, eyes darting furtively like searchlights always on alert, then without another sound melted back into the landscape. We never found out how he became a drifter, or what awaited him in Idaho. His wasn't an easy road, whether he'd chosen it or not. But he survived.

We ended the day in Grand Forks, after 97 miles, close enough to a century. On the way, another storm caught and drenched us. I got us lost trying to find the fancy B&B I wanted, called *511 Reeves*. My shoes squelched, my legs wobbled, my head spun from low glucose. I was ready to strangle someone when the curtains of rain parted, revealing a huge double rainbow, aglow in late afternoon sun. I remembered the one we'd seen at the start of our journey; this one marked its midpoint. Jane noted my condition and found a pay phone at a gas station. Within minutes she had better directions from Bill and Wanda, the innkeepers, and before the sun set we were showered, dried, dressed and walking to dinner.

During our after-dinner stroll, we came to a street where every house was boarded up and abandoned. On the next street it was the same. A

---

[10] Proof of my theory: too much sanitation weakens us. We have to inoculate ourselves with small doses of filth every now and then, so we're ready when civilization collapses.

whole neighborhood appeared to have been condemned. What had happened here? A plague? Back at the inn we asked Wanda about it and heard the story of the great disaster two years earlier, when the Red River rose twenty-five feet above flood stage. That neighborhood and others still awaited demolition. Ironically, fire destroyed a large section of downtown because the water was too deep for the fire engines to reach it. Fire and flood: Grand Forks had them both at once. I wondered where all the people went. To higher ground, I suppose.

That night, in the inn's bird-themed "Audubon Room," sprawled on the surface of a bed large enough to land a helicopter, high luxury after many nights in our coffin-sized tent, I thought about the Hidatsa brothers and Robert the Drifter, our "Wild Men" of North Dakota.

"Jane, when those Indian brothers got out of their truck, you didn't seem worried."

"No, I wasn't. Were you?" Jane was still awake, but fading.

"Sure I was. They could've been anybody, you know? And what Ed said about reservations, so, yeah I was nervous. But you're usually the skittish one. I was surprised how you just went with it."

"I guess I can sense people's intentions. I could see they were genuine right away."

"You were right. We didn't even get their names. They didn't want anything from us. Now, that drifter, Robert? He didn't scare me at all. I wanted to hear his stories."

"Interesting," Jane said. "I was so hoping he wouldn't come up to us. I didn't want to be around all that pain; that loneliness."

"Funny, that didn't bother me," I said. "I kind of admired him. He was a real survivor."

"I'll never forget those eyes," Jane said, as her own closed. "The depth and clarity. Like gazing into another universe."

Robert didn't ask for our names either, but he wanted our food. So who was I: Brother or Drifter? What did I need from others? I envied the Hidatsa brothers' close bond with each other, their sense of community and connection to place, while Robert filled me with sympathy because he was alone. I understood his independence, opportunism and his need to keep moving. I drifted too, not just literally from place to place but most everywhere in my life. In my career I'd hold out in a job only until I could no longer tolerate the exploitation, the boredom, or both. Yet I kept searching, hoping the next one would capture my imagination and feed my passion. Friendships with other guys were difficult. I had lots of acquaintances, but nothing approaching brotherhood, even with my actual brothers. Most guys had their jobs, their families, their sports and their beer and that was enough. At the moment, Jane was my best friend.

All you need is love, sang the Beatles, although I doubted that. Love is essential, but I also needed belonging, and a sense of purpose beyond making myself comfortable while waiting for the Grim Reaper. I wanted to know that I didn't waste my life. Perhaps love allowed all those other things to come in. And if I didn't resist it, maybe one day I'd find the place that felt like home; I'd find satisfying, useful work that didn't suck the life out of me; and find those among whom I didn't feel like an outcast. Find my place in the world; my tribe. Though I identified with Bob the Drifter, I longed to be a Brother.

I awoke to the age of thirty-six the next day; no longer young, not exactly old. Maybe old enough to know myself, and with enough time left to BE myself.

A warm late spring breeze fluttered the gauzy bedroom curtains, sunlight poured through the window and splashed onto the bed as a flock of robins chattered outside. The little table for two downstairs was set with a gourmet breakfast that included lefsa; a Norwegian flatbread; and Swedish pancakes; homage to the Scandinavian origins of many of the original settlers of North Dakota. Jeffrey from the nearby *Ski and Bike Shop* collected our rear wheel and rebuilt it while we took in the matinee of *Star Wars – Phantom Menace*; us and four other people. He delivered the rebuilt wheel that afternoon.

At a liquor store down the street from the inn, I plunked a couple of cold St. Pauli Girls on the counter.

"Can I see your ID?" the female clerk asked.

I blinked at her, then smiled. This hadn't happened in five years. "Really? Of course you can! Thank you!"

She looked at it, raised her eyebrows and handed it back. Perhaps she checked everyone's ID, but in addition to getting healthier, I was also feeling younger. Pretty good trade for getting poorer.

In the evening we found the best restaurant in town, an Italian place called *Lola's*, and carbo-loaded on twin mountains of pasta infused with garlic, sun-dried tomatoes, and goat cheese; topped by fresh basil leaves and shaved parmesan. Lola's owner stopped by our table to tell us that he'd seen us on the road the day before, and that our desserts were on the house. I didn't even mention my birthday. I was already overwhelmed and by this time getting loud with Chianti.

Beyond our booth, out the window, down a gulley, glistening black in the fading light, swirled the Red River. Minnesota, another state I'd never visited, lay on its opposite bank. The only associations I had with Minnesota were cold winters and Vikings, and I doubted we'd encounter either on this visit.

I was about to make some new associations.

MINNESOTA

In 1898, the Kensington Rune stone was found, entangled in the roots of a seventy-year-old tree, on the farm of Olaf Ohman, near Alexandria, Minnesota. The carvings on the stone allegedly tell of a journey of a band of Vikings through the region in the year 1362.

Many, but not all runeologists and experts in Scandinavian linguistics consider the runestone some kind of elaborate hoax with no discernable motive. Who ever heard of Minnesota Vikings?

19 MIRRORED SHADES

Scotland, 899 AD: *"Why did they call him Haakon White-Beard?" Hild asked. After a day among the natives, she and Eyvind were on their way to Skið, now accompanied by an escort of a dozen hunters. Broichan had insisted, for their safety. The summer sun beat down; humidity plastered damp clothes to their backs.*

"I don't think these people live long enough to have ever seen white hair," Eyvind said. "My father was already old when I was born. He and Broichan's people were allies. They traded for a long time and then when Ivarr Lothbrokson and his sword-Danes came north to plunder, Father sided with these people, brought weapons and men. They fought together until Ivarr went south again. I never knew Father was a great warrior. I always thought he was just a merchant." Eyvind grimaced and shifted his seat. "By the gods, I'll be glad to be back at sea again. I was not made for riding."

"I wonder what they'll call you, my hero husband," Hild said with a laugh. "Eyvind Red-Arse?"

"If my suffering amuses you, then at least it serves a purpose."

"Do you not enjoy this journey? Finally we are warm! Lush fields and thick forests all around us! Is not this the Land of the South that you imagined?"

Eyvind slapped a mosquito on his sweaty neck. "NO! Not this vermin-infested bog! I want to see the turquoise ocean and white sands; the trees like giant flowers; the lands of endless summer."

"Good!" Hild said. "I want to see great cities, built by the Romans. I want statues and paintings and music and places of learning. I want…civilization."

One of the hunters jabbed at Eyvind's arm and pointed ahead. They had rounded a bend in the road and emerged in a grassy clearing. At the bottom of the heather-covered slope lay the sea. And in its midst rose a large, mountainous island. "Skíð," said the hunter.

Bagley, MN, June 1999: BA-BOOM….BA-BOOM….BA-BOOM…

"What's the deal with this road?" I yelled back to Jane. "It feels like riding up a freaking staircase!" We had just entered Minnesota, and we were feeling the shift that happens at state lines in a very tangible way. Regular cracks spanned the road about every thirty feet; miniature chasms heaved open by repeated winter freezes, forming bicycle-sized speed bumps. My butt was kicked every five seconds. My seat had become less comfortable lately, probably due to depletion of the buttock fat that had built up from too much business travel and a sedentary lifestyle. This road brought matters to a head; or a tail, to be exact.

We hadn't seen such flat terrain for a while; farmland lay in every direction, cottages scattered here and there, oak and maple trees stood in little clusters, ponds and small lakes occasionally broke up the green and brown checkerboard land. High steel towers draped with thick power lines flanked us and, with the road, stretched away to the horizon. Fewer pickups and more minivans passed us. We hadn't crossed the Mississippi yet, but clearly we'd left the Wild West behind. This was the Mild East.

Midday we rolled into Bagley, Minnesota, after doing thirty-two miles on a little county road that paralleled Route 2. I had visions of purchasing one of those wide, cushy office-chair bike seats. We still had over 2,000 miles of cycling ahead of us, and I wasn't going to make it without some additional padding. We pedaled through town in five minutes. No bike shop. We pulled over at a manicured city park by a lake shore that also had a campground.

"That place looks nice," I ventured. "We could camp there tonight." Jane had been mostly silent that day, which usually indicated a foul mood, which over the years I'd learned not to try to fix but accept, like the weather. Her storms were beyond my control and passed through soon enough. The morning's ride had been less than pleasant. The truck drivers in Minnesota appeared to delight in seeing how close they could come without hitting us as they passed, unaware that their bulk created an air-wake that shoved us aside anyway. A convoy of five or six flatbeds, all carrying pre-fab houses and "Wide Load" banners seemed to say, *Get off our road, insects. We'll squash you.*

Jane barely gave the park a glance. "We can't stop yet. It's too early. We can do another twenty or thirty, at least. Let's get out of this *Podunk*." She knew as well as I that we were still behind schedule.

I sighed. "You're right. But let's get some food and then find the post office. I want to mail some stuff."

"Idon'tcarewhatever," Jane muttered.

After lunch, we found the tiny post office. Jane waited outside while I took care of the packages. When I came out the door, there he stood: Smokey Bear hat, shiny gold badge, mirrored wrap-around shades, tan shirt, brown trousers, both pressed with sharp vertical creases that seemed to perforate him into thirds. Officer Curt Backer, Minnesota State Patrol, smiled and talked with animation. Jane stood mute, arms folded, jaw set. I approached and introduced myself.

"You know," said Curt, "if you want a place to camp tonight, there's a great park just up the road here. You'll have really nice neighbors who will make you popcorn."

"That's a *really nice* offer," Jane said with tight civility, "but we're planning on going a little farther today, maybe to Bemidji." I thought: *Hmm, popcorn.*

"Great town, Bemidj'," said Curt. "I can tell you how to get to the bike shop there." Jane's arms uncrossed. His shades mirrored our expectant faces. He grinned. "But why don't you just come stay at my house tonight? We love having bikers over."

Yes, yes, yes, I thought. But Jane was on the fence. I'd come to rely on her intuition about where to stay, but also knew that stress could throw her off, make her go numb and insensible. She'd told me so when I'd once suggested we go to Vegas and try out her intuition there. Now she said "Hmmm," as if reconsidering.

Curt persisted. "Clean sheets, a real bed, good food…"

"We would love to!" I said.

"Great," said Curt. "Just follow me. It's not far."

"Part of the adventure?" Jane said, not quite on board, but willing to follow my lead.

"Definitely," I said. We saddled up and followed the patrol car to a white clapboarded ranch-style home that seemed to stand ready for inspection, with a fairway front lawn and the lake as its backyard, where we met his wife Malotte and their two boys, Kyle and Kevin. With military precision, Curt oriented us as we marched through the house. We sensed that this was a well-practiced drill.

"Here's the kitchen, help yourselves to anything." Down a hallway, he opened a door. "Here's the bedroom, Kyle will be moving out for you. Here are some towels." He flung open the last door at the end of the hall, to the garage. "And here's the hot tub."

Jane cheered up a bit in the hot tub, especially when I imitated her crouch from the month before, the lifetime before, in Washington. She recounted her introduction to Officer Backer. "He came up to me wearing those mirrored shades, strutting like he was something special, and I'm thinking: Just get me out of here. Those guys think they can do whatever they want."

"All state troopers wear mirrored shades," I said. "It's required. That's how they intimidate people: you can't see their eyes."

Once we'd dried off and dressed, we followed our noses to the aromatic symphony wafting from the kitchen. Malotte had dinner ready: sautéed chicken and herbed vegetables served with local wild rice that grows unrestrained in the Minnesota marshlands. For Jane that hot meal completed the thawing process started in the hot tub. I have never known Jane to complain about heat, except a lack of it. She exuded the warmth absorbed from the water: complimenting Kurt on their home, thanking Malotte for the meal, and never mentioning the morning's crappy ride. Kyle and Kevin were absent, probably off doing teenage activities, so we had a relaxed, adult dinner with Curt and Malotte.

Curt had taken off his shades and we could now see his eyes in the dim evening light. He must have sensed the question on our faces. "I have to wear them at all times right now. I had a …" he paused as his eyes met Malotte's "… procedure done on my brain a couple of weeks ago. It was kind of complicated. So my eyes are extra-sensitive to bright light. Temporarily; it's not permanent." Jane and I exchanged an abashed glance.

Kurt enjoyed helping people as a state trooper, but sometimes the work was gruesome. Often he'd arrive first on the scene at traffic accidents, and his most painful duty was informing the families about fatalities, which he did in person at their homes. Since Bagley was a town of only a thousand people, he knew most of the victims; sometimes teenagers he had watched grow up. "Those are the hardest," he said. "Nobody wants to see me on their doorstep, even if it's a social call."

Malotte was a social worker devoted to at-risk youth and troubled families in town, counseling abused women and children as she tried to keep the teens from ending up as another sad duty for her husband. "There is such a need around here, and I feel like I'm doing some good," she said. "I worry about Kurt, the dangers of his work. But it's important to him and nobody's better at it."

They were the heroes, the ones worthy of celebrity. We should have been treating them to a dinner.

I heaped more chicken and rice onto my plate while Jane told the grizzly bear story, and I wondered about who my engineering work served. Unknown people in far-off factories, I assumed, but I'd never met them, or knew if what I did mattered to them. I'd gone into my career full of hope, that I'd solve major problems, patent my inventions, feed the hungry, make clever, life-altering gadgets smaller, faster, cheaper. At least make a tangible contribution; be able to point out my creations to others and say, "That's one of mine." Five years on and all my work is buried deep inside jet engine compressor and turbine casings. Maybe on an army base in Kuwait a maintenance sergeant overhauled a T700 turboshaft engine from a

Blackhawk helicopter, nudged his corporal and said, "Man, look at this bolt head design; it's impossible to put it in wrong. That engineer really put some thought into this." Or a Navy S3B pilot on take-off, at full power, looked out at the wing where the TF34's fan is hitting 20,000 RPM and thought, "Thank God the engineer who did the stress analysis on the compressor blades knew his business, or we'd all be dead."

During my time at GE I had two wake-up calls, one at each end of my time there: After two weeks on the job, a senior engineer tells me that once a turbine designer, you'll never do anything else. Five years later an older colleague a year from retirement and ten feet from me collapses in cardiac arrest and dies on the way to the hospital. A month later I depart for a small startup software company, where the employees are young, active, and rarely eat doughnuts. I'm not even making real stuff anymore, but writing programs, ultimately 1s and 0s arranged on magnetic media, virtual stuff for the machines that make the real stuff.

I did that for another eight years, and now I didn't even write the virtual stuff anymore; just put together presentations to help sell what others create. How did I get here? It's like with money; once we carried bags of gold, then we had stacks of paper, then plastic, and now just electrons in a computer. I could no longer put my hands on an actual product of my labors. I made smoke and sold vapor.

We told our stories: of climbing mountain passes, getting parasites, meeting large animals, and of making new friends. Anonymity seemed impossible in a town like Bagley. Kurt and Malotte belonged here and played vital roles in the community, but also sought connection with outsiders, as if it reassured them of a world existing beyond their daily labors of intervening in their neighbors' struggles.

That night, lying in Kyle's bed, we talked about the day's events.

"When I first met Kurt, I couldn't see his eyes," Jane said. "I couldn't see the man behind the shades. I had no idea who he was."

"If the eyes are the windows into the soul..." I mused. "That's why they're called shades; shades for the soul's windows?"

"We wear them when we don't want to be seen," Jane said. "Our inner selves. It's hard to tell what someone is thinking or feeling when you can't see their eyes."

"Yeah," I said. "Because who wears them, typically? Mafia hit men, fighter pilots, CIA agents, movie stars...and state troopers."

"Maybe," Jane said. "But I'm glad we got to know the man behind the mirrored shades. Curt has a big heart."

The next morning Curt and Malotte posed as I snapped their photo in front of the patrol car. "I'm sorry I only have one of these," Curt said, whipping out a folded Minnesota State Police t-shirt emblazoned with the outline of a correctly worn seat belt, "but you two can share it."

"Perfect," I said. "The t-shirts we started this trip with are threadbare. We wear them every day." After hugs and gratitude we set off down the same stretch of road from the day before, in a much better mood.

The practice of welcoming travelers into one's home was not "European" or "West Coast." It seemed to be everywhere.

Except where we lived, of course.

20 BLOOD SUCKING BASTARDS

We slogged through Minnesota in the moist June heat. The state slogan is "Ten Thousand Lakes," no exaggeration, with a hundred times again as many ponds, creeks, ditches, birdbaths, puddles and discarded tires filled with stagnant water; perfect conditions for breeding mosquitoes—trillions of them—and they all loved me. Some would fly kamikaze into eyes, nostrils and ear canals, keeping our hands occupied while their friends lanced into meaty legs and pulsing necks. Minnesotans, via natural selection, seemed to have developed a biological repellent. While camping I did not see any use of bug spray, yet whole families could gather outside in t-shirts and shorts, not slapping at all. I tried that and a dark, living cloud descended and tucked into the blood buffet as I danced the Funky Chicken before retreating indoors.

In Bemidji I picked up a gel seat pad, which felt squishy, like sitting on fresh road kill, but gave instant relief to my aching buttocks. In a tiny village called Remer we tired of the day's splash through the rain and soon found the only lodgings in town. A sign out front read *No Vacancy*. We looked at each other with knowing smirks: *Is that a fact?* Jane went into action, using tactics perfected in Montana—which now didn't work. Even her best forlorn puppy expression failed. There was a big wedding that weekend and they were literally full. We were told to continue on to the next town, Hill City. *We must be heading east*, I thought, to have come to our first "no vacancy" that really meant it. After cycling the requisite seventeen miles we found neither hill nor city, only a small jumble of houses and shops and a motel with vacancies; and luckily screens on the windows.

At home I had a black five-piece Pearl drum kit and cymbals that I loved to bang away on. The repetitive action worked like cycling as a kind of meditation that stilled the mind. The next morning I awoke thinking about home and how little I missed it, except for those drums. I lay in bed as a groove I had worked on before this journey ran through my head when I noticed a faint, rhythmic tapping. Intrigued, I followed the noise to the motel room's window and looked close to see swarms of mosquitoes massing on the screen like a tiny Zulu army, wings beating a screen-rattling war groove. They had followed my scent and knew I'd have to come out sometime. I breathed on the screen and it shook with their blood-excitement. Come and get it.

"I hate mosquitoes," I said. "They take my blood without permission. They spread diseases like malaria, encephalitis and yellow fever." It wasn't hard to put a face on each little bugger: a relative here, a teacher there, coworkers, bosses, whiney customers, bitchy ex-girlfriends, telemarketers, Jehovahs ringing the doorbell at dinnertime; everyone who needed something from me. Each one took a tiny bite of my time and energy, of my life essence, and I allowed it. "They're useless. What would happen if every mosquito disappeared from this planet? Does anything depend on them? You could say the same thing about humans, I suppose."

"They don't bother me too much," Jane said as she rose from the bed with a yawn. "Mosquitoes, I mean."

"That's because they always go for me. I'm sweatier. Do you know it's only the females that bite?"

"They do seem to love you. You could put on some bug deodorant." Most people would have either laughed at this or not understood what she meant. Jane admits to having brief bouts of word mangling, and that it runs in her family, like a private dialect. One time Jane's mom told her she had to take the car to the mechanic because of "square brakes." Jane understood the issue immediately, and replied that it seemed to come out of "left blue." I had been around this long enough to develop an internal decoder ring, so I knew that the car had a warped brake disk, and now she meant bug *repellent*.

"I hate putting toxins on my skin even more; especially when I have to leave them on all day. How about if you bring the bike inside, we'll load it up and then ride out the door?" I personally tracked down and nailed the eighteen little bandits that flew into the motel room with the bike. I cannot bear to hunt or fish, but delight in ending mosquito lives. Perhaps their evil little souls return as something more evolved, something with a more noble purpose, such as an earwig, a maggot or a termite.

Twenty minutes later the door swung open and our fully-loaded rig burst out into the warm, languid morning, pedals churning. A gaggle of the beasts drafted us, biding their time. I tried not to think about getting a flat tire. We ate while moving, easy on a tandem bike because Jane's hands were free to pass pop-tarts forward. The gaggle diminished as its less-determined squadrons peeled off in search of easier prey. We still had a sizable following when it came time for the inevitable pit-stop. We screeched to a halt and jumped off as one, leaned the rig against a tree and ran behind separate bushes. On the way in I noticed a small sign that said "Mississippi River," beside a creek I could have stepped over. Peeling out, we slapped off the hangers-on and I got off with only a dozen or so bites. We didn't stop again until Duluth, where the cool winds from Lake Superior drove the last little bastards off. They tailed us for seventy-eight miles that day, pushing our total over 2,000.

I will never cycle that stretch of road again, ever.

WISCONSIN

Wisconsin Law once required serving a small amount of cheese and butter with meals in restaurants (effective from June 1935 to March 1937). I can think of no dish that a little cheese and butter would fail to improve.

21 MISS INFORMATION

Isle of Skye, 899 AD*: Two Norse youths rowed the dory that carried them to the island of Skíð. A jumble of thatched houses, shops, inns and a tavern clustered around the semicircular harbor. They walked the length of the wooden pier, looking for Olaf's ship, Wulf Sang, among the row of tied-up longships. "Which one is it?" asked Hild. "They all look alike to me."*

"I cannot tell," Eyvind said. "I know it from the carved wolf's head on the prow, but none of these have figures on their prows. They take them down in friendly waters so as not to frighten the good spirits."

As he scanned the row of prows, he now noticed one that appeared to still have its beast-head mounted and strode toward it. As he gazed at the hideous dragon head, it transformed into Mother's head.

"Now you listen to me," it shrieked. "You will take the next ship home. You will marry a rich, sensible girl and stop all this running around nonsense!"

He looked at Hild. "You do not see it?"

"The dragon?"

"It is Mother. It spoke to me."

"I did not hear it speak, either. Eyvind, we must find a way to get rid of her."

"That beast would frighten away any good spirits." Then they both had the same thought: "The tavern," they said together.

Noise, darkness, and wood smoke mixed with the smell of stale ale assaulted them as the tavern door creaked open. Loud laughter came from a back corner. Eyvind shooed a cat off a nearby table so Hild could sit. Suddenly a familiar voice, very drunk, boomed from the dark. "Swordsman!! Bane and terror of Freezin pirates! That scrawny Scot didn't kill you?" Olaf slapped the rump of the wench on his lap, heaved himself upright, belched, and staggered over to throw his arms around their shoulders. "At las' yer here! We have a-ventures ahead, Liddle Ones!" Hild turned her head to inhale.

A few days later: on a sparkling sea, sail bellied out, Wulf Sang ran with a fair wind. Hild strummed her harp and sang a popular ballad about heroes voyaging home. Eyvind stood with Olaf astern at the steering oar. "You ought to come Viking," Olaf said. "Join my crew. Get rich and fat like me. We will be home long before Yule."

"Home?" Eyvind said, staring at the horizon. "What home have I?"

"Mine, of course. In Dubhlinn, Eire, in the land of the Gaels. Big city, Dubhlinn. The natives can be bastards, mind, but your wife will be content at my hall. She will find much to amuse her, while we go south, far south. To the Golden Lands. To wonders you cannot imagine."

Superior, WI, June 1999: "Here you are," said the young woman behind the desk of the Wisconsin tourist information office in downtown Superior. She handed me a slick catalog. "This has maps of all the bike trails in the state. As you can see, cycling is very popular in Wisconsin." She flashed a sunny smile and returned to her magazine.

I flipped through the catalog and noticed it only listed mountain bike trails that mostly went in circles. I was done with going in circles. "Excuse me, miss," I said. "Thank you. This is great, but we're touring, riding across the state? We'd like to avoid Route 2 if possible. Do you have any maps that show back roads or bike paths that'll take us east?" By now Route 2 had become the major thoroughfare that we were familiar with in Boston, with four lanes, speed limit 60 and a shoulder narrower than the painted white stripe.

Her smile evaporated, replaced by vacancy. "Other than the trails in there, I don't know of any other way except Route 2. Sorry." End of conversation. I laid the catalog on the counter and walked outside into the morning sunshine and checked the sign again. Yes, it said Tourist Information.

"Any luck?" asked Jane as she held the bike upright. Commuters whizzed past on Route 2 a few yards behind her. By now we were far off our mapped route, which would have taken us through Iowa corn fields and manure piles.

"None at all," I said. "Apparently Wisconsin has only one road going east."

"There's a nice park next door. Let's check it out," Jane said. We walked our bike over to the park and nearly bumped into a large sign which read "Bike Path Entrance – Osaugie Trail." The shining bulk of the tourist information building, resembling a giant aluminum Bundt cake pan, had eclipsed the sign.

The trail, though unknown to the state tourist board, led us exactly where we wanted to go, due east, alongside a river bank. A few miles out of the city it deposited us onto County Route 13, a peaceful lane that ran along Lake Superior's southern shore straight to the Bayfield Peninsula and the Apostle Islands.

Being the first day of summer, the weather gods sent us oppressive heat and humidity. The farther we pedaled the more irritable I became. My shirt plastered itself to my back and sweat trickled into my eyes. Then somebody turned on the AC. In the space of perhaps a quarter of a mile, the hot wind at our backs died, reversed direction, cooled by thirty degrees and rushed into our faces. We had reached the southern shore of Lake Superior, with "lake effect" winds that outstrip any sea breeze I'd ever felt. Within minutes my sweaty body was as dry and chilled as one of 007's vodka martinis. We broke out the jackets. The cool dry air defused my irritability, but as the afternoon wore on, after pedaling fifty-three miles in unceasing headwinds, a heaviness entered my mind. Emotions are not my forte. I'm much happier suffering in silence. Maybe not happier, but it's less work. I hoped my mood shift would go unnoticed so I could deal with it alone, like a man.

We stopped in a little lakefront village called Port Wing, a quiet place of shady lanes, picket fences that fronted prim, white-washed saltbox houses, and a steepled church on nearly every corner. At the general store we picked up spaghetti fixings and directions to the campground. After setting up, I brooded over the maps at the picnic table as the stove's tiny blue flame heated a pot of water for tea. Jane tossed the sleeping bags into the tent and zipped the door shut, then sat beside me.

"How are you doing?" she asked in the significant way which meant that an answer of "fine, how are you?" would not suffice; this was an opening for a real conversation.

Busted. I'd have to share. I sighed and laid my head on the table. "It's the summer solstice," I began. "We've had a great day riding, perfect weather, and we're camped in a beautiful spot. But I'm depressed."

"Do you know why?"

"No, why?" I brightened, hoping she would just tell me and we'd be done.

"I'm asking."

I'd rather scrub toilets than analyze my feelings, but there was no ducking out of this one. After a few moments of hard reflection, I saw the answer staring back at me.

"Look at this." I had hoped to get us back on the Adventure Cycling route, since we'd lugged the maps 2,000 miles already. I spread out the ones for Michigan, Indiana and Ohio, and pointed out phrases like: dangerous, congested, heavily trafficked, use extreme caution, avoid commuting hours, poor visibility, we assume no responsibility, and beware of manure piles.

"Manure piles?" Jane said.

"Where the Amish are."

"Oh. So it's not all back roads and cycling paths?" she said, rubbing my shoulders. I bowed my head and grunted. "Well I feel the same way. The east is a lot more crowded than the west. I miss the prairie, the mountains and the open spaces."

"Yeah, the Hi-Line in Montana; that was bliss," I said, chin in palm, gazing at the western sky. "Remember that Midwest boondoggle we did a couple years ago?" Somehow I had arranged a business trip that consisted of meetings with four different customers in the Midwest over a two week period. Then I convinced management that it would be a lot cheaper than airline tickets and hotels if I rented a minivan and drove the whole way, camping out between meetings. We packed bikes and camping gear and I got paid to be a tourist, with only brief interruptions for work. No wonder that company went under. Twice.

"That was fun in a car, but I wouldn't want to ride it," Jane said. I agreed. The mapped route would have us traverse Michigan from the Upper Peninsula, keep south of the Great Lakes and hit New England by way of Ohio, Pennsylvania and New York. I knew that territory from my sales calls: a few Amish farms and horse-drawn carriages and a lot of freeways connecting cities with suburban sprawl. There had to be a better way. I looked at the drawing of the USA on the map's cover and it hit me: north of Michigan lay not the world's edge, but another entire country, named Canada.

I jabbed a finger into the map. "Why can't we cut across Ontario?" I said. "Wouldn't that be a whole lot shorter? And less traffic? Doesn't Canada have a population of like, fifty thousand?"

"Oh," Jane said. "Canada? Well, nothing says we have to stay in the U.S., right?"

"No," I said. "It wasn't the plan, but we're making this up as we go."

"Then let's do it."

"I've never been to Ontario; except Toronto one time when I was four, but I don't remember much, so..."

"So it'll be an adventure," Jane said. "And...Rita Dom lives near Toronto. We could stay with her."

I remembered the good beer and sausage I had with Rita and her daughter back in Washington. "Wonder if she meant it, inviting us?"

"We'll find out. I've got her phone number and address. OK, now I'm excited. How about you?"

"Stoked," I said. "Totally." And I meant it. We were going back into the unknown. We had adventures ahead.

It all seemed so obvious, so simple. In one brief discussion we had gained a week, and would avoid all those dangerous roads. We both cheered up, because we had never cycled in Ontario. If we had, we would never have considered it as an option now. Ignorance is not really bliss. Only a tiny percentage of it is. The rest is pretty miserable. For the moment our dinghy of bliss bobbed merrily in a sea of ignorance.

22 DELUGE

We crawled into our tentling as Orion and the Great Bear sparkled overhead. By midnight the thin fabric shuddered under a heavy downpour. Booming thunder shook us awake. Lightning flashed lurid shapes on the tent walls. It was the type of storm we'd seen in North Dakota: very intense, but blows through fast. Our sleeping bags were still dry, and the towels we'd hung outside were already saturated, so we went back to sleep.

In the morning we discovered that this was a different type of storm—the Lake Superior kind—intense and doesn't budge. By morning the rain still beat a staccato on the sagging tent fly and funneled off the edges in four unbroken streams. The ground squished under our feet, the dirt road a wide swath of sticky mud as we tip-toed to a nearby diner. A friendly young couple there, also camping, noted our drowned rat demeanor and sodden clothes and offered us a lift to the Laundromat in the next town, since they were headed there anyway. Back at camp we shoved everything that could be washed into the B.O.B. bag and minutes later we fed quarters into the machines while the storm raged on. As our last load spun and dried, the clouds spent themselves and moved out, much lightened after dumping four inches of rain.

Wearing clean, still-warm clothes, we packed up and rode sixteen miles to Cornucopia, where we checked into the "Village Inn," one of those throwback Victorian inns like in the westerns with a saloon downstairs and rooms upstairs. The special tonight was fresh-caught lake trout, which answered the question of whether we'd be camping. I'd spend an extra fifty bucks to not waste all those quarters and let everything get wet again. We checked in and hurried downstairs to dine on the last two fillets remaining.

Next morning, we prepared for departure in front of the inn. "What do you do when it rains?" rasped the old lady, ready for the weather, encased in a clear plastic raincoat.

"We really haven't had to ride in the rain much at all," Jane said, and that was true. Almost two months on the road and I counted only a handful of days where rain had soaked us through. Now threatening gray clouds filled the sky, but I figured they'd been well wrung out after yesterday's drenching and we'd enjoy a dry day on the road. A light rain began as we set off. A passing shower, nothing more, I thought. We WOULD go to Bayfield that day. The skies darkened. The drops increased in size, frequency and pace. Drivers turned on their lights and switched wipers to high. Impossible. It rained four inches yesterday. We would not stop. The rain would stop soon. But nothing stopped until we splashed into Bayfield, on the shores of Lake Superior and the jumping off point for the Apostle Islands, our first islands since Washington.

We'd only gone twenty-one miles, but the well-timed rain saturated us. Water squelched out of our shoes with each pedal stroke. A fountain like a rooster's tail flew off the rear wheel. We didn't leave tracks; we left a wake.

Rounding a bend I raised my eyes, water dripping from my helmet rim, and there on a little knoll stood a vintage farmhouse, like something painted by Norman Rockwell. I imagined grandma inside, setting down the platter of golden roasted turkey onto the long, polished, shaker-built dining room table ringed with eager young faces, eyes shining with reflected candlelight.

In the front yard, an oval wooden sign hung between two elaborately turned posts, and stood in a bark-mulched petunia bed. Carefully painted creamy white with dark green trim the sign announced *Red Raspberry Inn*, and *Vacancy*. I hit the brakes as if a grizzly bear had stepped in front of us. Frictional forces prevailed after half a minute and we slowed to a stop before the gravel drive.

"It IS now raining," I declared, "and I think we need to stay HERE." I pointed at the inn. Jane nodded in numb agreement. She hadn't spoken in a while and her blank expression told me she had "checked out." Although physically present, her mind had most likely long since departed for Elysium, where I imagined she danced in the sunshine in a field resplendent with spring wildflowers.

We separated ourselves from the sopping bike seats and squished up the steps to the front door. No answer. We squished around to the back door while desperate hands smoothed matted hair and flicked mud, grass clippings and small clinging insects from our legs as if to improve our chances of welcome. Someone was in the kitchen. I tapped on the screen door's frame.

"Hi," I said, wondering if pathos might work to our advantage here. "We were wondering…"

"Oh, hi, come on in! I'm Carol, and this is Jon." Carol had a round, soft face, like a shining bun straight out of the oven. This reception was as if Jon and Carol had expected us, and we were old and cherished friends who had arrived right on time. We squished our way through the door, conscious of the small puddles forming beneath us.

"We…" I began again, but my input was not required. Carol peppered us with questions. "You probably want to change into something dry. Where did you ride from? Do you want to see the rooms? And how about some tea?"

When we explained our reluctance to walk on her spotless gleaming floors, Jon said, "Anyone who can cycle through that rain is welcome to walk on our floors." We walked. The kitchen enveloped us in heat and light, and was filled with bakery scents: yeast, butter, brown sugar and cinnamon. Jane nudged me, indicating a photo on the wall we recognized as the Chalice Well in Glastonbury, England. We had an almost identical photo at home. Next to it hung a handmade leather medicine pouch with fringe and intricate beadwork on it, similar to the one Jane carried.

After we'd cleaned up, Carol had tea ready, accompanied by still-warm sticky buns; our sweet reward for plowing through the deluge. Jane is a connoisseur of sticky buns. If she were a fish, you would catch her with a sticky bun lure. She took a bite then leaned close to whisper: "These are as good as mom's." We sat around the kitchen table, bone china cups steaming in saucers. The rain, powerless to reach us, hissed against the window glass.

"Have you been to the Chalice Well in Glastonbury?" Jane asked. "I noticed your photo. We were there last year." There are two wells: red and white. They symbolize blood and seed: fertility, birth, and the intersection of human and divine.

"Yes, we love England," Jon said. "So civilized. We go every couple years."

"So do we," I said. "My Dad's from there, and my sister lives there so we go a lot. And we've always had afternoon tea. Even my German mom was converted." Laughter. We all think coffee is for barbarians.

"Glastonbury is such an interesting place," Carol said. "For thousands of years it's been a place of mystery and of healing." We'd gone there on a journey to England and France with our spiritual teachers a year before. We'd learned about Avalon and the Holy Grail. In Glastonbury, ley lines converge at an entrance to the Otherworld.

"At Avebury, at the standing stones, is where Ian asked me to marry him." Jane said.

"Now that's romantic," Jon said. "Avebury's another special place. Everyone goes to Stonehenge, but Avebury is more ancient, and to me feels more powerful." I'd felt it too. Thousands of years ago, the cycles of life were rendered in stones weighing up to forty tons. Astronomical observations and sacrifices to ancient gods were made in such places. To me it seemed the perfect place to make a lifetime commitment.

The conversation progressed from travel to food to books to movies, with hardly a point of disagreement. I felt like we were conversing with older versions of ourselves. An hour, perhaps two, passed without needing to excuse myself or feeling self-conscious about revealing too much. In the morning we booked a second night, garaged the bike, and made plans to explore the Apostle Islands.

Unlike the New Testament Apostles, the islands number more than twelve; there are twenty-two; all are forested and most are uninhabited. The largest, Madeline Island, contains a village and a state park. Hordes of summer tourists make day trips via the small ferry boats from Bayfield. In winter when the lake freezes over, the ferry boats are replaced by ice boats, a sled/fan-boat hybrid that can both skitter across the ice and plunge into the frigid water as needed.

The sun had returned. Jane and I basked in its rays as we stood on the deck of the Madeline Island ferry. Nearly two months on the road had given us interesting tan lines: brown faces, necks, forearms and mid-thighs to mid-calves. Everything else was stark white, except for the brown ovals on the backs of our hands. This was known as a "biker tan." We tried in vain to even things out on the beach, with the result that our white sections turned red. I watched the small children and dogs splash in the shallows and being a hardy New Englander, strode down the sandy beach and waded in. I would not stop until I was afloat. In thigh-high water I could no longer feel my feet, and the numbness crept up my legs turning the family jewels into a coat button and a pair of navy beans. I swung my arms a bit, made a few splashes, about-faced and stumped back to shore. Enough Misogi for today.

Late that afternoon, Carol summoned us to Wisconsin-style high tea out on the deck. The freshly baked scones with jam and clotted cream were accompanied by smoked trout and a selection of local cheeses. A white tailed doe with a spindly spotted fawn browsed at the edge of the yard. We continued the previous day's conversation, and then discussed our work. Jane said she missed the children she taught.

"Are you planning on kids of your own?" Carol asked. Ah, that question. During our eight years together we never seriously explored this topic, which partly explained why we were still together. Many of my previous girlfriends had this high on their agenda, if not the primary motivation for dating: to evaluate my potential as provider and father. I could provide all right, but didn't know about the fathering part. I wasn't sure if I could suppress my gag reflex like other parents seemed to do. I already had nieces and nephews to borrow. I expect my exes found me too ambivalent and dumped me. Or I pre-empted them. And now I was clearly in love with Jane, and I'd even take on parenting if she wanted a family, but I believed she didn't.

Jane taught young children, as did Ann, her married but childless older sister, and this satisfied her "kid fix." She'd come home from work exhausted and all given out. In those first years together, when we were both in our twenties she'd told me she never wanted children and I'd said that was fine and that settled the matter. No pressure. Now eight years later, she at 34, our decision approached irrevocability. Was the matter still settled? I let Jane answer Carol's question.

"Oh," Jane said, shooting me a glance. "We, ah, haven't got there yet. No plans. Do you have children?" We'd guessed they had grown children who were lucky to have had such cool parents.

A cloud's shadow passed over us. Our easy conversation took a hard turn. Jon shifted in his seat. Carol looked down.

"We lost our only son a few years ago," Carol said in a quiet voice. "A car accident."

"Oh, gosh," Jane said. "I'm so sorry." I was stunned. They were so upbeat. My mouth had dropped open. I closed it.

The story poured out of Carol. On a deep winter night she awoke from a vivid dream in which their teenage boy died in a car accident. That week he had been planning a road trip with some friends. Was the dream a message, or just the heightened worries of a protective parent? When it came time for him to leave on his trip, she told him of her dream and pleaded with him not to go, but he would not be dissuaded: "I want to go with my friends," he'd insisted. He left, and that night their car hit a patch of black ice. All four boys died at the scene.

I thought of Officer Backer's Wisconsin counterpart delivering the unbearable, the news no parent should ever have to hear. How does the mind absorb it? You expect to bury your parents one day, and your pets, but never your children. How do you go on? Yet here were Jon and Carol. They'd appeared to have found strength to go forward and continue to engage in life. They traveled, watched movies, read books, baked sticky buns, loved each other and welcomed drenched strangers wandering to their door. They had every right to be bitter and cynical—and they were not. I didn't know what their healing process looked like, or what support they had, but they could still embrace the present, still see a future. My admiration for them went through the roof, because they lived my deepest fear: to give life; to pour one's heart and soul into another; to see them grow tall and strong and beautiful, and begin to make their way in the world, to wonder who they will become, to look forward to grandchildren, and begin to believe that all the sacrifice was worth it; and then everything is ripped away in an instant. You're left with the memories, the silence, the guilt, the emptiness, the ache that never stops, and you wonder who they *might* have become. To go on with life after this can only be called *valor*.

The next morning we had to leave, though we didn't want to. Jon and

Carol helped us linger. They sat down with us for a breakfast I wished would never end: homemade waffles with fresh-picked strawberries and clotted cream. But it ended, and Jane went upstairs, presumably to pack. I took care of the bill with Jon. Music drifted down the stairs. Jon listened a moment. "Do you have a radio playing?" he asked.

"No. That must be Jane on her backpacker guitar," I said. When Jane came down Jon asked her if she would play a song for them. She agreed and they settled themselves on the sofa, smiling, holding hands.

"I wrote this about six years ago," Jane said. "It's called *You Can Cry.*" Her fingers picked the soft slow melody as she sang:

"Somewhere deep inside of me,
There lies a crystal pool.
Quiet like a starry night,
Offering me the fool.
Saying child, don't you go away,
Trust yourself, you know what to say.
Saying child won't you play,
Learn how to live it's the only way.
For you can wish upon a star.
You can be who you truly are
You can fly by the moonlight,
And you can cry if that is what
You need tonight…" [11]

The song has a few more stanzas which I won't repeat here but they're just as evocative. Jon and Carol wept quiet tears. My eyes glistened too, even though I'd heard this song countless times. It just gets me.

Jon brought our bike out of the garage. We let them take it for spin around the block before we hitched the trailer. As I watched them ride, the song *Daisy* came into my head: *You look sweet upon the seat of a bicycle built for two.* We must look sweet on that bike, too. Carol handed us a wrapped package for the road: scones and a jar of homemade raspberry jam. Jon presented us with a book that was meaningful for him, *The Education of Little Tree* by Forrest Carter. "For you," he said, "and your children, if you have them one day."

If we had them one day.

I had just turned thirty-six and Jane was thirty-four. Though engaged for a year we had no wedding plans. We never rushed anything in our relationship, but maybe we needed to pick up the pace now. We'd get married "one day," until which time my own earthly line was doomed. If nothing changed I would wander my way into extinction; the dead branch of the family tree. Did I even want to be a parent? I'd be crap at it. I was

---

[11] "You Can Cry" ©1993 Jane Justice

too self-absorbed, yet still hadn't figured out who I was. How could I guide another? I didn't want to be one of those parents thwarted in their own dreams, who then live vicariously through their kids. But how much longer could I put it off? I knew I didn't want to change diapers at fifty, and have people mistake me for my kids' grandpa. I could imagine my future son's or daughter's friends saying, "Your old man is OK, but...*he really is an old man.*"

Jane's biological deadline was nearer still. Was this door closed? None of her three siblings had any, while my side of the family was hip deep in kids: I had eight nieces and nephews. But why do I keep asking myself this question? Why did I want them? Was it ego? If I ever have children, I want it to be because of love and not fear.

We pedaled on and let the day go where it would.

It would go downhill, though it seemed all uphill, against the wind, unbearably hot, and in heavy traffic. We ran out of water in the afternoon and ended the day in a glassy-eyed staring contest in the restaurant of a Ramada Inn, while an organist played "Tie a Yellow Ribbon" or something equally annoying in the background. Most days on the road did not end as they began. Too often, I wanted to stay when we had to leave, and stop when I wanted to keep going. Since we left the Washington coast, no place had stirred the same yearning, the same veiled memory of home in me, yet there were many places I'd wanted to linger, because we'd connected with people there. Although realtors would disagree, perhaps there was more to a home than its location.

Concord, MA 1991: "Dis one needs too much work," Mom said, after a cursory inspection. "Forget it, you'll never be able to sell it. Ein Stück Scheisse."

My parents and I stood outside of the admittedly small and plain ranch house I had put an offer on, and after months of looking, my patience had gone. "First of all, I'm not selling, I'm buying. Secondly, you said the last house was overpriced and had no potential because everything had already been done to it. 'Get the worst house in the best neighborhood,' you said. So here it is. It's got two acres..."

"Of swamp land. And there's a huge crack in the foundation."

"Two acres, in Concord, at a price I can afford."

"No one else will touch it, det's why it's so cheap."

"All we're saying," Dad said in his gentle way, "is we want to see you in a home you can be proud of."

That did it. I turned my back to regain my self-command.

"All right. Fine. Let's just go," I rasped.

In time I decided home-owning wasn't meant to be and gave up looking. I moved in with Jane, which apparently was meant to be.

MICHIGAN

Although Michigan is often called the "Wolverine State" it no longer contains any wolverines. Numbers have declined steadily in the US since the 19th century due to trapping, habitat fragmentation and climate change.

23 BEAUTY PARLOR

"You're next, sir." I put down the January 1999 issue of *Country Living*, walked across the thin industrial carpeting and eased myself into a monstrosity of chrome and black vinyl, a veritable throne of a barber chair. Joanie, a smiling and buxom woman of middle years wore an XXL white tee shirt emblazoned with Mickey Mouse. She draped a black sheet over me and snapped the top of it around my neck. In the mirror, my disembodied head floated in a shiny black sea. Tan-skinned and wild-haired, it stared me down.

"This is my first time in a beauty parlor," I said. The décor was straight out of 1970: the walls a mixture of faux brick, dark plywood paneling and textured wallpaper with a pine tree theme. On every countertop sprouted a miniature cityscape of spray bottles, tubes and jars. Tacked to the walls were photos and local news clippings, yellowed and curling at the edges. Behind me lurked a bank of ancient hairdryers; the huge space-helmet kind you sat under. The whole anachronism was lit from two rows of suspended fluorescents, casting an unflattering, jaundiced light. Joanie's Beauty Parlor was undeniably ugly, a throwback, and only seven bucks for a haircut.

"Not to worry," said Joanie, hosing down my head from a spray bottle. "I do men's hair all the time."

"Well then, make me beautiful," I said. After two months on the road, my hair had taken on the shape of the inside of my helmet, all ridges and valleys, with the surplus sprouting from the air vents like weeds through an old sidewalk. My hair has won awards. When I was in high school, the soccer team seemed fascinated by the bulk and un-governability of my hair in high winds. The varsity goalkeeper, Skillet Haskell, urged on by my brother Dave, who was team captain, fashioned a special award plaque in shop class just for me: *The Hairdoo Award*, which they presented at the annual banquet. At least I got recognition. Growing hair is one of my gifts, and as time passes I seem to gain the hair that other men lose. I wish I could donate to those less fortunate. Meanwhile Jane had added two heavy inches to her shoulder-length brown tresses. With the rain pelting down this afternoon, we sheltered at Joanie's while shedding some of that extra weight.

We had crossed the state line into Michigan's Upper Peninsula two days earlier on June 27, once again feeling the combination of anxiety and anticipation of new adventures in a new state. The last day's ride through northeastern Wisconsin was a pleasant country ramble through light and airy pine and birch forest, beside frequent small lakes where the odd summer home or tiny fisherman's camp seemed to beckon with a siren's song of quiet, relaxation, and solitude.

A pair of fellow cyclists had appeared on the other side of the road, heading in the opposite direction. They were the racing type of riders, carrying nothing, who remind me of dragonflies with their neon jerseys, hard-shell helmets, eyes hidden behind bulbous sunglasses, slender bodies atop stick-like bicycle frames, whirring past at high speed. We waved as we always did when meeting other cyclists. They raised their hands in an efficient, aerodynamic acknowledgement. Soon a few more dragonflies appeared and we waved at them. Then there was a big group of them, so we waved some more and then I noticed the numbers pinned to their chests.

"We can stop waving now," I said to Jane. "This looks like an organized event."

"Good," she said. "My arm's getting tired." We had stumbled upon the annual R.A.W., the Ride Across Wisconsin, with over 1600 participants, I found out later. That would have been a lot of waving.

We passed our first night in Michigan in a little Upper Peninsula town called Stambaugh. The sign outside of the Wales Inn featured a spouting sperm whale. This confused me because we were nowhere near the ocean or the small but fierce country to the left of England. In the morning I consulted our proprietress while she replenished our pancake stacks.

"Wales is our family name," she said.

"So the whale on the sign is…"

"A play on words, I guess."

"Ha, now I get it," I said. "Very good, indeed."

"I hope you don't mind," she said, "but I called the local paper and told them you were staying here. You guys are big news. Would you be up for an interview?"

I turned to Jane. "Are we taking interviews today?" She answered me with wide eyes and tight lips. Jane shied from the spotlight, while I enjoyed attention. "Yes, I think we can work that in."

"I'm Lynn Perry from the *Iron County Reporter*." Young, pretty and serious, the Lois Lane of Stambaugh presently arrived and sat across from us, notepad at the ready. When she asked me what made me want to do this ride, I tried to sum it up without being too personal and this was my answer:

"We wanted to see small town America up close. From what you see and hear in the media today, you get the impression that everybody in this country lives in fear, not knowing who their neighbors are, alarming their houses and cars, not looking anyone in the eye. We wanted to discover if a different way of life exists. We're finding out that it does."

This was all true enough, and would probably help *IC Reporter* readers feel good about where they lived, but my real reasons for the journey were complicated. As a human being, my progress towards enlightenment, fulfillment and a sense of personal power had ground to a halt. I hoped this journey would change that, that it would somehow make me a better person: more courageous, healthier, and more self-aware. Earthly terrors I had in abundance: failure, poverty, marriage, children, pot-luck dinners, name-tag events, mosquitoes and now canned beets. Most of these were easily understood, but why did I fear marriage? Was it related to the fear of failure? And why wasn't I OK with not being married?

Part of me longed for the appearance of normality my parents and three older siblings had. My parents had married, cranked out four of us in five years, toiled and sacrificed to raise us, get us educated and into careers so we could have things and save up money like they did. My siblings all married, bought houses and had children, for whom they now toiled and sacrificed. This looked like an infinite loop, and infinite loops are bad. Hence, I was stuck at the marriage step. I didn't see the point in all that toil and sacrifice, unless I did something beyond repeating what they did. We were more than halfway home and I still had no answers.

Back at the beauty parlor, cool air hit my scalp as the layers of untamed growth—the last of the hair that I wore before the journey—fell to Joanie's shears and lay in a fuzzy circle around me. Every seven to ten years virtually all the cells in one's body have been replaced. Except for our brains we are literally new people every decade. Human skin cells only live 3-4 weeks. Although my insides would take years more to replace themselves, the outside that I had worn back home—the cells comprising skin, hair and nails—had now been completely shed, like a serpent's skin.

In the waiting area, Jane was in animated conversation with another woman who looked about our age and had a small child in tow. I admired Jane's ease with people; how she could strike up a conversation with almost anyone and keep it going; a skill I never mastered. Casual socializing has always been hard labor for me. I go at it clumsy and brusque, like cutting someone's hair with hedge clippers, trying to get it over with fast. Years ago my employer, in an effort to bolster my people skills, had sent me to the *Dale Carnegie Course on Effective Speaking and Human Relations*. I'd enjoyed it immensely, because we role-played. I hammed it up and got big applause. I can play a role no problem. I can be whoever the person I'm facing wants me to be. But my true self likes to hide. My true self is scared silly of being singled out as different and laughed at, which happened often enough during my awkward years, i.e. birth to present. The trouble was, by blending into the background, nobody really knew me.

Once again, thanks to Jane, we were invited to spend the night in the home of people we'd just met: Juan and Holly Jasso and their three young daughters. I'd half expected that once we got east this would stop happening, but it really had more to do with being in small towns versus big cities. We found people in small towns friendlier and less fearful of strangers. The larger the population of a place, the less likely it was we'd be invited into someone's home.

In the morning we enjoyed croissants and Danishes around the kitchen table with our host family, exchanging stories of how we got to be there. Juan was originally from Mexico, met Holly in southern California, and together they moved to this quiet spot among the birches on a lake in northern Michigan. They needed a safer and more affordable place to make their living and raise their daughters, the eldest of whom had cerebral palsy. I wondered if they had relatives nearby. None were mentioned. I admired their courage in starting a new life in a new place, and remembered that my parents had done it also, from Europe, a generation ago.

Later that day, we crossed into the Eastern Time Zone and lost an hour. Home suddenly felt much closer. Once again, the thought prodded at me: "What happens when you get home?" I know, I know! No job, no plans. What was my future? As much as I wrestled with the question, no clear answer emerged. I couldn't know what I was going to do until I did it. Mornings we couldn't plan where we'd spend the night, much less how we'd spend our week, because we never knew where we'd end up that day. It depended on the weather, on who we met, on how we felt, on the quality of the roads. I'd been used to that since Washington and now Jane was comfortable with it too. Maybe this was how we'd operate from now on.

24 SEUL CHOIX

By July 1st we had ridden over 2,400 miles, with approximately 1,600 to go. Sixty percent home. We ended that day near the fog-bound northern shore of Lake Michigan, in a Lilliputian village called Gulliver, which offered only one choice of lodgings: 10' x 12' garden sheds fitted with windows and billed as "cabins" fronting Lake Gulliver. They would suffice; when it came to shelter from the rain, clean, cheap and dry won over spaciousness and luxuries every time. The daily grind of packing, riding, eating, more riding, and unpacking for two months had worn us down. We needed a vacation from our vacation. The last few miles felt like pedaling along the sea floor, spinning hard to inch forward, compressed lungs always a breath behind the demands of straining muscles.

In the morning we awoke to the kind of rain that keeps up all day, not heavy but steady. I pried open my eyes and met Jane's, which dared me to make a move. After that we slept two more hours.

"You know, we've been riding that bike pretty hard," I said to Jane when we finally hauled ourselves upright. "We don't want to fatigue the metal. It should have a rest day, don't you think?"

"I was thinking the same thing," Jane said. "Except...what are we going to do all day?" We had *The Alchemist* by Paulo Coehelo, but we saved him for evenings. Jane practiced her guitar and I wrote in my journal until cabin fever set in well before noon. We needed to get out. We sought out our hostess, Marilyn Fischer, to book a second night and solicit ideas for a rainy day.

"You ought to see the Seul Choix (pronouncing it 'Sis-shwa') lighthouse," said Marilyn. "The name means 'only choice', because it's the only safe harbor in this part of Lake Michigan. What's interesting about the lighthouse is that it's haunted."

"Cool," I said. "It's a perfect day to go see a haunted lighthouse. Is it

147

far?"

"About ten miles. I'd be happy to take you there and give you a tour. I'm president of the Gulliver Historical Society, and preserving that lighthouse is our main mission."

On the drive, Marilyn told us some true ghost stories about the lighthouse, phenomena that she had experienced first-hand: unexplained cigar aromas, footfalls on the steps, lights turning off, heavy objects moving by themselves, and most hair-raising, the image of a face in the bedroom mirror, which she caught on videotape. A professional crew had also filmed this image, but their tape mysteriously disappeared afterward. One time a group of state and local police spent the night in the lighthouse, armed with sophisticated recording equipment, hoping to document the weirdness. Most of the phenomena happened while they were there, but over several hours while it happened, none of their equipment would function. They recorded nothing.

Another time, a séance with an Ouija board revealed the name of the spirit: W-I-L-L. The lighthouse keeper until 1910, Joseph W. Townsend had gone by the name of "Captain Will." He was still keeping the light, it seemed.

The lighthouse itself is a well-preserved tower of white-painted brick dating back to 1892. We climbed the spiral staircase to the top and looked out over the mist-shrouded lake, the world beyond as veiled as our future. I imagined old sailing ships and steamers, storm-tossed, following the light to safety. Jane and I have always been interested in stories of the supernatural, and have each had experiences that have confirmed our belief in other planes of existence, in life forces beyond the mundane realm of our five senses.

When I was six years old, having moved to Massachusetts from Pennsylvania, I awoke suddenly in the middle of the night to see a young man standing beside my bed. He was dressed like an 18th century colonial: a long dark coat with many buttons, vest, breeches, stockings, and shoes with buckles. His hair was pulled back into a short pig-tail. He looked like nobody I'd ever seen before, and I could see through him to my brother's bed across the room. The ghost looked at me and stepped backward, as if surprised. I called out softly to my brother, "Davy, wake up!" He was fast asleep. The ghost then vanished without a sound. I wasn't frightened by it; just fascinated. When I described the experience to my family the next morning they dismissed it as a dream—only back then I hadn't known what New England colonists looked like; it was only later that I could identify him as possibly the ghost of some young revolutionary, or an English ancestor coming for a visit.

Years later my Dad met up with a ghost of his own. On a visit to Ireland, he stayed at an ancient stone manor house. Oil portraits of previous owners in intricate gilded frames adorned the wall along the grand staircase. Whenever he walked past one in particular, a severe-looking woman in 18th century dress, the hairs on the back of his neck stood on end. His host told him this woman was a renowned recluse who despised visitors. Intrigued, my Dad took a few photos of the portrait. On developing the roll, a huge black smear, like an energetic storm cloud, obscured only these photos; the others turned out fine. Long after death, the reclusive ghost still protected her privacy.

More recently, Jane as an adult met a ghost in a Newton cemetery. One bitterly cold winter day she walked along a path from the grave of a relative toward her parked car. She glanced up to see an elderly woman coming the opposite way, wearing a light-weight tan jacket and carrying two bags of groceries. After they passed one another Jane was struck by how lightly dressed the woman seemed for January in Massachusetts, and with her heavy parcels...Jane spun around, mere seconds after they'd passed, to offer her a lift. She was nowhere in sight. Weeks later she told her friend Sue this story. Sue's eyes got big and her mouth formed an O. On a different day Sue had seen the same woman, in the same part of the cemetery. And the woman had also vanished.

These first-hand experiences convinced us that spirits exist, that a life-force continues after our bodies die, and that it is sometimes possible to interact with spirits of the departed. We believed in ghosts.

Back in the lighthouse, Marilyn, Jane and I were not alone. I would feel a vibration, a sound just beyond hearing, or catch a small motion, a shadow out of the corner of my eye, where I wasn't sure whether I'd seen or imagined it. Jane felt it too and we agreed that it was not malevolent. It felt like it watched us but kept its distance like a reluctant host who ensured we disturbed nothing and hoped his uninvited guests would soon leave. Maybe Captain Will was annoyed at having tourists tramp through his home. Being up in that tower reminded me of castles I'd visited in Europe, and it struck me that like those castles centuries ago, lighthouses now fell out of use, replaced by better technology, and perhaps the spirits inhabiting them did not want to be forgotten. Maybe these spirits have unfinished business on earth. Maybe they died before attempting their Big One and now lived on in eternal regret, envious of those with time yet to manifest their dreams.

25 TWO BRIDGES

Dublin, Ireland, 899 AD*: Wulf Sang, with prow again bereft of its wolf's head, glided into Dubhlinn's harbor. Never had Eyvind and Hild seen so many ships at once, nor had they ever seen a real city before. The rowers stood the oars in silent salute. Ropes were thrown and a plank lowered. Olaf marched down it, followed by Eyvind and Hild.*

"Welcome home, my scoundrel," said a contralto voice. They turned to see Olaf's female counterpart, a perfect match in girth and hair color: coppery braids framed her formidable bust. A brass ring, heavy with keys hung from her waist. She walked up to Olaf, grabbed two fistfuls of beard and kissed him hard.

"My wife, Frieda," Olaf said. "These are our guests: Eyvind the Sword-Master, and Hild the…uh… Enchantress. They're my good luck charms." He turned to shout orders to his crew.

A younger woman, also a red-head, stood near Frieda, scanning the ship. Hild stared. "Anja? You live here? I never thought to see you again." She advanced and embraced her old friend.

Anja, frowning, patted Hild's shoulder, then stammered, "Yes…Helga…you look well."

Hild broke the embrace. "Anja. It is Hild. Am I so altered these two years since we parted?"

"Hild. Of course. Forgive me. I am looking for my husband, Bjorn. You must have met him on your journey?" Their awkward reunion ended when Anja spotted Bjorn and rushed to him.

"We were like sisters once," said Hild. Frieda took their hands and led them away from the wharf, along a cobbled street thronged with people: Norse people. There were shops of every description, musicians, jugglers, birds of scarlet and

bright yellow, vendors of bread, cheese, fish and roasting meats. Strange smells wafted over them: pungent spices, colorful fruits impossibly large and sweet-smelling, jewelry and silks from faraway lands. Harlots in the shadows beckoned to Eyvind, whose eyes were wide, expecting to see his mother's face around every corner. But she did not appear.

Hild's brow was yet furrowed. "She did not know me. Am I so altered?"

"Not to me," Eyvind said. "Come, it seems we have found your civilization at last."

St. Ignace, MI, July 1999: The eastern end of the Upper Peninsula lay within a day's ride from Gulliver. The steady overnight rain relented next morning, leaving a thick fog blanket on the landscape. Most days we rode whatever mileage felt right, but today we were committed to ride seventy-five miles. Matt and Karen, our old friends from Boston had flown out to meet us in St. Ignace for the July 4 holiday weekend. They wanted to be the first to celebrate the end of our journey, a month early.

St. Ignace is where the Mackinac Bridge, five miles of freeway, towers and suspended cables – a super-sized Golden Gate Bridge—connects the Upper Peninsula to the rest of Michigan and the Midwest. We wouldn't cross it; I didn't need to see Detroit again, although it might have been fun to visit the airport and show Jane the bench where I spent the snowy night that snowballed into the Big One.

Afternoon sunshine dissolved the fog as we pedaled eastward along Route 2. The day off had done us all good; the bike hummed along with so little effort the miles rolled beneath us unnoticed and we focused on the scenery. On our right Lake Michigan sparkled indigo beyond long stretches of white sand beach. Within half a mile, another blue horizon loomed ahead: Lake Huron. The road narrowed to two lanes and swooped northward to hug the shore as the Upper Peninsula neared its eastern end. Grassy verge gave way to sandy beach civilized with park benches, play structures, picnic tables and gazebos.

"I'd swear we were on the Cape," Jane said. Up ahead a stubby promontory jutted eastward, forming East Moran Bay. Another elegant white-washed brick lighthouse stood sentinel at its point.

"I never knew there was so much inland coast," I said. "We should be just up past that lighthouse."

We pedaled through the heart of St. Ignace, then pulled into the plush hotel our friends had booked for the busy holiday weekend. Jane and I had both known Karen before we'd found each other at her birthday party. Because she brought us together she held a special place in our hearts. A keen traveler, she had been my sister's college roommate, a close friend of Jane, an avid cyclist, and now an ardent supporter of our journey. Matt provided a good balance for Karen; reserved and technical like me and also knew his way around a kitchen. If not for the guys, these ladies would subsist mainly on cereal and toast.

The bike stowed, the four of us played sightseers that humid weekend: a packed ferry disgorged us onto Mackinac Island, the tourist magnet and location for the film *Somewhere in Time*. Cars are forbidden on the island as there is nowhere to park, in favor of horse-drawn carriage taxis. Hence everyone walks, and sweats in the summer heat. Bodies of strange pedestrians pressed in from all sides, adding their unwanted warmth to my own. Artificial perfumes and stress-induced body odor made my stomach lurch. I felt bad for the horses, surrounded all day by the stink of humanity and wondered if they daydreamed of galloping through green, sun-drenched pastures. Crowds make me nervous. I like the *concept* of large gatherings, but often find I'm lonely in a crowd. After two months of blue skies, endless vistas and the open road, a day amongst the masses shocked my system, dulled my senses and left me ponderous and exhausted.

"Oh boy, oh mighty. That was rough," Jane said that night in the hotel room as we turned in.

"Yeah," I said. "It started out fun, playing mini-golf and that, but all that crowded touristy stuff took a lot out of me."

"Me too. Just our axe to bear, I guess."

"Axe to…ah, you mean cross…our cross to bear."

"Whatever. I'm wiped."

On the Fourth Karen and Matt treated us to my belated birthday *Moët* and strawberries on our hotel room balcony as the night sky bloomed in a riot of color, smoke and noise. Both great talkers, our friends regaled us with story after story of their own adventures, as if in friendly competition with ours. Karen had survived cancer, cycled around the world, started a business and I'd always looked up to her and been content to listen and wish for my own adventures. We all slipped into the familiar pattern we'd established and always enjoyed, but now I found myself feeling frustrated. I told our stories but couldn't seem to convey the power of our experiences, or how those two months had changed us. Maybe we didn't need to explain ourselves. Maybe they already understood, but I began to feel out of place with these old friends, whereas I'd felt instantly at home with Jon and Carol in Wisconsin, Ed and Margaret in Montana, and Kurt and Malotte in Minnesota. Connection was far easier without the prejudice of history, to see others and be seen with "baby eyes."

My frustration turned into sadness when the thought struck me that maybe I no longer belonged at home. Was it the people or the place that didn't fit me? Perhaps both. Maybe places attracted certain types of people; sub-cultures and philosophies borne out of topography, climate, flora and fauna, and history. Maybe I wasn't meant for New England and that's why I could never buy a home there.

Presently our friends bade us a good night and retired to their room. Jane and I stayed out on the balcony, grateful for the quiet, watching the night sky. A wall of storm clouds gathered on the heels of the fireworks. A dark gray wave curled overhead. Nature would not be outdone by man's puny fireworks: she threw down sheets of rain and cracked the sky with many-limbed bolts that thudded and echoed in our chests and flashed our retinas with glowing images of scarlet, lime green and even purple.

I saved the champagne cork as a memory from that time for many years afterward, but we would never spend another weekend with these friends. The road we'd chosen claimed its toll.

The next day found us fifty miles north, gazing at the Sault St. Marie International Bridge. Nearly two miles long, its narrow, two-lane road rises 123 feet above the St. Mary's River, which connects Lake Superior to its sister Great Lakes and ultimately the Atlantic Ocean. The largest of freighters pass under its span with ease, while crosswinds have been known to blow trucks off its tightrope of a road; the road we chose to travel today.

"See you when you get home!" our friends had said when we set off that morning, their voices and images already a distant, fading echo. I didn't know where home was anymore. The thick cords that moored us to New England, woven over two generations, each strand a relationship, had begun to fray and unravel.

Jane read my thoughts. "Now do you see why I had to come with you?"

"To do my socializing, of course." My attempted humor failed this time, my fake smile dissipating under Jane's steady gaze.

"I knew you'd come back a different person, and I wouldn't have understood why unless I'd gone with you."

I took a deep breath. "So you know I might not be able to live in Newton anymore?"

She looked away a moment, then locked eyes again. "I don't know if I can either."

This was big. Jane's family was tight-knit. They still all gathered for Christmas, Thanksgiving and birthdays. Unlike my family, who hadn't gathered since the last wedding five years ago, they had traditions. Although she had a life invested back east, apparently Jane and I had been thinking in tandem, wondering if we'd be happier making a new life elsewhere. And she would come with me to find out. This journey was hers as much as mine.

I faced the bridge. "It's narrow, and blowing like hell up there. No bike lane. No way to turn back."

"Let's get across," Jane said.

ONTARIO

The longest street in the world is Younge Street in Ontario. It stretches over 1,178 miles. They must have house numbers in the millions.

26 TEA TIME

Up on the "Soo" bridge we leaned left into a stiff crosswind, our heads almost in the traffic lane. The wind whistled through my helmet's vent holes and clawed at my arms and legs. For three miles we threaded our way along the two-foot wide pedestrian corridor, separated from the traffic only by a low steel rail that presumably arrested the tires of any vehicles blown sideways. I didn't look down or enjoy the view, and if Jane did, she didn't talk about it. Keeping our rig upright and moving commanded my full attention.

We crested the midpoint and began the descent into Canada. At three-quarters across, the winds relented and we could relax and coast to the gatehouse. A bored border official gave our Massachusetts driver's licenses the briefest of glances, handed them back and said "Welcome to Canada." At the Ministry of Tourism office we found no road maps available, nor did they seem necessary. Only one road joined each population center; you could not get lost. We went east on the *Trans-Canada Highway*, straight and level with a decent shoulder. A tailwind pushed us from Sault St. Marie into pleasant countryside forested with pine and hardwoods. After twenty miles we spotted a mobile home converted into a café—kitchen inside, tables outside—and pulled over for our first Canadian refreshment: tea and sandwiches.

"Now that's a good cup of tea," Jane said, refilling her cup from the pot. "Almost as good as in England." I agreed, and filled mine. A stream of liquid copper hissed into my cup, sending up steamy curls of aromatic vapor. I tilted the milk jug and a thin white jet plunged into the steam, dove to the bottom of the cup and exploded upward. An undersea cloud suffused the clear red-gold, forming an opaque, tanned creaminess. Bubbles gathered on the surface like tiny pearls that danced and broke with the stir of a spoon. I raised the steaming cup to my lips, paused to inhale scents of pungent leaf, tropical flowers, fertile black earth, and equatorial sunshine. I closed my eyes and sipped, anticipating the flavor that would carry me back to a thousand peaceful afternoons. The warmth spread downwards, throat to belly, all the way to fingers and toes. Unlike coffee, which zaps me awake with a caffeine cattle prod, the stimulus of tea is subtle, a beautiful lady who whispers in my ear, cradles my body and mind in warm soft hands and gives a firm but gentle lift.

Jane and I were tea connoisseurs. Our families of origin retained the English tea-time tradition, and we never broke the four-o'clock habit. At home the only problem was supply. Domestic brands such as Lipton and Red Rose were stale and insipid, so each trip to England we stopped at a Waitrose or a Sainsbury's and filled our cart with absurdly cheap yet robust and fragrant packets of Assam, Kenya, Darjeeling and English Breakfast, fresh from the four corners of the British Empire.

Although part of North America, Canada is not American. America and Canada were sister colonies, bastard offspring of England and France, that couple driven together and apart throughout history by mutual alternations of lust and loathing. America was the favored one, with such potential, so like her ambitious parents, yet destined for even greater achievements. England secretly feared America, guarded her with jealousy, exploited and taxed her while treating her as minion, an inferior, unrefined and ignorant. America, desperate for recognition, became the bad girl, the rebel. She smoked and wore leather, hung out with gangs of Germans. England tried discipline, slapped her around, until America pulled a gun and said, "Liberty or death, you old bitch." England screamed, "Just you wait! You'll see how it is to civilize aboriginals, fund civil wars, crush revolts, fend off foreign invasions. See if you don't come crawling back when Spain rams a dreadnought up your arse! You're just like me!" "I'm nothing like you," America shouted. "I'll never have your rigid class structure, your imperialism, your snotty arrogance! And you know what? Tea is for wussies and old farts! Coffee from now on!"

Canada, meanwhile, got on rather well with mother England. She limited France to one province. She took tea, dressed her police in bright red coats, paid homage to the sovereign, joined in when England picked fights with the neighbors; all the while taking small steps towards the independence her sister colony had only achieved at gunpoint. Eventually England allowed Canada a place of her own: a flag, a Parliament, and money; dollars bearing the face of mother England. Canada had grown up, yet remained firmly within the tea-drinking Commonwealth.

In time, America grew up also. She saw the truth in England's admonitions; the pitfalls of slavery, the cost of civil war, the difficulties of empire-building and how irritating Spain could be. She saw the striking likeness to her mother. They spoke the same language. And England could see America now as a peer and not a servant. The two clasped hands, embraced, and together pummeled Germany. Twice. But England never forgot the "wussies and old farts" comment, and in secret organized her tea-growing friends to send America nothing but the dregs.

Which is why small town America proved to be a tea-drinker's purgatory. Typically we'd get a coffee mug full of tepid water, a bag of scentless, pulverized brown dust, and a useless lemon wedge. Whatever tea flavor we could extract from the stale leaf remnant was overpowered by the mug's acidic coffee residue. We could do a tad better with our camp stove and plastic mugs. This Canadian potful was the first in two months anywhere near as strong and hot as we liked it. The tea was fresh and flavorful, the water had truly been boiled, and it arrived with bone china tea cups, matching saucers, a small pitcher of milk, and no lemon whatsoever. Civilization at last.

A spaciousness like the Montana prairie surrounded us: wide open expanses of grass, occasional farmhouses, white pine and birch woodlands, and plentiful lakes. None of it was familiar; until we reached New York we could stay in denial about our proximity to home. We let the subject of where we'd be living post-Big One lie undisturbed for the time being. That idea needed more time to gestate. Instead, I recalled our discussion in Wisconsin.

"Looks like we made the right choice," I said, unable to keep the smug out of my tone. "We would have been in Kalamazoo by now, headed for Fort Wayne, with Cleveland to look forward to."

"Aaah, the traffic, those fumes," Jane said with a shudder. "Cheers to Canada." We clinked teacups.

"Is this still the Trans-Canada Highway?" Jane said, indicating the road by the café.

"I think so," I said, finishing my last bite of sandwich. "It's also called Highway 17 around here. It seems to be the only way east. Why?"

"When I talked to David on the phone yesterday, he said to avoid the Trans-Canada at all costs. He was pretty insistent about it." David is Jane's older brother, quiet and thoughtful, and someone with whom I can easily dominate the conversation. He only says what is truly worth saying. When he's emphatic, I pay close attention. But this didn't jibe.

"I don't see how we can avoid it," I said. "At any rate, this road seems fine. What were his objections?"

"He said it was dangerous. Narrow, with lots of big trucks. 'It's the worst road I've ever driven,' he said. 'It's a death road.'"

"He called it a *death road*?"

"That's what he said."

"Well it's the only road going east. He must be thinking of another road. That busy one in Idaho was a lot worse than this, and I used to commute through Lynn every day and had more than insults hurled at me. This is nothing, trust me."

After tea-time, we knew David had made no mistake, and we were the fools. His professional expertise is GIS systems. He doesn't just read maps, he makes them. Within the next twenty miles, a skinny band of loose gravel replaced our paved shoulder and the road narrowed to three inches in excess of two truck-widths; the extra three inches occupied by the center stripe. Road crews here did not waste materials, and posted no speed limits.

27 TRANSPORTS

Dublin, Ireland, 899 AD: *Thorvald, twelve year old red-haired son of Olaf and Frieda, begged Eyvind to teach him the sword. They practiced every day with wooden staves while Eyvind and Hild stayed as guests in Olaf's lodge. Hild admired the finery collected from Olaf's travels: silks, jade, ivory, bright-glazed stoneware. The city enthralled her with its music, foreigners, strange foods, bazaars and slave markets. She loved to go out riding on one of Olaf's sturdy dun ponies, twins named Freyr and Freya, along the narrow lanes crisscrossing the rolling hills and tilled fields outside of the city.*

Today she urged Eyvind to come along. *"You must practice your riding, my love. That is how you improve."*

"Perhaps it will give my sword arm a rest," he said, and they set off together, Eyvind on Freya, the gentle mare, while Hild rode Freyr, the frisky stallion.

After a peaceful ride through the countryside, they walked Freyr and Freya along a narrow lane, a path between plowed fields bordered on one side by a rough stone wall, on the other by a wide, water-filled ditch. A deep rumbling from behind made them turn. An empty hay-rick, nearly as wide as the lane and drawn by two galloping horses, charged toward them at high speed. At first Eyvind thought it was a runaway, but its Irish driver whipped his horses on, a gleam in his eye. *"Go, Hild, go!"* Eyvind slapped Freyr's rump and urged Freya into a trot, down the lane, to where it hopefully opened out and they could step aside.

"What does he mean to do, run us off the road?" Hild said, glancing behind.

"It appears so. Olaf did say the Irish can be bastards." Eyvind said. *"I should have brought my sword. Do not these ponies go any faster? That mad waggoneer draws closer."*

The wagon rumbled onward, looming larger. Hoofs thundered, throwing up clods of dirt from the track. The mad Irishman now keened and howled, a wolf scenting sheep. Yet Freyr and Freya merely trotted, oblivious to any danger.

"Hild, the ditch!" Exasperated, Eyvind turned Freya around to make a stand. Hild turned Freyr toward the ditch, made a run, and leapt it nimbly. But her grin of triumph became a gasp of horror. Freya, now spooked by the wagon, shied and skittered sideways, stumbling at the edge of the ditch. Eyvind toppled forward and hit the water with a splash. As the wagon roared past, there was Mother's ghost, scowling next to the mad driver who shrieked: "To the devil with ye, foreign filth!!" The wagon careened onward.

Eyvind stood, hip-deep in ditch water, pulling wet weeds from his hair. "Irish bastards."

"Oh, Eyvind, are you all right?" Hild said.

"Clumsy horse," Eyvind said. Freya tossed her head.

Trans-Canada Highway, Ontario, July 1999: Canadian transports are very much like our semi-trucks, only without brakes. At least it seemed that way. We spent the rest of our day dodging them, as they sped by in both directions in excess of 100 kilometers per hour in increasing numbers. We only had the air wake to contend with when a single transport passed us. The drivers were good about moving over a foot or two to give us space. But when they bore down from opposite directions, which happened every ten minutes or so, something had to give, and that something was us.

To avoid being splattered on the grille of a thundering Peterbilt, bits of torn lycra and Goretex flapping between the bars like the crushed wings of some huge pastel moth, we ditched into the loose, tire grabbing gravel road bank. A sudden stop could launch us over the handlebars if we didn't brace for it. Like in Idaho when I had my gas issue, we worked out a system. When I saw transport grilles filling up both my forward field of vision and rearview mirror, I yelled "DITCH!" We braced, then ditched into the gravel. The first time, we stopped four feet from the lane. A blast of air ahead of the transport shoved us away, then as it passed by, a suction pulled us toward the churning wheels. The ground shook and the roar of converging diesels rose to a crescendo, battered us like a thousand tiny fists, then faded in a cloud of gray fumes. It was over in two or three seconds.

This wasn't nothing. But we could get through it. I looked back at Jane. "All right?"

Her mouth was a thin line, jaw set. She nodded. "Let's go."

We pedaled with a will until the next meeting of the transports. During one of these pedaling intervals, Jane heard me laughing. "What's so funny?" she shouted.

"Ironic, isn't it?" I said. "We came this way to avoid dangerous traffic."

Jane didn't see the humor. I can be such an idiot. What a meaningless, embarrassing death it would be, crushed by a transport on a road we had no business being on. I'd hate to be our parents, if this went badly. I'm truly sorry for your loss, Mrs. Owens, Mrs. Justice; but cycling on the Trans-Canada? Maybe Darwin was onto something. I thought of our brush with the grizzly bear, the lightning storms, and all the other intense traffic situations we'd faced and emerged from, unscathed, when we could have been killed. Was it destiny or luck? Now I had to believe in destiny. Statistics dictate that luck runs out, and I wasn't ready to die.

After eighty miles, nerves frayed, shadows creeping across the road, we pulled into a nameless roadside motel. According to locals, we had another sixty miles on the Trans-Canada before we could turn off it forever.

In the room that night we made what seemed a simple and clever plan: get up super-early and beat the traffic; get our sixty miles done before 9 o'clock. Exhaustion dragged us into fitful sleep once the excess adrenaline discharged from our twitching limbs. Still better than a business trip, I thought; except I don't get paid.

At first light we set off, taillight flashing, and found that the traffic beat us again. We had indeed beaten all the car traffic. At this hour nothing but transports filled the road. Headlights seemed to search, fix on us, pin us down in their glare. Then came the jake-brake roar, like a great carnivorous beast scenting blood. Ready to pounce, air horns shrieked, obliterating all other sound. Blinded and deafened, we sidestepped the charges again and again, like a two-wheeled matador in a weird, pre-dawn mechanized bullfight. After an eternal hour, the sun peeked over the eastern hills. We settled into the rhythm that comes from doing a thing so many times it happens without thought. I didn't need to yell "DITCH" anymore. We'd learned the dance. In only a day we'd adjusted from terror to tolerance of the transports.

In early afternoon we reached Espanola and whooped for joy at the final turn off of the Trans-Canada. My sphincter unclenched as relief washed over me. I made a silent prayer of thanks to whatever unseen guardians had come to our aid, with a vow to make better choices. Guardians tend to abandon those who refuse to learn.

A thunderstorm's growl and pelting drops sent us to shelter at a fruit stand covered by an enormous blue tarp. The smiling young couple who ran it had emigrated from Ireland. We selected bananas, apples and peaches as we told them of our harrowing ride. We asked about Route 6, the only road to take us south to Manatoulin Island. Was it any better? They told us the Trans-Canada was "the good road." *Fabulous*, I thought. But a good road for a car is not the same as a good road for a bike. We stowed our fruit and pulled on rain jackets.

28 THE ONLY ROAD

At 415,000 square miles, Ontario is immense; larger than the states of Texas and Montana combined. It stretches from Hudson Bay to Lake Erie and spans New York to Minnesota. Nevertheless, it is only the fourth largest Canadian province. It is also the most crowded one, home to more than a third of all Canadians. Its border with the U.S. is over 1,600 miles long, most of it formed by the Great Lakes and inland waterways. We would keep to the southern edge of Ontario, hug the northern shore of Lake Huron, then hop onto Manatoulin Island, skirt Toronto and finally cross the St. Lawrence River into New York state. We would only see a tiny sliver of southeastern Ontario, not to sight-see but merely to short-cut through the neighbor's back yard. We had three weeks to get home and my latest ATM slip revealed an alarming balance, with one decimal place fewer than I'd expected. I told myself I'd have a new career when I got home. I'd start a business, use my vast computer experience to help the underdogs: the small businesses, artists and non-profits without the knowledge to leverage the internet. I'd never give anyone else the power to bore and exploit me; I'd do it for myself.

Route 6 from Espanola to Manatoulin Island was a big improvement from a cyclist's perspective. Drivers preferred the Trans-Canada because with its long empty straightaways they could go 120 kph and hardly ever use their brakes. In contrast, Route 6's narrow and crumbling surface slithered and wound a torturous path through undulating, boulder-strewn wilderness. It led to nothing of interest to most drivers; no shopping malls, gas stations, liquor stores, casinos or Tim Horton's donut shops. To us, however, it felt like the eye of the storm, a welcome interlude of peace in a chaotic world.

Two roads diverged in a wood and I,

I took the one less traveled by,
And that has made all the difference [12].

Jane's mom often recited Robert Frost and these lines now recalled themselves. Here the choice of road was easy. How would it be when we got home? The smooth, straight freeway I'd been traveling fast on before the Big One, alongside all my friends and colleagues—the high-stress high-tech job and grandiose big-city living—*had* not, and *could* not lead me to Blissville. It would detour and drop me at Cardiac Ar-Rest Stop, Obese City, Pharmacoepia, and Singletown, midway between Misery Island and Point of Despair. By riding the Big One, we'd taken an exit, a bone-jarring, ramshackle road, abandoned and forgotten, with a signpost so faded and obscured by tall weeds we couldn't make out its destination. Yet it felt right. I hoped it would lead to a place where we didn't feel like weirdos for being late bloomers extraordinaire. It was our only, lonely road. Maybe not quite lonely, because I knew in my heart, since we crossed the Soo Bridge, that Jane and I would travel it together to its end. She knew how to love unconditionally, and I would learn how.

To be married now felt right. Of all the questions I'd been trying to answer these past nine weeks, this was the only one I could be sure of, and it was the one that mattered most. I'd done this journey out of love, not fear. "What is your heart's desire?" Jane had asked me. My answer then had been "to ride the Big One." I'd done that, except for this final stretch. My answer now, thought but unvoiced, would be to marry her, to make a home and a family. The first seemed probable, the second difficult but possible, the third, still a dream; but no longer a fantasy.

Manatoulin, largest lake island in the world, lies on the Canadian side of Lake Huron. It contains over one hundred of its own lakes, many with their own islands. On empty roads we pedaled among towering natural rock formations streaked with muted shades of ochre, violet, avocado and harvest gold; colors that give this area the nickname "Rainbow Country." Pristine ponds left and right looked better than expensive landscaping, complete with lily pads, turtles, dragonflies, weeping willows, ornamental grasses, and blood-red wildflowers sprouting between the rocks. A series of bridges between smaller "stepping stone" islands connected Manitoulin to the mainland. We wouldn't need a boat until we got to its eastern end.

Since we'd spent the past few nights indoors we kept an eye out for camping opportunities. In Sheguindah we stopped at a large grassy field, sodden from recent rains, on which row upon row of campers and popup trailers squatted. A large sign indicated that we beheld a campground, not an RV storage lot. I turned to Jane and said "I don't think so" just as she said "No way."

---

[12] "The Road Not Taken" by Robert Frost

A few kilometers – le Système international d'unités prevailed here — further on, the sign *Island Oaks Bed and Breakfast and Antiques* caught my eye. Retirees Stan and Barbara Arnelien met us at the door. Stan, wheelchair-bound since a stroke a few years ago paralyzed his left side, kept the antique business going. His wife Barbara ran everything else and asked all the questions. She immediately found out my profession.

"Computers, eh? Maybe you can fix my printer," she said. "I'm ready to strangle it."

"I specialize in antique technology," I said, recalling antique dealer Ed in Montana, and anticipating a future client. I performed CPR (Crappy Printer Repair) and it wheezed back to life.

The next morning Jane and I sat in a borrowed car outside a bank in town. Heavy rain rattled the roof and sheeted down the windows. Barbara had handed us her car keys, in the way that grateful proprietors always seem to do after I fix their computer equipment, so we could get some cash. I was soaked through just from the dash between car and ATM. Miniature class 4 rapids coursed down both gutters of the street, forcing even Canadian drivers to turn on their headlights and slow down. We looked at one another and chuckled, knowing how ridiculous it would be to ride that day. Back at the inn we told Barbara we'd be staying another night. She clapped her hands and invited us to dinner that evening, "as our guests."

A strapping young man named Brian, an engineering instructor with the US Navy, was the inn's other guest. He'd arrived on a motorcycle and also elected to wait out the rain, and would join us for dinner. I wondered what he had repaired. Since Stan and Barbara had two of their grandchildren visiting, we formed a family circle of sorts around the dinner table: three generations. The dinner table…

Marblehead, Massachusetts, 1973: "It's ready. Now," Mom declared, raising a hand to smash the little brass wind chime that hung from the kitchen ceiling light and served as our dinner bell. In 1973 I was ten.

Our dinner table was an oval of dense maple: stained, stripped, painted and refinished many times, bumped and scarred from long use. The table came with spindle-back wooden chairs, seats polished smooth and spindles worn white, loose or missing. One chair, a ram among the tired old sheep, was larger and sturdier than the rest and equipped with arms, meant for the family's head.

I remember that year because the war in Vietnam ended, Dad turned fifty, and I learned what "laid off" meant. It meant you lost your job, but it wasn't your fault. Mom started working for a realtor's that year, and would take the Mercedes out to show houses. Dad stayed home and tried to sell burglar alarms. It seemed like a lot of houses were for sale, and not because of burglaries.

Dad and my teenaged siblings shuffled in and took their places at the dinner table. I, youngest, sat at the "tail" end, backed into the bay window. From there we sat in order of age: Dave and Wendy either side of me, Alan and Mom either side of Dad at the "head" end. Except now, Dad slumped in one of the lesser chairs, thighs crossed, like he'd been hit in the balls. "I like having my back to the wall," he'd said when I asked about the seating change. "I can keep an eye on everyone." Mom placed the casserole in the center of the table, threw off the oven mitts and sat herself cross-legged in the ram chair, at the head of the table, hands fisted on the arms.

"Go ahead," she challenged, glaring all around.

"What IS that?" my brother said, studying the dish, the surface of which was crusted over and blackened, with bits of broccoli sticking up, like a battlefield diorama that had been fire-bombed.

"Just eat it and shut up."

The three months of this journey were the longest I'd ever been out of work, but I'd chosen unemployment. And none of our dining room chairs at home had arms.

"How far away was that grizzly?" Jane had been telling that story and her question snapped me out of my reverie.

"Thirty feet or so," I said. "Initially. But when we passed by him, no more than twenty." Satisfying gasps from our audience.

We traded stories of the road for Barbara's anecdotes of quirky neighbors and island living. We must have got on the subject of death— maybe it was hearing about Stan's stroke and paralysis—when Brian opened up about his head-on car accident a few years back. Rescuers approached the wreckage with little hope, his car twisted and crumpled like a smoking ball of tinfoil. They pried it open and gathered him up. Miraculously brain and spinal cord, his tree-of-life, were undamaged. Months of surgeries replaced shattered bones and joints with titanium rods, screws and other hardware. He learned to walk again. In a year he could live on his own. Now he no longer feared death. He'd accepted his death in the moments after the crash. Since then, every day was a miraculous, unexpected gift.

I wonder if we as humans need to know death in order to embrace life. Maybe that's the attraction of thrill-seeking, death-defying pursuits: to silence the mind and allow ourselves to feel our blood course through veins, our breath surge into lungs, our flesh, resilient yet fragile. I imagine ancient people always lived on that twilight edge, with threats from predation, starvation, exposure, and battle with their neighbors as daily realities. Maybe this journey was my way of an introduction to death at a distance, to make me see the tragedy of the road not taken, to see the life I'd lived as a predictable sequence of fear-based, avoid-the-pain choices. That stuff catches up with you. Eventually all your choices are painful and it takes a death threat to face the fear of the unknown.

We were all silent a moment. Then Barbara asked Jane if she would play a song or two for the kids. We gathered in the living room. Jane started with one of her quiet lullabies, and the little boy was asleep before the second verse. After Barbara put the grandchildren to bed, she came downstairs smiling.

"It's never that easy, usually," she said. "They often can't get to sleep and have horrible nightmares. Their father's a drunken bastard who beats their mother, sometimes so bad she has to be rushed to the hospital."

"That's so sad," Jane said. "Those poor kids."

"But that music," said Barbara. "Something in that music gave them peace. They were asleep instantly."

Jane's eyes shone. "Well, thank you for letting me share it." *She'd make a great mother*, I thought.

"I hope you will continue to share that gift," said Barbara.

As we pushed further east, the journey became less like flying and more like crawling. The physical challenges we had mastered. We liked the cycling. Our bodies were lean, hard and enduring. The demands now, near the finish, were mental and emotional, and like our bodies back in Washington, our minds now needed to strengthen or we'd be plowed under when we got home and wanted to make life changes. Since entering Ontario, death seemed to surround us. First, we faced being run over by transports. Then we encountered a man paralyzed by stroke, a battered family, an accident victim re-animated with power tools and metallurgy, and the near-trashing of an innocent printer. We were in the dark; plunged into a long tunnel of uncertainty and doubt, straining to see if a distant glimmer marked its end.

29 THE LAST RESORT

"Where are you headed?" I asked the slim young woman as she cycled past us on a mud-spattered mountain bike close behind that of a matching slim young man. Four water bottles hung from her frame, front and rear panniers bulged, and camping gear was bungied on. "New York," she threw over her shoulder, voice dropping in pitch due to the Doppler effect, and they were gone.

"Great," I said to no one. "Nice talking to you." My guess was that this couple probably hadn't had lunch yet in their rush to catch the 1:30 ferry to Tobermoray. We cornered them on the boat and coaxed a little more out of them. They were Swiss and lived near Geneva. Their Big One was halfway around the world, Australia to Switzerland, crossing the US from Los Angeles to New York. Our enthusiasm to hear their stories far exceeded theirs in telling them. They fidgeted, darted their eyes around, distracted. They wanted to be elsewhere. We let them go. We'd met few other touring cyclists on this journey, which surprised me. More surprising was how most of the ones we met were in a great hurry and avoided us, like they were in the middle of a race and we slowed them down. That wasn't our style. We traveled, and now lived, in the slow lane.

We stood on the deck, near the bow, sun warm on our backs, breeze ruffling our hair. Memories rekindled. "Remember that ferry ride in Washington, from Whidbey Island?" I said.

"Seems like ages ago," Jane said. "Those were the days. We had this whole journey ahead of us. It was so beautiful there."

"I loved the sea and the mountains; the fresh air. Not taking too many pictures anymore."

"This is hard labor. I'm just counting the days," Jane said.

"You're not having fun anymore?" I said with mock surprise.

She glared at me. "You're joking."

"Yes." The wonder of the journey had worn thin as my threadbare and faded tee shirts. We'd lost some of our good humor, especially since the ordeal with the transports. We spent more time in silence, counting the days, counting the miles to home. The ship plodded across Lake Huron. We stood silent on the deck, looking ahead, looking east.

From Tobermoray we picked up Route 6, once again the only road, after all the eastbound ferry traffic and the racing Swiss cleared out. As we rode I looked up in horror to see a car in the wrong lane, bearing down on us, head on. The driver accelerated past six slower vehicles in an attempt to make the ferry. *Head-on crash, twisted wreckage, months of surgeries, titanium rods, learning to walk again, lucky to be alive* flashed through my mind. Reflexes engaged. "DITCH!" I yelled, and we plowed into the roadside dirt as he rocketed by. I doubt he'd seen us, or if he had, just didn't care.

Late in the day we turned off of Route 6 with relief onto the unpaved road that led to Lion's Head, an affluent community of large waterfront homes which on this summer Saturday night had filled all its decent accommodations. Our last resort hove into view as dusk descended. Nick's Cabins benefitted from the failing light, having been constructed primarily from dumpster scraps. Nick was pleasant enough, well into a six-pack of Molson's, and we weren't so fussy by now.

While attempting to cook dinner I found an earwig rummaging in our food bag. I ran with the bag into the bathroom with the intention of flipping the harmless fellow into the toilet. Instead, the earwig leaped free of the gyrating bag and scuttled to safety. The uncooked spaghetti slid in a golden cascade, missing the toilet to bounce and scatter like pick-up sticks across the bathroom floor. Did she see? I couldn't get them all up before Jane stuck her head around the door and saw everything. That spaghetti was our only food, and local stores all closed. Our eyes met and for a split second we hung poised on the edge of a pit of righteous rage, suppressed frustration and mental exhaustion, so easy to dive into and wallow. Instead we both collapsed in whoops of laughter. We laughed until the tears flowed. It had been a while since our last good laugh, and fortunately, we laughed together.

"Oh, honey," Jane said. "What are we doing? Where are we going?"

"We're living the dream, of course," I said. "I hope to own a cabin like this one day." This started the laughter all over again.

We ate the spaghetti. Boiling kills everything, right? We were lucky enough to have both olive oil and salt for it. At home, I'd make a simple tomato sauce: chopped onions and plenty of pressed garlic sautéed golden in extra virgin olive oil. Add generous pinches of dried basil, oregano and sea salt. Then chopped roma tomatoes, a splash of merlot and a few twists of black pepper. Finish with a drip of molasses or two, if the tomatoes need some extra sweetness. Let that simmer a while. Let the garlic and herbs flavor the walls for years to come. Let the scent seduce you, obsess you with visions of your plate, mounded and steaming; the grated parmesan melting, forming little rivulets down the flanks. You plunge in a fork and turn, winding up the perfect bite…

I missed cooking in our tiny galley kitchen at home, too small for a table. With all we'd been through, on this trip and over the years, I knew we could be happy anywhere together. We'd gotten good at taking up no space. But I'd lived four years in that little house in Newton, comfortable, but under someone else's roof. Now I wanted our own roof, and room to grow. I wanted to be terrified, not comfortable; terrified and alive like I was when we started on the Big One.

"I meant what I said in Michigan," I said.

"About not living in Newton anymore?" Jane said. "I know. I meant it too. I haven't forgotten how it was before we left. It wasn't working anymore." *Relief. We were together on this.*

"I want to have it all figured out, though, by the time we get home," I said. "I feel like we should know what we want by now."

"Should?" she smiled. "That sounds like your mother. Ian, this is huge. This is about where we're going to live, what we're going to do for work, what sort of community we want. It's going to take time. Hopefully not years, but months at least."

"You may be right. A few months anyway. We'll take it one step at a time." If you want to do something big, you do a little piece every day. Life is one big … Big One.

30 SHE AIN'T PEDALIN'

Dublin, Ireland, 899 AD: *After a month in Dubhlinn, Eyvind felt confined and was restless. And as Olaf's crew prepared for the autumn voyage, Hild again would not be left behind.*

"I saved your life once," she said to Eyvind. "This is my journey as much as yours."

They both boarded Wulf Sang for a voyage further south, beyond the Saxon realm to the Golden lands, as Olaf envisioned. Brisk trade winds brought them to an azure sea, sun-sparkled and warm. Dolphins raced alongside the ship. Land appeared, with fine sand beaches the color of snow, and trees without branches that grew like giant flowers and swayed in the breeze. The sun bleached the tiny mud hovels white and burned coppery the skins of the rag-swaddled natives, who scurried like animals whenever the ship came close to shore. "I have never seen such poverty," Eyvind said.

"Nor I," said Olaf. "Where are the churches and temples stuffed with gold and silver? Do not these people worship the nailed god?"

Days stretched into weeks. The only shining gold was the pitiless sun. The winds died. They turned the ship around. And rowed. They rowed until backs blistered and oars rubbed hands raw.

One day Eyvind, at the oar, noticed a dark spot on the horizon astern. It seemed to grow as he watched. "Is that another ship?"

"Coming straight for us, no matter how I alter course," Svein said, then shouted "Olaf!"

Olaf came aft and squinted where Svein pointed. "Trouble?"

"Could be. They're large and moving fast. Longship."

"Arm yourselves!" Olaf barked. His warriors and Eyvind donned whatever

mail or leather they had and pulled weapons from beneath benches. Olaf pushed his own helmet down over his unruly red hair and took up his battle axe. "Be ready. They may try to break our oars as they pass."

Hild took up a rusted sword plundered from a dead pirate and stood with Eyvind at the stern.

"Hild," Eyvind said. "What are you…"

"We fight together, husband. Remember the Shield-Maidens?"

A bright painted dragon head could now be seen on the approaching war ship. At the bow stood a blond-bearded Dane, resplendent in fine mail but missing his left arm. Olaf lowered his axe and motioned to his men to do the same. "Thorfinn! Still out looking for your arm?"

"Olaf, still bobbing about in that old tub?" the one-armed Dane replied. "We would plunder you, but you ride so high in the water I think it not worth the effort."

"You are welcome to try, but how will you scratch your arse when I take your other arm?"

Thorfinn laughed, then caught sight of Hild, who still held her sword. "If you want to get home by Yule, make that girl row! She looks like the best man you have!" Thorfinn signaled with his remaining arm and the dragon ship, with twenty oars churning, veered off and left them behind.

"I never liked that bastard," Olaf said.

Presently Wulf Sang eked its way past Cornwall, riding high in the flat sea. They had little to show for two months of trading with the filthy, jabbering people who inhabited the barren, sun-blanched southern wasteland. Its fabled riches, if they ever existed, had already been picked clean by the Danes.

Ontario, Canada, July, 1999: We reached the town of Barrie, fifty miles north of Toronto, on July 12. The odometer read 2,944, and I figured we had about a thousand to go over the next twenty days: fifty miles per day, average. That sounded familiar, and now so much easier a prospect than the first time I'd said it. Hot, sultry weather had settled in; the combination of blazing sun, sudden rains and oppressive humidity that marked high summer in the east. The air hung thick and heavy with moisture while cicadas buzzed. Here the road demanded little else from us than to keep pedaling. Flattish, grassy farmland, small clusters of beech, oak, birch and maple, the occasional forest of wispy eastern pine, very few cars and plenty of sky reminded us of the prairie.

Now one of the few cars whipped past us at high speed. I saw no smoke on the horizon. "Jane," I called back to her, "I wonder why the locals drive so fast? They're pretty laid back when you meet them in person, but put them in a car and they're possessed."

"Maybe it's because they're so spread out," she said. "It takes a long time getting anywhere, so you go fast and save time."

"Okay," I said. "So with all this space why do they pack themselves together when camping? Every campground we've seen is like a parking lot."

"I suspect it's because they like to socialize on vacation, since they live so isolated."

I was about to agree with this reasoning when a silver minivan pulled up beside us, matching our speed. The window lowered and a red unshaven face with a round, balding head poked out. "Hey, she ain't pedallin'!"

We rolled our eyes. We didn't get this joke the first time we heard it, nor the twentieth time, and it was just as unfunny this time. Our entertainment grinned at me and waited for me to look behind. "Hey, mister, tell us one we haven't heard," I said. Up went the window while his accomplice hit the gas. Anyone who has ridden a tandem bike, or thought about the principles behind it, would see the impossibility of a Stoker not pedaling and the Captain unaware of the fact. The loss of power is dramatic. Would our clever friend, I wondered, not notice if half of his engine's cylinders stopped firing?

From Barrie, we went north of Simcoe Lake, crossing the Trent-Severn waterway, a 240-mile-long system of canals and forty-five hydraulic locks that connect the lakes and rivers in a continuous water route between Lake Huron and Lake Ontario. At Fenelon Falls we paused to watch for the twenty minutes it took for Lock Number thirty-four to raise a cabin cruiser twenty feet. Then it went on its way at a new level. Jane was right. Change takes time. It begins with questions. The answers come later. I'd need patience for the coming months.

We camped in Stonyridge that night at a place called "Pilgrim's Rest." Next door was *Petroglyphs Provincial Park*, which held the largest collection of aboriginal rock carvings in Canada. Ancient stories etched into stone excited Jane more than me, so she planned to visit it on her own after phoning her younger brother, also named Ian. Call completed, she sat beside me and looked into the orange glow of our small campfire.

"Well, what did Ian J. have to say?" I said. I was Ian O, her brother was Ian J.

"He had a really good idea. Fly a small Canadian flag from our trailer mast."

"I'll try anything at this point." The problem of narrow roads and aggressive drivers was not going away, and we felt like targets out there. Maybe the issue was nationalistic. Maybe flying the maple leaf would help. Strangely enough, it worked. Drivers slowed down and kept their distance. Fly their flag and no matter who you are, Canadians will stand on guard for thee.

The mercury soared ever higher, over 30 (Celsius) most days, yet we managed our fifty miles (80 kilometers) per day average by starting at dawn and ending in early afternoon. In Consecon, an air-conditioned inn provided welcome relief from a day in the sun. We had settled into the room when we noticed the smell.

Jane's nose wrinkled. "What is that smell?" A pungent, rotten, toxic fume, like the forgotten blue cheese from Christmastime found in the back of the fridge the following June, permeated the room.

"Yeah," I said. "It's worse than wet dog smell. More like wet, two weeks' dead dog smell. Do you suppose we've turned into people who smell bad and don't notice it? God I hope not." We followed our noses to my damp sandals. They'd been packed wet in plastic and subsequently incubated mildew during the day's heat. I took them outside before other guests complained. After eleven days in Ontario, we looked forward to leaving it like one looks forward to leaving the dentist's chair. Even a strong, really hot cup of tea didn't compensate for the crazy-dangerous roads.

The next day we stopped in Bloomfield at what looked like an indoor/outdoor roadside bike shop. The overhead sun and our growling stomachs indicated lunchtime and sweat soaked us from another scorching summer day. We wanted to see about a gel seat pad for Jane, who had succumbed to the same affliction I had back in Minnesota: a sore bum. We parked and climbed the steps of the capacious porch. Bookshelves lined its one wall, all of them filled with not bicycling books, but literature. I recognized many authors: Dickens, Hemingway and Dostoevsky stood with Asimov, Clarke and LeGuin. I'd been forced to read a few classics in school, but science fiction I read for pleasure. It took me far, far away in both time and space. I loved the technology, and the message of hope implied: that humanity would one day resolve all differences, create a utopia on Earth, work together to reach the stars; there to exploit galactic resources, wage interstellar war and slaughter sentient but icky-looking aliens.

The sagging sofa, threadbare loungers and milk crates furnishing the porch brought back my college years: being young, unworried, surrounded by friends and equals, and my future a white canvas before me. "I've never seen a combination bike shop and library," I said, addressing the youthful tie-dyed couple occupying the aforementioned furnishings. "You're our kind of folks."

"A pair of overgrown teenagers; that's us," said KT, co-owner with husband Rick of Bloomfield Cycles. They saw our Ibis tandem and got big eyes. We were hip. We were a class act. Would we like some lunch? Being cyclists, they knew this question was mere formality. In a few minutes KT brought out the food while we browsed the library, looking for light-weight but substantial reading.

We cooled off in the shade of their outdoor lounge—munching a Mexican-themed rice and bean salad with tomatoes, corn and cilantro in it, accompanied by flatbread—and got acquainted. Rick and KT traveled everywhere by bicycle. When not cycling, they read. We traded travel anecdotes for a good hour. My favorite one of theirs had them cycling through Alabama. Well-meaning white folks told them to avoid the town of Pritchard. It was poor and run-down. And black. They would not be safe. We knew where this was going. As luck would have it a downpour caught them, they lost orientation, and found themselves very wet, and very white, in the center of downtown Pritchard. Hoping to escape undue attention and wait out the rain, they ducked into a diner, despite the multiple taped-over bullet holes in the windows. The place went dead silent as none but black faces turned their way. In a small, quavering voice KT said, "Is it okay...if we eat here?" The room erupted in laughter. An hour later, fifty new friends paid for their lunch. We had similar tales of misguided fear to relate, among them the story of the Hidatsa brothers coming to our rescue in North Dakota, after we'd been told to avoid Indian reservations.

Rick added, "Whenever we need our faith in humanity restored, we go on a bike trip."

We agreed. The last few months set us straight on some of our own prejudices. In every state, the people we'd met, swapped stories with, helped and been helped by, who fed us and sheltered us from the storms, who we laughed and cried with; none of them cared about our income, where we'd gone to school or our job titles. We wouldn't have met them in our former world. People I'd thought of as "poor" were rich in ways I'd never considered. They were known and loved by others, happy in their work, *content*. I felt my own poverty now. I had money, I had Jane's love, but I had no community and no purpose.

I saw Rick and KT as intelligent, well-read, well-traveled and well-matched. They did what they loved every day, and finding these kindred spirits and others like them gave me hope for the future, that here were people who had arrived at and lived by the same truths we were discovering. I'd been trying to fit myself into someone else's suit and tie, until it slowly strangled me. Maybe tie-dye would fit better. An alternate path lay open to us, if we had the strength of mind to follow it.

On purpose we passed through Kingston because the Dutch friend we'd made in Washington, Rita Dom, lived there and probably had air-conditioning. She greeted us at the door of her immaculate suburban ranch-style house with reserved joy, and refrained from hugging our sweat-soaked bodies.

"Well, you're only a half hour late. I was thinking maybe you were in hospital; it's so hot today," she said, motioning us inside before we let too much of the nice, cool, costly air out.

"No, we're fine. We just had to stop every ten or fifteen kilometers to cool down," I said with a seamless switch to metric units. Like most Germanic people I know, Rita gave organization and tidiness a high priority. The floor of her garage was painted pale grey, and nothing stuck to my bare feet when I walked on it, unlike our kitchen floor at home.

I left my stinky sandals outside until I found some bleach for them. Rita was a model hostess and tour guide for the following two days. She shuttled us around the sights of Kingston, including a fort, a cathedral, and a steam museum. We laundered our threadbare and stained clothes, ate frequent and abundant meals, stayed off the bike, and forgot about where we were going next.

Rita's accent, decided opinions, thrift and preoccupation with housekeeping all reminded me of Mom, who met Dad at the Canadair factory in Montreal in 1955. Both had immigrated to Canada from Europe soon after the war. Mom worked alongside other young women on an electronic component assembly line, while Dad was the dashing young line engineer. She stood out from the other girls, with her movie-star face, big chest, small waist and shapely legs. Her dimples appeared whenever her earthy hazel eyes met his Atlantic blue ones.

One evening Mom had worked late to sort out some assembly issues and Dad saw an opening, and offered her a lift home. He thought: *Here's a simple, uneducated but fine-looking German girl, who will know how to cook, clean and look after children.* She thought: *The English are so refined; here is an educated man who makes lots of money and will help me get an education too.* A year later they married. Their generation had seen whole cities in flames, long lines of fresh corpses, entire families laughing together one day and dead the next; what must have seemed the world's ending. They lived fast.

In the next six years his career took them to New York, where my two oldest siblings were born, then Pennsylvania, birthplace of my second brother and me. In 1967 another transfer moved us all to Massachusetts.

By about the same ages we were now, my parents had married, had four children and four different homes in three states and two countries. We would retrace their Canada to Massachusetts steps now as an unmarried couple, without jobs or plan about where we'd live or whether we'd have children, or really any definite goals at all. We saw this as complete freedom, no attachments, a world of possibilities and a great gift.

But to my parents, the wartime generation, we had no ambition.

NEW YORK

There is more to New York than the Big Apple. Adirondack Park is larger than Yellowstone, Yosemite, Grand Canyon, Glacier, and Olympic National Parks <u>combined</u>.

31 THE CAT'S ASS

Dublin, Ireland, 902 AD: *Eyvind and Hild lived in Dubhlinn for three years. They built a cottage on a plot of fertile land, and in March of 902, Hild gave birth to a son they named Leif. Eyvind learned the merchant's trade and how to handle a longboat on subsequent, highly profitable voyages with Olaf's crew. When Svein got a ship of his own, the Heron, Eyvind served as first mate. But the Gaels, urged on by Christian priests, had wearied of their pagan overlords. That summer, the smoldering sparks of rebellion ignited...*

In the dead of night, a fist pounded the cottage door. Hild woke Eyvind and gathered up little Leif and their valuables. Eyvind unbarred and opened the door. Three armed crewmen waited, bathed in the wavering orange glow of distant fires. "Leinster and Brega have joined forces. It is hopeless. We must go," the one named Bjorn said. Eyvind stepped outside, dressed for battle in mail with his sword buckled on. "Bjorn. See my family safely on board Heron. I will alert the rest of the crew. We will hold them off... but if it goes wrong, do not wait. Get the ship away." He drew Fotbitr and disappeared into the fire-streaked dark. The insurrection had begun in earnest.

By the time Eyvind and his cohort arrived at the wharf, a line of men had formed a wall of shields across its narrow entrance, Olaf and Svein at its center. It opened as Eyvind led the last of the crew in a mad dash to the wharf, ahead of the first wave of armed Irish. Sling-whipped stones cracked and bounced off the arrayed shields. Thrown torches had started numerous small fires that illuminated the thin Norse line. "Master Olaf, you must withdraw now," Svein said. "Your ship is the larger. We can hold these gutless...poets." Olaf nodded as if they had discussed this already.

Behind them, an overturned hay-rick served as a crude barricade. "Once Wulf

Sang is away," Olaf said to Svein and Eyvind, "we'll send an arrow storm to cover you. The fire arrows are your signal. Light the barricade and go." They embraced, raised their weapons, then the whole line screamed "O-din."Eyvind took the place of one of Olaf's men in the line, his shield covering the man to his left. His mouth went dry and his knees quaked. He touched the silver Thor's hammer amulet at his breast. The lead skirmishers of King Brega drew closer, not yet mad enough or drunk enough to rush a shield-wall of trained warriors, but nearly so…

Suddenly, a figure on horseback cantered down the Irish line, bellowing challenges and taunts to the Norse. He dismounted and stood before the shield wall. "Norse vermin! You cower behind your shields! I challenge your best to single combat! Is there not a man among you?"

Eyvind saw not this fierce Irishman, but Mother's ghost. And it taunted him. "Go home, go home, little boy, or all of your friends will die! We will kill them all!" His fury kindled white-hot. He roared and burst from the shield wall, sword raised. Momentarily surprised, Mother side-stepped the challenge, parried Eyvind's wild cut and chuckled. "You're a weakling, like your father! I should have drowned you at birth!" Eyvind felt warmth trickle down his arm. Mother's blade had slashed his shoulder.

Mother attacked, stabbing low. Eyvind brought his shield down just in time, but the thrust was a feint. Mother's sword now arced high and downward, and would have split his skull had he not pushed back with his legs so that the blade whooshed past. Eyvind staggered backward, but kept his balance.

"You would kill your own son?"

"To be together in death, yes. You do not know what it is like, to be left behind! Your father left me, and now you! You will come home now."

"So be it." Time slowed down. Eyvind noticed the sudden silence in which he could now only hear the beating of his own heart. He raised Fotbitr's blade to his lips and kissed it. His next attack was much like his first, and Mother easily parried. But this time Eyvind pulled up his stroke just before the blades clashed, spun his body so his blade whipped around in a lightning-fast backswing, slicing through leather and deep into neck. Mother put a hand to the mortal wound, looking at Eyvind, mouth moving wordlessly, then pitched forward and was still. Immediately Mother vanished, replaced by the dead Irishman. The Norse line cheered. The Irish now roared and surged forward. Eyvind turned, leapt over the fires and rejoined the shield wall. He was free, and the battle for Dubhlinn had begun.

Cape Vincent, NY, July 1999: Two small ferries took us back to our own country: the first from Kingston to Wolfe Island, at the northern end of

Lake Ontario where it narrows into the St. Lawrence River, and now the second from Wolfe Island to Cape Vincent, NY. This one pulled itself along by an underwater cable, could hold six cars and cost us a dollar each.

An American man (his car had NY plates) in matching Nike athletic wear stood on the deck, arms folded. He was of average height and build, medium hair color, about forty-five years old; average looks, average pot belly. He drove a late-model dark blue Ford or GM midsized sedan. He was, in every way I could see, exceptionally median. Our rig leaned against the gunwale and he eyed it with a smile. Before us stood the Average American Man, and I wondered what he thought about on this day, July 19, 1999. Then he spoke.

"That thing is the cat's ass!"

Welcome to the U.S.A. Cat's ass? The language had already changed during our absence.

"Thanks, it works very well," I said, wondering if we'd been complimented or insulted. The A.A.M. had nothing more to share, so we resumed watching the details of our homeland's shore appear. In a few minutes we would be stateside again.

From Cape Vincent we pedaled into upstate New York, first passing through Watertown, the smallest city to have a park designed by Frederick Law Olmstead. In the early 20th century, Watertown had more millionaires per capita than any other U.S. city. Now at century's end, despite inflation, most of those millionaires had died, gone broke or left town. Brick warehouses stood abandoned and boarded up, dark empty storefronts with dirty windows distorted our reflection, ragweed grew tall from cracked sidewalks. Crumpled pages of yellowed newspaper, dead leaves and fast food Styrofoam tumbled in the wind and choked the storm drains. What one generation built, the next allowed to crumble. Only a matter of time, I thought, before a new generation moves in and renovates these old buildings. History lived here too, in the east: soaring stone churches, statues and fountains, gracious colonial and ornate Victorian homes. These places endure.

We camped in Natural Bridge, next door to Fort Drum, an army base where they seemed to be engaged in nighttime artillery practice. We bedded down while big guns thundered in the dark. I listened to the distant thumps and wondered how it must have been to live through a war.

Antoniew, Eastern Germany, April 1945: *"You can't take those books, Ida, they're too heavy," Hulda, her eldest sister admonished. "You're walking. There are no more horses, so anything we bring, we carry. We'll come back as soon as the war is over."*

"But this is our home," Ida said. "Why should we leave?"

"Mein Gott, how does the child get so stupid in fourteen years?" her father Gustav said. "Because Hitler lost the war; that is why."

"I still don't understand. We're farmers, not Nazis. Won't the English…"

"Because the Russians are coming here and they like young girls," her mother Adoline said. "Do as you are told! You look after Linda and stay together! You will be safe with family. Trust no one else. Keep walking west until you find the English or the Americans."

"And what will you do when the Russians come?"

At this Adoline turned away and pressed her apron to her face. Gustav held her, his eyes gray steel. "We're too old for the Russians to bother about," he said. "It will be better for us without you here. So go, now. And may God go with you."

When the Russians came, they sent my grandparents to a Soviet labor camp to help rebuild what the war had destroyed. Their farm, vacant and emptied of everything of value, became a collective of the Soviet state.

Mom and her sister walked some five hundred miles west. She spent her adolescence somewhere in post-war Poland. Through the Lutheran Church she located her brother Ferdinand in Oldenburg, West Germany and through the German "Right of Return" law was allowed to move there. Then she traced her sister Frieda to Alberta, Canada, and Frieda sponsored her emigration. On the way to Alberta, Montreal's bright lights and cosmopolitan air captivated her. She got off the ship in Montreal and started a new life there.

It wasn't until 1955, ten years after she left home, that she could travel to Oldenburg to see her repatriated parents. At first her mother did not recognize her grown daughter. I imagine old Adoline had more pressing concerns during her years in the Gulag than daughter number six. Mom never spoke about those early post-war years, except to admit she lived with a family, cooked, cleaned and looked after children. And learned to speak Polish.

Dad entered the war in 1945 as a 21-year-old sub-lieutenant in the Royal Navy, which he'd joined to avoid the Royal Army. Assigned to North Sea duties in Scotland, he oversaw maintenance on a squadron of Supermarine *Seafires*. Though he could speak at length on nearly any subject, he shared little about what happened in that corner of the war.

He returned to an England reeling from the crippling costs of victory in another world war.

Blackpool, England, March 1949: *"How did it go, then, Alf?" Fred Lord, my father's stepfather, folded the newspaper he was reading and looked at his stepson. He saw a dashing young man of twenty-five wearing a baggy grey* *business suit and a very long face.*

"Not so good, Dad, I'm afraid. It seems for every job posting there are a hundred other chaps just as keen." He turned to face the window, which admitted a dreary grey light that was somehow damp and cold. He put his hands on his hips. "I...just don't know anymore."

Fred lifted the newspaper. "Says here that sweets are being rationed again. Four years since Hitler and we're still short of sweets? It's like the bloody war never ended!" He slammed the paper down. "If I were you..."

"I know, I know. Go to America. Uncle Jack tells me the same."

"No, Alf. Go to Canada. You'll have an easier time getting in there. They speak English, of a sort, and they don't care if you're Catholic or Irish or bloody Hindu."

"And what about Mum? I'll just leave her then?"

"I'm looking after her, not you. Don't worry, we'll never move, we'll never change. England will carry on, and you're a fool if you hang about here for the rest of your life. Like that Yank once said: 'Go west, young man,' while you still can."

I'd never been in a war, never lost my home, and only on bike trips did I ever wonder where my next meal was coming from or where I'd sleep. Apart from one night in Detroit Airport, I'd never been a homeless refugee in a strange country, so of course my parents couldn't tell me what it was like. How could I ever understand? They were foreigners with accents. They didn't move here out of boredom. My wanderlust puzzled them, especially Mom. What was I looking for? Didn't I already have everything? They'd given us a safe home, an education and a work ethic. We would become professionals. To do that they'd left their parents behind. Things were different back then. Europe was holes in the ground, colorless cities mounded with rubble, awash in blood and sorrow, while America welcomed anyone who worked hard. In return you'd have three bedrooms and two baths, a Rambler or Chevy with chrome and tail fins, and a neat patch of green lawn. The sun would shine, the newspaper would arrive every day, and no-one would come in the night to take it all away.

Dad was seventy-five now and starting to forget things; Mom was sixty-eight. Old age worried them. Two of their children had already moved far away. Only my brother Dave and I lived nearby. They wouldn't be at the finish of my Big One, celebrating. Of that I was certain.

Somehow I thought the Adirondacks would be easy mountains after the Cascades and the Rockies but the reverse was true. To cross those big western ranges we steeled ourselves for two days of steady climbing, reached the pass, then coasted to the bottom and we were done. The

Adirondacks had been rounded and stooped by millions more years of wind, water and gravity. They undulated across six million acres of white pine and hardwood forest, and seemed endless, hill upon hill. Day after day we never reached the peak, just a level place from where the road rose some more or made a paltry descent before it rose again. The worn-down mountains wore us down.

After our first day in the Adirondacks we had completed more than 3,300 miles, and had ten days to reach the Atlantic. I knew we were right on schedule, but Jane still believed us a long way from home.

"No more than five hundred miles to go," I told her, "In ten days. That's still fifty miles a day, *average*." I echoed her words from before the journey, words that struck terror in our hearts back then.

"Oh," Jane said. "Well, that's not much. We can even take a rest day if we want." I agreed. Fifty miles made for an easy day now, a day of coasting and sightseeing. Our tanned thigh muscles stretched the black spandex of our bike shorts. Calves bulged like turkey drumsticks. We could have been leg models. We'd been forged and galvanized, welded into a unified, well-tuned and powerful machine.

Another day brought us to rest in Newcomb, a little town on a lake, like most other little towns in upstate New York. Aunt Polly's Bed and Breakfast looked inviting, fronted as it was by bark mulched flower beds. As we walked through the white trellis of climbing red roses, the proprietress approached us with something in her cupped hands. "Look what I just rescued," she said. We looked into her hands and there lay a ruby-throated hummingbird, iridescent wings folded, crouching there and blinking up at us. Strands of spider silk still clung to the tiny quivering body.

"Where was he?" asked Jane.

"Caught in the web of the biggest spider I've ever seen," said the woman. "About the same size as this hummer." I liked spiders, but a three-inch one made me nervous. And it was still out there, hungry.

We stayed the night. I checked the bed before we climbed in. The next morning another animal visitor woke us. Excited barks and shouts came from the back yard. We threw on some clothes and hurried outside. Our host was there already.

The little pug-nosed black and white Boston terrier wagged his stubby tail and yapped with equal enthusiasm as he danced around the big maple tree in the back yard. His pal, a golden retriever added his barks every now and then and also looked up. We followed their gaze, expecting to find a chattering squirrel, chipmunk or maybe a 'coon. Instead, an adult black bear hunched itself into a tight ball, lodged in a V of branches eight feet up, looking miserable.

"That's the kind of bear I know," I said. "Scared of that little Chihuahua."

"It's true," Jane said. "We didn't know grizzlies were so different from black bears."

"You ran into one out west?" asked our host. "A grizzly in the wild?"

"Yeah, and he nearly ate us," I said, and I smiled at the memory as Jane recounted the story. In Montana we'd met a bear and plenty of hummingbirds, in the wild, free and powerful. Now back east, the bear and the hummingbird reappeared and they were trapped, threatened, and cowering. A Native American shaman would say that when animals approach you in the wild, or come to you in dreams, they can be messengers and guardians. We saw the hummingbird as a spirit messenger symbolizing love, beauty and intelligence. And the bear can symbolize the cycle of life, death and renewal.

Seemed about right.

VERMONT

Montpelier, Vermont is the only U.S. state capital without a McDonalds.

32 THE ATTITUDE STATE

Dublin, Ireland, 902 AD: *"Take her home, boy. Take—." The weak voice choked itself silent. Eyvind staggered under the weight of Svein towards the waiting Heron. "Go, now!" he ordered. Hands reached out to drag Svein, semi-conscious, from Eyvind's back before he leaped over the gunwale. Stones, bricks and arrows crashed into raised shields as rowers bent to their work. He scrambled to the steering oar and leaned into it. Heron slewed away from the jetty and followed Wulf Sang out to sea...*

Dawn broke on a gray sky thick with clouds. It had been a near disaster last night, but both ships still floated, lashed together in the gently heaving sea. Men slept in gruesome postures on the benches where they had collapsed, exhausted. Women tended the wounded. Hild stared at nothing where she sat by the steering oar, next to Svein's inert body, her hands caked with drying blood. Frieda knelt by her, touched her shoulder. "He was pierced inside," she said. "There was nothing to be done."

A rasping call echoed across the water. All eyes looked up to see a raven alight on the masthead. "Odin's messenger," Eyvind said. "Svein has entered the feasting hall." Svein's dead hand still clutched the hilt of Fotbitr. Eyvind had curled the convulsing fingers around it as life fled the body. Now he eased the sword free and sheathed it. "'Take her home,' he said. Who am I meant to take home?"

Men stirred and woke. They saw Svein's body and looked to Eyvind. "Where now, Master Eyvind?"

Eyvind realized the command was his, and Mother's ghost would plague him no more. "Away from here. That way." He pointed north.

That night, Olaf touched flame to the largest of the pyres they'd built on the deserted shingle beach. Twigs crackled and orange flames leaped up to engulf Svein's body. "He was a vicious bastard," Olaf said to Eyvind. "No sense of humor. I never knew where he came from. No family. But he was loyal. He lived bravely, and died well. With honor. Heron is yours now, lad. It is what he wanted. Steer her true."

The guards posted around the camp's perimeter wrapped their cloaks about them as a chill fog crept in from the sea, feeling its way around the smoldering pyres like the tentacles of some huge vaporous sea creature. This would be their last night in Ireland. They were going home, to Norway.

Near Pittsford, VT, July 1999: We trundled down a narrow country lane, flanked and shaded by ancient oaks and maples that reached to spread their full-leaved summer boughs overhead. Behind barbed wire, black and white heads of Holstein cows, ears twitching, rose above the long grass to look at us.

"Ben and Jerry's!" Jane said.

"Soon," I said.

Beyond the pasture, arrayed corn stood man-tall and heavy with dark-tasseled ears. We passed the barn, rough boards unpainted and weathered silver, then the village, with a stark white one-room church, general store, and a stately red-brick colonial home, where ivy climbed up the facade and towering magenta hollyhocks leaned over the white picket fence. We heard a rushing stream, coasted to a crossroads, and there, crafted from hand-hewn timbers, painted burgundy with white trim: the covered bridge, unofficial icon of Vermont and the epitome of New England romance.

In years past we'd go north for the fiery crimsons and brilliant oranges of October foliage, for hot air ballooning in June, winter skiing at Pico, Stratton or Killington and horse-drawn sleigh rides. We went for apple picking and mountain biking. Recent gentrification fueled by wealth from New York, Stamford and New Haven turned many of the old farms, mills and orchards into tourist destinations: big city amenities with bucolic views. When we crossed the state line from New York, accommodation prices doubled for no other reason than the cachet of Vermont.

Here the Appalachians continued as the Green Mountains, now lumpy and forested but 350 million years ago must have loomed tall and jagged when present-day North America slammed into what's now Europe to form the supercontinent Pangaea. Glacial melt 12,000 years ago formed Lake Champlain, and today the temperature and humidity climbed with us. That morning, a gray haze obscured the distance as we screamed down the five mile descent into Ticonderoga. We could have easily broken our 46 mph speed record, but I feared overheating the brakes, blowing out a tire, or hitting a stone, so I kept it below 40, still a white-knuckler.

As we progressed east, white man's history reached further back in time, to the mid-eighteenth century. Before heading into Vermont, we'd stopped for a tour of Fort Ticonderoga, where in 1758, French and Canadian defenders totaling 4,000 beat back 16,000 British regulars and American colonists. British General James Abercromby was replaced, recalled to England, promoted and eventually became a Member of Parliament. Incompetent generals notwithstanding, England would eventually wrest Canada from the French, and Americans and Canadians would thereafter only fight each other on skates.

After our tour, the smart move would have been to spend the night at a cheap air-conditioned motel in Ticonderoga. Instead, we doggedly pressed onward into Vermont, lured by romantic memories rekindled. Our enthusiasm for crossing the next to last state line wilted in the sultry July heat when we discovered that Vermont has no cheap air-conditioned lodgings. We slogged onward. An hour later, an inn, an authentically-restored colonial saltbox house with tiny windows, wavy clapboard siding and huge central chimney appeared. We entered: wide pine floors creaked under our steps and antiques for sale lurked everywhere. Antique dealers still rated high in our esteem. Maybe I could fix or program something and bag another client, a dinner, or even a free stay. We hoped for the best.

Inside, a palpable, heavy silence enveloped us, like we'd intruded on a church service. Candles were lit and sunlight was somehow denied entry. Our hostess, a somber woman of middle years, clad in gray and black, soon informed us of her dear husband's death a year ago. A year ago? It seemed like the wake was still in progress. After preliminaries, she ushered us out of the showcase main house and into the much smaller carriage house, where we would share quarters with the antique inventory. The room, more like a cell, was period authentic without modern conveniences like ventilation. It had a single window too small to fit through in the event of a fire. Not a breath of air stirred the price tags dangling from the lamps, end tables, mirrors, chests, chairs and bedstead as we lay sprawled and sweating on the lovely $850 Jenny Lind spool bed.

"You sleeping?" Jane said.

"You kidding?" I said. "I wish we had an antique air-conditioner, even one that rattles and drips all night."

"The water here looks yellow, feels greasy and tastes like sulphur," Jane said. "I almost gagged brushing my teeth."

"I saw bottled water in the main house," I said. "Not out here, though."

"I feel bad for the lady, losing her husband, but why do we all have to suffer?"

"Yeah, we could have camped at Lake Bomoseen and gotten our sauna for free." Early in our relationship, I took Jane camping to this remote Vermont lake for some quiet romance and we found ourselves surrounded by a Harley Davidson convention. And it rained enough to float Noah's ark. That night was about as fun as this one, but a lot cheaper.

To pass the time, my thoughts returned to this idea of "Home." My adult existence had been a nomadic one, with home a series of rented digs in the Boston area, always with one or more housemates, always temporary arrangements, as I endeavored to save money for the home I would eventually buy—had tried for many years to buy—but the ones that weren't total crap-holes always seemed out of reach of my single income, or possessed of some irredeemable flaw in my mother's opinion. Get a big house, she would say. Get the worst house in the best area; you can always fix it up. Don't get one that needs too much work, you'll never sell it. Make sure it has a big lot. Offer them very little. She had been a realtor and so I followed her often conflicting advice and got nowhere, it being the early 1990s and a seller's market. Gone were the days when family-sized houses sat for months without offers, only cost twice your annual income and came with 5% mortgages.

When I was four, my Dad got a transfer to the GE in Lynn, Massachusetts. He wanted to be near the ocean and get us kids into a better school system. We moved to Marblehead, into the house on Mohawk Road, a modest four bedroom on a quarter acre in a neighborhood filled with kids. I walked or rode my bike everywhere: to Bell School, Abbott Library, Sergio's house, Chris' house, Pete's house, the Tracks, Tent's Corner, Redd's Pond and of course Devereaux Beach, my gateway to the Atlantic. We played street hockey, or neighborhood hide 'n seek on the long summer evenings, and waged all-out snowball wars in winter. The neighbors all knew me. I delivered their Boston Globe every morning.

After ten years there, and after Dad was recalled to GE after the big layoff, my parents snapped up one of the few remaining buildable lots on Marblehead "Neck," an island bastion of mansions, yacht clubs and elitism separated from the mainland by a half-mile causeway and a whole lot of entitlement.

Marblehead, Massachusetts, 1975: "We'll have the house set back to about here," Mom said. We stood in a field of high grass, trying to imagine where our future home would sit. "A long driveway, and a big two-car garage on this side. You will be able to see the ocean from upstairs. There's a private beach across the street we can walk to."

"I don't know anybody who lives on the Neck," I said to Wendy. "Do you want to live here?"

"Doesn't matter much to me," Wendy said. "I'll be in college by then."

"HEY! That's private property." A bent old man who'd crept out of the small castle next door glowered at us over the split-rail fence.

"Yeah?" Wendy said. "Well we just bought it!"

"Wendy, shhh, he's going to be our neighbor," Dad said, and walked over to apologize and introduce himself.

"What a jerk," Wendy said to me. "God!"

"Yeah, but what about me?" I said. "We have no friends out here. We don't have a boat or play tennis. We're, like, the poor people. I'll probably have to ride the frigging bus to school."

"I'll be driving by then. And when I turn eighteen I'll buy you beers so you can get hammered."

"Yeah, but you'll be gone to college by then."

"True. Dave will do it, then."

"Until he leaves the next year."

"It's just a few years. You'll survive. You'll have an ocean view. Mom and Dad always wanted to live on the Neck. Let them have their dream, if it makes them happy."

Five years later, I'm seventeen. It's just the three of us now, rattling around that 3,000 square foot colonial with the two-car garage and ocean views. In the kitchen, Mom is crying bitterly. She won't say why. I go upstairs and pass my parents' bedroom. The door stands open. Dad sits on the edge of the bed, his back to me, head bowed, his face in his hands.

They lasted four more years there and then sold it and retired to Virginia Beach. I packed up my childhood treasures into cardboard boxes and kept them in my room at college, so they wouldn't get lost. I was happy for my parents. They didn't need a big house. Maybe moving would fix their marriage.

The next year I graduated university and went to work at the same GE that laid off Dad twelve years earlier. I inherited his stapler with the GE logo and three-hole punch and moved into an apartment house in old town Marblehead, built in the eighteenth century and last updated in the early twentieth. By then my parents had already moved again, from Virginia to Maryland. Now they wanted to return to Massachusetts. They said the problem was the south; too hot in summer and too many black people year round. I drove a fully packed Ryder truck north, to the rental house I'd found them in Marblehead. They'd move again, locally, to get away from something or other that wasn't right. It kept them busy, but I wished they had normal hobbies like quilting and model railroading.

With the exception of Jane's sister in St. Louis, her family all still clustered in the Boston area, and gathered for holidays and birthdays without fail. Her mom still lived in Jane's childhood home, kept the bedrooms unaltered, put the Christmas tree in the same spot every year. They kept everything the same, year after year, while my family kept nothing the same and never gathered. I wanted neither and both. Where was the happy medium between unchanging traditions and nothing at all?

We would spend one more night in Vermont, as the heat, humidity and hills did us in after sixty miles. Despite the expensive sauna, Vermont had its moments. During the day we ground our way up and down Route 40, heading south for Massachusetts. At a non-covered bridge over a small stream an orange "Detour" sign pointed to an unpaved road. The bridge looked fine, in much better shape than the bone-shaking dirt road. We saw no reason for the detour. Jane hailed a passing motorist, who stopped and lowered his window.

"Do you know why this detour is here?" she asked. "The bridge looks fine."

"Oh, they're supposed to be working on another bridge further down, but you can still get through. I don't know why that sign is still there," replied the motorist.

We figured the sign guy arrived before the bridge workers, crossed the little bridge and enjoyed four traffic-free miles when we came to the second bridge, truly closed by a crew of yellow-vested workers, but still intact enough to cross. We didn't want to backtrack. I sought out the foreman.

"If we're super careful," I said, "and walk our bike, do you think you could maybe let us across?"

"I'm sorry, the bridge is closed," he said. "We'd be liable if anything happened to you."

I could see he was in a legal bind. I looked up at the noon sun.

"I understand," I said. "We wouldn't want to get anyone into trouble. But what time do you break for lunch?"

In a second or two a smile broke across his tanned face. He picked up the striped sawhorse and moved it aside. "All right, go on across. Just be careful."

"Thanks," I said. "You saved us ten extra miles."

We skirted east of the Green Mountain National Forest, tracing its edge along Route 155, more of a meandering country road than the popular Route 7, which also went south but swung further west than we wanted. Though we didn't ride through the national forest, we missed none of the Green Mountains. The ribbon of grey asphalt shimmered in the afternoon heat, rise after rise bisecting the dark green pine carpet, the colors melting into the watery blue haze of humidity well before the horizon. Our shirts were soaked through; we couldn't get the water, Gatorade or whatever yellow or blue bottled sweat we could lay hands on into us fast enough, and stopped every hour to refill our bottles. "It doesn't usually get this hot here," everyone said.

The day we tackled Okemo Mountain, we'd drunk plenty but neglected to eat. We pulled into an inn, shaky and exhausted. Almost seven and the sun hadn't set. Bereft of provisions except for some dry cereal, we asked the innkeeper clipping the hedge where we could find the nearest food source.

"There's only the general store that's close, about a half mile that way," he pointed down the road. "They close at seven, but you might just make it."

We dug down into our energy reserves; the extra ten percent that high school coaches are always asking for; and pounded down that road, screeching to a stop five minutes later in front of the store. The female clerk was outside, just putting key in lock, having already hung up the "Closed" sign.

"Excuse me," I said, feeling a bit like Oliver Twist asking for more gruel, "I know you're technically closed, but we've been riding all day and haven't eaten anything since lunch. Could we just buy a couple of things real quick?"

She ran her eyes up and down me, finding neither threat nor reward. "Sorry. The register's locked." She turned the key and the bolt slammed home. This roadblock wasn't moving aside.

"Is there anywhere else…" ventured Jane, but her voice trailed off because the intended target already had its car in reverse. I rationalized. Maybe she had to be somewhere, maybe she'd worn her happy face all day for rude tourists, maybe she struggled with a failing marriage, a troubled teen, or a rare and terminal disease; maybe she's not really a nasty sweat-bag, but I was still hungry.

We pedaled, adagio, back to the inn and saw the innkeeper again. "How'd you make out?" he asked.

"All we wanted was some milk for our cereal, and she wouldn't sell us any," I whined. His eyebrows lowered. He frowned and grunted.

"That's ridiculous. If you need milk, come on in. I've got a whole gallon. And bananas. Just help yourself. Make yourselves at home." We had breakfast for a late supper which was better than nothing, and rested up for another dripping day on the road.

That night, as we tucked into bed, Jane said, "You've changed, my dear."

"Have I? How?"

"You talk to people more. You can ask for help. You let them see more of your true self, and draw them to you instead of pushing them away."

I thought about that a minute. "That part of me, that doesn't need anyone's help and has to do it all myself? I think it died somewhere on the road back there. Maybe with the parasites. I hope I have changed. Otherwise what would be the point of all this?"

"It's like your true self, the one you keep hidden from everyone except me, is coming forward. I love it, because now everyone can see what I see."

The heat, hills and increasing tourist traffic continued to prey on us. I had to get to the ocean before spontaneous combustion, so we rode with a will, thinking that if we just got out of Vermont then everything would change, as it always had done at state lines. The next day we missed lunchtime after eating nothing but sun-warmed pop-tarts all morning, and finally found the sense to pull over at a café in NewFane at 2:07 pm, where they served lunch from 11-2. The owner, with extreme politeness was explaining this to us when Jane suddenly dropped to her knees, clasped her hands and commenced to plead. The owner, whether amused, embarrassed or eager to avoid a scene, hustled us to a back table. Later that day, the mercury crossing 100 as we crossed 3,500 miles, Jane hallucinated. Somewhere near Brattleboro we dogged past a small coffee shop. Jane's head swiveled and she commanded a stop. "Ice cream," she squealed. "That's what I want right now."

I looked at the coffee shop, then across the street, where they installed mufflers. "Where do you see ice cream?"

"Right here," Jane said, indicating the coffee shop. "I saw the counter through the window. Let's go in."

Jane usually has great food intuition, but inside the coffee shop was simply the inside of a coffee shop: a few pastries under glass, but nothing creamy, frozen and delicious. She looked left and right. "I saw it through the window; a marble counter, twelve flavors and a stack of cones. I was positive."

"Sure you did," I said. "It's probably time for a little break. We need to cool down." We approached the counter and I explained how we were cycling across the country and my "wife" had just hallucinated ice cream in this shop. The lady thought this very funny and shook with laughter.

"Oh, honey, I think we can find you some ice cream." She went back to the kitchen and in a few minutes returned with two large bowls heaped with vanilla. "Enjoy," she said.

When we crossed our final state line into Massachusetts, our odometer read 3,530 miles. We lived nearly our whole lives in Massachusetts, and I had cycled its length and breadth many times. I knew what to expect: same old potholed roads, heavy traffic, and aggressive, multi-tasking drivers. I expected that we'd be ignored, cursed at, run off the road, or all of the above.

I expected all of that, and didn't resist it, because you always get what you resist.

MASSACHUSETTS

There is a house in Rockport built entirely of newspaper.
You could say it has more stories than any house in the world.

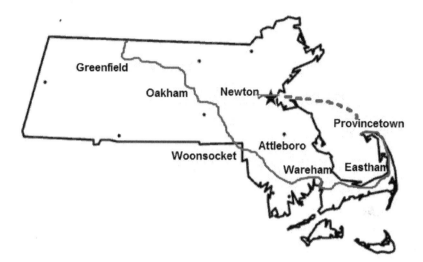

33 LOST

Norway, 902 AD: *There was no wind, no sound at all. Oars raised, Heron glided towards shore. "Strange," Eyvind thought, "that no one welcomes us. A ship of any size coming into the village was a rare event when we'd left home. Had so much changed in three years? It looked the same as ever. Except, where was everyone?"*

The bow crunched gently onto the gravel beach, not far from where Eyvind had sat with his brothers and made his decision to leave. Wearing helmet, mail and his sword, Eyvind leapt over the side with Bjorn. His men secured the ship. Two ragged figures he recognized now came down the beach to meet them. Eyvind and Bjorn waited. The ragged ones shuffled, clutching one another, to stop three paces away. Eyes down, Ragnar spoke: "Good Masters, you are welcome. I am Ragnar, son of Haakon, and this is my brother Gudrik. May we know your names?"

"Brothers," Eyvind grinned and removed his helmet. "I have returned. You smell the same, Gudrik."

"By the gods," Gudrik said. "Is it truly you? Eyvind? We thought you dead. Hild! And..." Hild now strode up from the ship, holding little Leif.

"Leif, meet your old uncles, Ragnar and Gudrik," Hild said. All five embraced and talked at once. The adults laughed and wept; Leif grabbed Gudrik's beard and tugged at it.

"What has happened here?" Eyvind said. "Where is everyone?"

"They fled when they saw your ship. You know not of Harold Finehair?" Ragnar said. "He would rule all of Norway. Every day, he masses more men, ships and gold. None can resist him. We thought you were his men...one day they will come, and then..."

"Then come with us," Eyvind said. "Another ship follows, a larger one. You remember Olaf?"

"But where would you go?" Gudrik said. "Nowhere is safe anymore."

"A good, rich land called Caithness, just across the sea, a few days' sailing. Gather your people, brothers. Bring provisions, your silver and your weapons and tools. We have adventures ahead."

"Our home is here, Eyvind," Ragnar said. "It is your home also. We will not leave it for unknown foreign perils. It is your duty to stay and defend your family, your home. Now is when we need you most. Would you abandon us again?"

Greenfield, MA July 1999: With eight days and under three hundred miles to go before August 1, we could afford a day off. We stopped in Greenfield, a small rural town near I-91 in northwestern Massachusetts where our friends, Lenny and Sue Weeks and their three boys lived. As we labored up the hill towards their house the rear tire hissed and thumped—our first flat since North Dakota. We repaired it in minutes and hove into the Weeks' driveway to receive a spirited family welcome, déjà-vu of a similar family farewell all those miles ago, in Washington at the Freimund's.

After much hand-pumping, back-thumping, hugs and a terrifying ride in the Connecticut River on Lenny's new jet-ski, the Weeks' went back to their activities. We'd been lucky to catch them at home; the next day their relatives would swing by in a minivan and all would depart in a mini convoy for Quebec. Sue took charge. Armed with numerous lists she issued orders to everyone but us. The thermometer climbed past ninety and we were glad to be off the road. We laundered clothes, ate and wallowed in their above-ground pool. We hooked our arms over the side and watched the Weeks, who reminded me of ants around an anthill.

"How do you feel about going home?" Jane asked.

"Strangely, I'm not dreading it," I said. "I think I'm ready for a change."

"I admit it'll be nice," Jane added, "to be in a home again, to sleep in our own bed and not have to pack up every day, find food, and figure out where to spend the night. That was getting old."

"I'm getting excited to start a new career, helping people like Ed Hencz from Montana," I said. "I want to do something fun for work, or at least have it be on my own terms."

"I'd like that too." I knew she meant to turn her music into a career. Her tone told me that this was a prospect both thrilling and daunting. For me, what had been adventure was now routine, comfortable, even tedious at times. I wondered if being at home would be uncomfortable now.

The next morning we tried to stay out of the way as chaos ensued. Suitcases and backpacks fell into heaps outside. Sue marched to and fro, crossing items off her list. The cat made two unsuccessful escape attempts.

The relatives arrived, and somehow everything and everyone found their place and the expedition lurched down the drive, horns honking, arms out the windows, waving like the legs of an overturned beetle. We savored the silence a few moments, then set off as well. After three miles I noticed the cool draft on my back. No Camelback! We turned around; it waited on the Weeks' doorstep. I strapped it on as a huge iron-gray cloudbank rolled in and big drops fell. We used the hidden key to re-enter the house and wait out the rain.

I called my parents to let them know where I was and that I'd be home in a few days. Mom answered.

"You're in Massachusetts? Good. Come home right now. We're in a crisis here."

"What sort of crisis?"

"We sold our house, but we haven't bought another one yet. That realtor was such a bastard! We have to be out this weekend, can you believe it? They're forcing us out!"

"How can they do that? You have somewhere to go, right?"

"We got an apartment in Salem. Just get on a train and come home and help us."

"Did you know you can hire movers? They'll do all that for you."

"YES, we have movers, of course. But we need you for moral support. You have no idea how hard it is. Det guy, he's useless."

"That guy? You mean Dad? Where's Dave? Did you call him?"

"YES, YES, mein Gott, he's here too. But you should help your family. You've been gone long enough. Can you be here tomorrow? We're desperate."

They needed me? This was new. All my life my parents had been fiercely independent, had admonished me to be independent and not put too much trust in others. Mom had been in real estate herself. She knew the business. And now my streetwise parents who always got the best of every deal had been victimized? The world changed since I'd gone away. My heart pounded. I began to sweat.

I wanted to cave in and say yes. I'd done it my whole life. I'd pretty much finished my Big One, accomplished what I'd set out to do, and was ready to come home. What difference would those last couple of hundred miles make?

But wait.

Maybe this was some kind of test to see if I'd really changed. Maybe I'd go back to my old pattern of pleasing everyone in return for approval. Mom wanted me to wear a suit, work my way up the corporate ladder, live near her in a big house, marry someone beautiful, thin, accomplished and white who would raise our children to be just like us, and we'd all vote the same way and be a big happy family. None of my siblings had done their bidding;

it was all up to me. I used to believe in this. I'd tried hard over the years, but I simply couldn't make that fantasy happen.

Change is work. I'd much rather surf the internet or read a science fiction novel than learn a new language, or an instrument, or improve my social skills. I resist change with a will like a force of nature. My "Resistance," as author Steven Pressfield describes, likes things as they are, and will throw up one obstacle after another to keep me from evolving my soul. I'd completed 98% of my Big One, and it was changing me. Now, at the finish line was desperation time. What form could Resistance take to make me quit on myself, give up my dreams, and return to living someone else's vision of the Successful Life?

It would take the form of Guilt.

This was not reasonable. Would Tom and Lorraine, Al and Dee, Ed and Margaret or Curt and Malotte have asked such a thing of their children? They would not. Would Jon and Carol give all they had to hold their son one more time? They would. Here was a problem without a correct answer. If I said yes to them, I'd have to say no to myself, and nothing would change. I'd return to the life that was a slow death. If I said no to them, everything would change, and that led to the unknown; and as an engineer I'd been trained to eliminate the unknowns. But I'd learned something about love on the Big One. Love isn't about being nice; nor does love employ guilt. Love is blind, love is a mystery, and love is truth. And what is true requires no deliberation. You don't need to think it through. You just say it.

"No, Mom, I won't do that. This is too important to me. Sorry."

An ominous silence. Then…

"What?" she shrieked. "No? You won't help us? I can't believe it! Damn these bloody kids! Who raised you? I knocked myself out for you and now you won't…" Then the tears came. "Oh, Gott, mein Gott in Himmel!"

"It's just a move, Mom. You've done so many. Dave will be there. You don't need me. I'm going to finish my ride."

"Fine. FINE! Just go! Go on your bicycle! I don't know you! You're not my son, OK! To HELL with you!"

The line went dead. A nauseous wave rose up, burned bitter in my throat. Mom knew just how to ruin my fun. Thirty-six years old and I still wanted my Mom's approval, and its sudden withdrawal sent me into despair. I cursed myself and obsessed over what I'd done. I fought the urge to call her back and recant, try to remake what I'd destroyed. If only I'd rebelled more in my teens, I'd be better at it. I wondered if she tormented her other children equally, or was I her favorite target? Even the strongest, hottest cup of tea would not fix this. But it wouldn't hurt. I filled the kettle and lit the burner.

Fine. Maybe I'm not her son. Maybe she's not my real mother. Maybe they made a mistake at the hospital and I wouldn't inherit her nastiness.

Where was Dad? When he lost the armed chair all those years ago, his voice went from active to passive. He opposed no one. Had we spoken, he would have said something like: It would be nice to have you here, but we'll muddle through all right. Don't you worry about us, just come when you can and we'll see you when we see you.

And I probably would have dropped everything and come running to the rescue.

34 FOUND

From long association with me, Jane knew what my dazed look meant: I'd been disrespected, dumped on and disappointed once again. Nevertheless I filled her in on the details. She shook her head slowly, encircled my waist with her arms and laid her head on my chest. "I'm so sorry that happened," she said.

"Me too. I just wanted to tell them where I was, and I end up as a lightning rod. I'm supposed to drop everything and come running, because she's miserable? Is that normal? Aren't parents supposed help you? I feel like she fights me on everything."

"I love you, and support you, whatever you need to do," she told me. Her body tense, jaw set, told me she had little patience left for my mother.

"What I need to do …" I began.

What you need to do is tell her to go f*** herself, was Jane's thought at the time.

"…is finish this thing," I said.

The next day I tried to put the previous day's conflict behind me and focus on the task at hand. We didn't talk about it. This was my axe to bear. We tried Route 2, the eastern end of Montana's "Hi-Line" for a few miles before choosing a quieter road, Route 122, which rewarded us with little traffic, a forest of long-needled white pines swaying in the breeze, gentle rises, and the sparkling Quabbin Reservoir. This was Massachusetts? When did it get so…woodsy? After stopping to consult our map, a Town of Oakham highway department dump truck pulled up alongside us and groaned to a stop. I'd never heard of Oakham. "Do you need help getting somewhere?" the passenger asked, his coworker grinning from the driver's seat.

"We want to get to 31 South," I said. Fifteen minutes later, we were on our way with a detailed itinerary. We saw our new friends again a little later.

209

They'd driven ahead and waited for us to make sure we made a crucial turn. Swinging south to avoid Worcester, we came to rest on the steep slopes of the town of Spencer, first settled by Europeans in 1717. Later that century passengers heading from Boston to New York along the old Boston Post Road would stop here to change stage coaches. The town exuded colonial history in its fine old houses and dry stone walls. We treated ourselves to one last B&B at the Red Maple Inn, where the room contained a four-poster bed, antiques that were not for sale, and a modern air-conditioner. I still felt a pang of guilt at being comfortable, at being without a job for so long, at spending money when I had no income. I couldn't help it; it's how I was raised. But guilt didn't stop me. I thought of my parents struggling with their move and couldn't figure them out. They spent their whole lives struggling; first for survival, then for prosperity. Now their kids were grown, educated and established. Dad retired with plenty of money. They should be enjoying themselves, living in a condo, traveling, enjoying their grandchildren, going to the theater, attending potlucks, playing golf. But they couldn't do that; they needed to struggle against something, and if nothing presented itself, they'd create it and enlist others in it. I didn't want to end up like that. I needed to be away from it. Far away.

I felt like I was far away. I didn't recognize vast areas of the state I'd lived in for thirty-plus years. I'd never cycled the route we now took, a meandering diagonal from northwest to southeast, and I'd never seen the towns along the way. Not many roads in Massachusetts are laid out in a grid pattern. They were built on top of cow paths between barn, pasture and market, established centuries before the automobile. This is as true in Boston as in Uxbridge, where we found ourselves lost once again, trying to get to the Cape. Many of the former cow paths were not on our AAA maps, so we took many wrong turns and asked directions often. One driver slowed to our speed, rolled down the window, and instead of the expected snide comment, yelled "You're going to live to be a hundred!" By mistake we left Massachusetts one afternoon and ended up in downtown Woonsocket, Rhode Island. A young man struggled mightily for ten minutes with the task of directing us to Attleboro before he concluded: "Attleboro? That's in Massachusetts!" We thanked him for his efforts and then Jane spied a firehouse across the street.

"Let's ask in there," she said. "They ought to know their way around."

Within seconds of arriving at the station, the on-duty members of Woonsocket FD Engine Company 2 surrounded us. Noticing their matching t-shirts bearing the WFD logo, I said, "Those are really cool shirts. Got any extras?"

We discovered a little late in our trip that firehouses are excellent places to stop. Not only can the firefighters direct you anywhere, but they generally have time on their hands as long as nothing is on fire that day.

The station was equipped with clean bathrooms and well stocked with drinking water and snacks. After our tour and briefing on how to get to Attleboro, they presented us with official Woonsocket Fire Department t-shirts. Ours probably horrified them: they were faded, holey and sweat-yellowed.

We made Attleboro shortly before dark in time to notice the complete lack of accommodations available. Summer in New England, yes, but why was Attleboro booked up? Remembering a certain Minnesota State Trooper we approached a parked Massachusetts State Police patrol car. We asked the driver, who introduced himself as Officer Brian Witherell, if he had any ideas.

"There's one motel and one B&B in town and that's it," he said. "And I don't recommend the motel; it's right on Route 1." We had passed the motel already and dismissed it. Brian continued.

"But I've got a tent trailer in the back yard you can use, if you get stuck." He directed us to the B&B, then gave us his phone number. We found a pay phone and called the B&B before cycling out there, and sure enough, they were full. Jane dialed Brian's number and introduced herself to his wife Mich. "We just met your husband and he said we could stay in your trailer tonight." Mich was so casual and gave such excellent directions to their house that we assumed she had already spoken with Brian and knew to expect us. It turned out she had not, but we were welcomed just the same. Brian told us later that we looked a lot better than the "Phish" concert attendees that wandered about the previous weekend looking for a place to crash. The tent trailer was as comfortable as anyplace we'd slept in the past three months, and probably more secure since it sat in a cop's backyard, but we tended to sleep well anywhere. I'd never imagined that we'd get invited into a stranger's home in Massachusetts. I thought it wasn't done.

I was wrong.

35 ATLANTIC OCEAN

The next day, July 29, we were on our last hundred miles. We would not make a beeline for the Atlantic, but leave the dipping of the front wheel in the Atlantic ceremony for the Cape. Our plan was to stop in Orleans, where Jane's great aunt Kate lived, then ride the curled-arm length of the Cape to its fist in Provincetown, entering Boston from the sea on one last ferry ride.

Massachusetts' friendliness surprised and delighted us daily. The natives noticed us and conversed everywhere we stopped. At the Rehoboth General Store we met a woman who looked our age, who turned out to be a grandmother who was also lead singer for the rock band Metaphor. She had a mustang; not the car but a wild mustang she had adopted from Montana.

We also met a man who left home at age sixteen with $15 in his pocket, riding a 1939 Harley "held togetha with shoelaces and wiyah." He roamed North America all summer, working odd jobs. We saw our home state with baby eyes, like tourists. We noticed the silent R's. Not having acquired the dialect ourselves, we'd been telling everyone across the country that people from Massachusetts don't have accents, but now everyone seemed to talk like a Kennedy. We were outsiders looking in.

Low on water, we stopped at the Freetown State Forest Fire Warden Station. I'd never heard of Freetown or fire wardens until that day. It's between Fall River and Buzzard's Bay, about twenty miles from Cape Cod. Mark and Kenny, who manned the station, served us iced tea, filled our bottles and taught us about what fire wardens do, which is to protect and manage an area of forest. Kenny asked us where we were going. "The Cape," we said, and Mark quickly printed out detailed topo maps of the area and directions to get us there. "We're here to serve the people," said Mark. If only everyone in all the world's governments lived by this code.

The hills diminished in size, the pine trees grew shorter in the sandy soil as we rolled towards the Cape. We got our first whiff of the fresh, tangy salt air near New Bedford. The unmistakable sea breeze cooled our faces in Wareham, and we crested a hill to see the patch of blue that marked the end of our journey: the Atlantic. No, not quite the Atlantic, but Buzzard's Bay. We still had to get to the Lower Cape to truly reach the Atlantic. We swung onto the Cape Cod Canal Bike Path and merged with the heavy summer bicycle traffic. Here our rear tire, installed in Minot, ND, finally gave out after 2,300 miles. We installed our skinny spare and crossed the Sagamore Bridge as the sun touched the horizon.

As we packed our gear for the penultimate last time outside of the inn in Sandwich the next morning, an elderly couple approached us; New Yorkers old enough to have survived the Depression and the war, tough enough to survive the Big Apple of today. "We heard all about you from the innkeeper," said the woman. "We're so impressed with what you're doing." The old man, tears in his eyes, shook both our hands. "God bless you. The country needs beautiful people like you." Little did he know how I'd left my elderly parents to supervise their in-town move with only one of their children lending moral support.

We finally found some heavy traffic on Route 6A near Sandwich, Bostonians heading out for a summer weekend at the beach. We turned off and picked up the Cape Cod Rail Trail, an old rail line converted to a bike path, a straight and level road among stubby pines and birches stunted by salt air and sandy soil. There would be no more getting lost; this was a road I'd traveled on many times over the years, our own backyard. We seemed to glide without effort all the way to East Orleans, where Janes's Great Aunt Kate, also known as Kape Kod Kate, had built her dream house by the sea. Jane's family would greet us there.

Despite the obvious evidence of having worn a t-shirt and socks all summer, my beach appearance had vastly improved from three months ago. At the beach I threw off my shirt, made a mad dash for the surf and dove in. Yes, the water was still only warm enough for small children and dogs, but this day I felt ten years old.

That evening Jane and I sat on Kate's spacious deck, eating lobster rolls and corn on the cob, surrounded by family and friends. Among them were Jane's mom, her brothers David and Ian, and her sister Ann who flew in from St. Louis. I admired how they all turned out for our homecoming, and their efforts to include me and make me feel a part of the family. We spent our final night of the Big One at Kate's, falling asleep to the cry of seagulls, the toll of the bell buoys and the distant roar of the Atlantic surf.

In the morning we packed up our B.O.B. bag one last time.

"Can we take anything home for you? The trailer, maybe?" was asked several times with my answer a resounding "NO," with a force that surprised me. Sure, I'd learned to accept help over the last three months, but that trailer full of stuff was like a part of me now. I couldn't let it go, not yet. We had one more day.

Tradition dictates that to complete a true coast-to-coast ride, the rear wheel must touch the ocean you begin from, and the front wheel must touch the ocean at which you finish. On May 1 we'd dipped our rear tire into Puget Sound at Orcas Island. Now on August 1 we rode the three miles to Nauset Beach, escorted by a pace car packed with family and friends.

"You can't ride in the parking lot!" The attendant rose from her beach chair at the little booth to scold us. During the Big One nobody had told us where not to ride. I looked at Jane and we shrugged and dismounted. Parking lots are dangerous places and it would not do to be flattened a hundred feet short of the Atlantic. We walked the bike along the boardwalk, rising until we crested the sandy berm and gazed upon our goal, the crashing surf and infinite blue of the Atlantic. We stepped down to the beach looking for a spot where the waves wouldn't knock us down, followed by our entourage and Ian Justice, who had his big professional camera out. We attracted onlookers, curious to know if we were anybody important. They stayed to watch a small wave dash itself into bits of foam and salt mist against our front tire as Ian J snapped the sequence with auto-wind.

Back in the parking lot we waved to our entourage and headed down the Cape: Eastham, Wellfleet, Truro, and finally Provincetown, where the ferry to Boston waited, the end of the line.

We had run out of land.

36 A PARADE

I knew something was up when I spotted our old friend Jack waiting for us on his bike at the pier in South Boston. We eased our loaded tandem down the ferry's gangway as crewmen wound ropes thick as a fire hose around the pier's huge aluminum cleats.

"I found a pretty good route to get us through the construction, if you don't mind going up a couple of one-way streets," Jack said. We looked around. Boston was in the throes of the "Big Dig," the largest publics works project in US history, which would eventually move 16 million cubic yards of earth, lay down 3.8 million cubic yards of concrete and run 190% over budget (only a couple of billion more than the Marshall Plan) while only killing one person. Instead of the usual potholed and winding city streets, a vast jumble of jersey barriers, orange plastic barrels with tiny flashing lights, detour signs, piles of gravel, chunks of old asphalt, dump trucks, diggers and backhoes greeted us. I recognized nothing.

"Wow, they've really gone to town," I said. "Lead on, man. I have no idea how to get out of here." Jack deftly threaded his way, leading us through the concrete canyons of the Financial District and over Beacon Hill. We hurried to keep up, laden as we were and with our city reflexes dulled from non-use. Our ten-mile-per-hour life was over. The world came at us much faster now. As we left the hulking grey blockiness of Mass. General Hospital as a blur on our right, Jack cut left. We followed him under the elevated tracks of the Green Line, up a pedestrian ramp and over the footbridge spanning Storrow Drive, now choked with the evening commute. It set us down on the Charles River Esplanade, with its bike path along the river bank to take us to Newton, west of Boston, for the final miles of the Big One. We could breathe again. Home lay minutes away. A ripe sun hung low and cast the day's final brilliance on our faces. I wanted to savor the moment, but Jack's legs pumped like pistons up ahead; he had become one of those racing dragonflies.

"Jack, hold up!" I yelled. We dismounted and I got the camera out. "How about a photo?" I asked as he circled back. He snatched the camera and clicked our "After" photo, then made to move off again. I felt a sudden pang of resentment. I didn't want to be hurried along. I didn't care about anyone's schedule. This was my...our moment. I turned to Jane. "Thank you for coming with me."

"Anytime," she said. We kissed as the sun touched the distant treetops. A moment later a gray twilight shadow crept upwards and seemed to veil the ruddy glow of Jane's face, like a color photo fading to black and white.

We saddled up and pedaled on at our normal pace, to the place where Jack noticed we weren't following anymore and stopped to urge us along. We caught on to the game when we met up with one friend and then others who "happened" to be out cycling, and joined us in an ever-lengthening parade— all arranged ahead of time as a welcome. Now we understood Jack's hurry as he was coordinating it all.

In Newton we exited the bike path, headed away from the Charles River and made the final turns toward home: Watertown St. to Lowell Avenue to Calvin. Approaching Walden Street, I noticed the big orange "Road Closed" sign and before we rounded the corner my imagination created a huge cheering throng in front of our house, TV cameras, police barricades and confetti. We would have our moment of celebrity.

We turned the corner. No throng. Apparently the city was installing new curbstones.

A few whoops and whistles accented the smattering of applause as we screeched to a stop at the house. Red helium balloons and a bed sheet hand-painted with "Hurrah" festooned its iron railing. Jane's mom, Drew and Margaret Hannah from across the street, and a couple other neighbors joined our mounted escort for an impromptu street party. Somebody handed Jane a bunch of stargazer lilies wrapped in cellophane. I wondered if somebody would hand me something too. The women always get flowers: a reflection of their creative apparatus. The men should get something suitably phallic. I suppose that's the magnum of champagne, standing tall and jetting its white froth far and wide. I would have settled for a cold beer. Instead, I received crushing hugs from the women, firm handshakes and high-fives from the men, camera flashes that made me see spots, and someone asking how it felt to be home.

I don't recall what I said then; something tactful, probably. But it felt like when you revisit your elementary school as an adult. The world I'd left in April had shrunk somehow. We'd been in big places. We'd crossed the Montana prairie, North Dakota, the Rockies and the Cascades; the sparsely populated rurality of Ontario. The house in front of us seemed to have compacted, pulled itself in somehow. The neighboring houses loomed over it in a threatening manner. We lost the sky behind walls, roofs, poles and overhead wires. Cars careened by, oblivious to us and insanely fast. What time was it? Where was the sun, the moon, the North Star? And what was that awful high-pitched whine that drowned out the birds and crickets like a behemoth mosquito? Why does anybody with a front lawn the size of a bath towel need leaf blowers, and a hired crew to wave them around?

I felt like we'd passed through a portal into a parallel universe, an alternate reality; similar, but a mirror to ours. In this universe, my alternative self was a fat, balding manager at GE with powdered sugar on my tie, who lived next door to my mother. Alternative Jane was a vacuous, tarted-up bleach blonde in high heels and furs. We didn't belong here and would soon be found out.

We had to get back to our own universe.

37 CRAPPILY EVER AFTER

Norwegian coast, Midsummer, 902 AD*: The elders, freemen and wives from all over the fjord had gathered for the Althing, the council, held in its traditional place, a natural stone amphitheater carved by a rushing stream of mountain snowmelt before it cascaded into the ocean below. The arrival of two ships added excitement and confusion to people's dread of Harald Finehair. There were matters to discuss, decisions to make. Many voices spoke out.*

"We cannot fight Harald," a white-bearded elder said. "He commands a thousand spears and would cut us down like rye."

"If we don't stand against him," Nils, a burly blond fisherman said, "then we live as his slaves and toil for his gain. I would prefer an honorable death to a life as a dog."

"Brave words, my friend. But the world has changed," a merchant named Bjarni said. "Foreigners threaten us. Harald seeks only to unite all of Norway so we can be strong. And he is a gold-giver. Better to accept the rule of one of our own kind than that of barbarians. Think of your sons and daughters. Would you condemn them as well?" At this, Olaf pointedly looked at Eyvind and shook his head. Loud mutterings issued from the throng.

"There is another way," Eyvind said. "Across the sea there is land and food enough for us all. We have been there and seen it. Many of our countrymen have left here, and live as free men in Caithness, Skye and countless other places. We welcome any who choose to come with us."

The fisherman spat in disgust. "Flee if you must. We have no power to hold you here. Desert us and go and be with your foreigners. But know that you will be numbered among Harald's enemies. Once you leave you can never return."

"There is a world beyond Norway," Hild said. "A world we can make our

own. And our children's. We can be our own masters. But you must have the faith, the vision, and the boldness to reach for it."

"And leave the land of your ancestors? Your fathers and mothers?" Ragnar said. "That we will not do."

Three days later, the Heron and the Wulf Sang departed for Scotland, never to return. Later that month Harald's mounted warriors arrived in the village to receive its tribute and oath of loyalty. In the end too few were willing to fight, and so all gave their oaths, and their silver, to Harald.

Harald became the first king of a united Norway, ruling until his death in 933. His son, Erik Bloodaxe inherited the kingdom, after slaying three half-brothers who might have challenged his rule.

Eyvind and Hild settled in Caithness, in the kingdom of Alba. They prospered as traders and explorers, owned a fine lodge with a large farm and many servants. Hild had two more sons and three daughters and was absolute ruler of the lodge.

In 917 Olaf returned to Dubhlinn to reassert Norse rule there, before his death at the hands of Friesian pirates during a sea voyage. Thorvald, his flame-haired son, avenged his father. At the age of fifteen, Leif, eldest son of Eyvind and Hild, went to sea with Thorvald.

They headed for Iceland.

Newton, MA August, 1999: "Happily Ever After" is not the human condition. After you rescue the princess, you marry her, become king and are weighed down with responsibility. After you slay the dragon, there is a hell of a mess to clean up, and then everyone asks you for more miracles. It never ends.

In our driveway, the small crowd stood around us in the gathering darkness. Our fifteen minutes were up. Attention wandered. I slapped a mosquito. Murmured side conversations broke out. Someone recounted the thrill of being backstage at the recent Lyle Lovett concert. Singly and in pairs our loose knot of well-wishers slipped off to their own concerns. We were no longer news. We opened the garage door and wheeled the bike inside. The odometer read 3,833 miles. "There will be more," I told it.

Of the months following I have no nostalgia. Our photo albums skip over this period. If I was dissatisfied with my life before the Big One, now I wanted to blow it to smithereens. The realization of one dream only revealed other, more inconvenient dreams lurking underneath. I wanted a home of my own. I wanted to do work that wasn't toxic to my soul. I yearned to be a husband and father. I wanted the life that a month ago seemed so natural and within my grasp, and now in the clamor and chaos of the life we'd put on hold, it distorted and faded like cloud pictures in the wind. Pretty normal desires, I thought, but they gnawed at me with a life-and-death desperation like a hungry wild thing, an inner beast awakened in the expansive west that I tried to chain up and cage for the genteel east.

There were piles of mail to sort through. Amongst the appalling mountain of unwanted catalogs and credit card offers were the packages we'd sent home, and we laughed and cried over these: the hats, gloves and fleeces no longer needed after we'd crossed the Rockies, the crystals and stones from Scott and Alyce, the cribbage board from Al and Dee, post cards, souvenirs, gifts and all our photos from the developer.

We helped my parents unpack boxes and position furniture. Now that I was back home and useful, I'd been promoted to son again. I asked them why they needed to move less than a mile to a house very similar to the one they were already living in. "Don't be stupid," Mom said, "that was a terrible house." Observing that I was still not working, she wondered, with sarcasm, if my life was going to be "one big vacation now." The beast strained against the bars. I might have felt like punching her, but I didn't feel depressed or ashamed. That was new, and liberating. Dad was happy to see us and wondered, without sarcasm, where we'd been all summer. He had truly forgotten. The problem with my parents is that they had no objectives beyond raising us and saving money for retirement. Their lives were about survival. Survive the War. Survive the post-war. Survive immigration. Survive marriage. Survive parenting. Survive moving. Survive being laid off. Survive retirement. Now they survived Mom's manufactured dramas.

At the house where we lived, everything felt wrong. While we were gone, yellow-jackets had built a nest in one of the walls. The sewer outlet pipe from the house blocked up and so we dealt with our crap in a very literal way, with a long pole. Helpful moths had eaten through four of my five suits. I had too many clothes. I filled trash bags. I made efforts to set up a consulting business, doing the type of work I'd done for Ed back in Montana, except for money. A few small projects drifted in and I made almost enough to pay for a new laptop. I hadn't netted such a small income since my paper route. Discouraged, I interviewed for a local job, just temporary, to generate some positive cash flow. I put on my remaining suit and caught a train downtown. The hiring manager was so eager to tell me all about the MUMPS programming language he practically leaped over the desk. The beast wanted to crush him in its powerful jaws. Mid-interview I did something I'd never done before. I stood up and excused myself, as the job sounded insanely dull, he was boring me to tears, and I'd rather pull my fingernails out with pliers than spend another minute in that room. I said it in a nice way. Walking home, the stiff leather shoes blistered my feet. They used to be so comfortable.

A week later a rock dropped and broke my foot in a freakish putting-out-the-trash accident. Trying not to disturb the neighbors by screaming my head off, I rolled around in the driveway doing a fair imitation of the song of the humpback whale. The empty coat hangers in my closet came in handy when a poison ivy rash bloomed underneath the cast. A few days later the police from a town near the New Hampshire line called me. They had my Dad there and would I come pick him up? He'd gotten lost driving to my brother's house, a trip he'd made a hundred times before. He admitted he wasn't thinking clearly these days, and gave me his car keys.

I was so self-absorbed I have little memory of what Jane did during this time. A beast had her too. She did not return to work. She wrote songs that would never leave that house. She worked on her own issues. We both stumbled through autumn's murk, unable to see the way forward, barely able to see one another, desperate to get back to where we'd felt whole. We remembered feeling happy in Washington State, near the coast, where mountains met sea. We dreamed of living there, where people would see us as we are instead of the people we'd always been. Moving would fix everything.

In November, the cast off my leg, we returned to Seattle to look around for a place to live. It rained nonstop. Nowhere felt right, although the sun emerged briefly and created a dazzling rainbow in Sequim, on the Olympic Peninsula. We returned with mold growing on our boots and no magical plan.

"What are we doing?" Jane would ask. "Is this right?"

"It can't have been for nothing," I'd say. But maybe it was all for nothing. And we'd swap roles; one doubting, unsure, the other determined, steadfast. Although no one else understood us, we were still in tandem, two hearts of one mind, chained to the same turning wheel of destiny.

We endured the holidays, the dark of the solstice, the dead freeze of a New England winter, down in our abyss of belonging nowhere. In January we visited Jane's childhood home in Wolfeboro, NH. At Lake Winnipesaukee's shore, looking west, she had a memory, and a vision: a town called Port Townsend, nestled between sea and mountains. We needed to look there. In February we flew west again to spend a glorious, sunny spring-like week in Port Townsend on the Olympic Peninsula where the rainbow appeared to touch ground. It was a weird, beautiful place, so eclectic that you only fit in by being different. Bumper stickers proclaim: "We're all here, because we're not all there." We looked for houses to rent and were horrified. We could tolerate a dumpster scrap house for a night, but not by the month. Our next to last day there we drove back from another housing disappointment. I braked at an intersection to let a couple of mule deer cross the road. Then I turned right. "We don't turn here," Jane said. "It's a dead end."

"You're right," I said, steering into a driveway. Before us, made of

Douglas fir logs that shone like burnished gold in the late sun, was the lodge of my fantasies. A "For Sale" sign hung, nodding yes in the light breeze. Jane just goggled, speechless.

"End of the road," I said.

In April, 2000 we surmounted the dual challenges of joblessness and one parent doing her best to disparage and disrupt our plans. We signed papers to make that golden lodge our first home together, and I had a new and exciting job where I was respected and valued. Before relocating ourselves west, we moved Dad into assisted living at Mom's urging. She was in no condition to look after anyone else.

We were not our parents. We would enjoy life from now on.

The following March, we jetted back east again to be with Dad, whose health had eroded severely since moving into assisted living. He now lived in a nursing home and greeted us with a warm smile, though he was shrunken and fragile; a wisp of the Dad I remembered. He knew our faces but not our names. I brought him a thermos of tea and sat with him. He regaled us with stories of when he was a young man in England, with absolute clarity; stories I'd never heard before. He said he'd done his best as a father and hoped he hadn't "mucked it up too badly." At the end of our week there, I told him Jane and I would marry next year.

"I'll be there," he said.

"We have to go now," I said.

"Well, see you next time, then."

As the elevator doors closed, I clenched my eyes shut to stop the sudden tears.

A few weeks later, after his Easter dinner, my father joined his ancestors. "Complications due to Alzheimer's" was what we were told. Mom blamed the doctors, the nursing home, and me, because if I "hadn't moved away he might not have died."

Bullshit. Maybe Dad depended on me for the love and acceptance he never got from his wife, but I had to crawl out of the "dying room;" as he had done, as Mom herself had done. A big difference between my parents is that Dad wanted all his children to go for their dreams, even if his own went unfulfilled.

I wrote a eulogy that seemed to hit home with my family as I read it at the funeral; with the line: "…his gift to his children was in being the father he never had," I glanced up from the podium to see their heads bobbing with the sudden release of decades of bottled up sorrow. At the time I thought maybe they were laughing at me; I was used to that.

My father wasn't a great man, but he was a good man. He deserved better.

The year 2001 held tragedy for all Americans; the loss of my Dad added a personal heartbreak on top of the lost innocence on September 11 that overshadowed that year. With time, with gut-wrenching hard work on many levels, with love for each other, we found our confidence again and the years following turned golden.

West of Seattle, WA, 2009: "Would you care for any champagne or shrimp cocktail?" The business class flight attendant had beautiful eyes and a sparkling smile. For the first time, I sat in the half empty upper deck of a 747, headed across the Pacific.

"Yes to both," I said. "Thank you."

As she laid the white tablecloth and set the "good things" before me, I reflected on how different my life looked now, compared with ten years ago. Memories flooded in:

I'd landed a part as an extra in a movie being filmed in Port Townsend. During a break on the set, a passerby asks if I'm playing the lead. "Not this time," I say.

We have simple hand-fasting marriage ceremony on our front lawn, under the blossoming plum tree. Jane is radiant, all in white, crowned with a wreath of flowers. Standing with us are dear friends who had married for life.

Our son John is born, one fist raised, as dawn's rosy fingers touch the snow-capped peaks of the Olympic Mountains. My line would continue.

I set down my drink to applaud and notice Jane's tip jar is stuffed with bills after a concert with her band at the Upstage Restaurant. The audience wants more.

On Mt. Kurama in Japan, I bow to my uke after the test for green belt, which concluded with defense against knife attack. Sensei JC Husfelt looks pleased. "What matters most is not technique, but how you move, and the purity of your heart."

On the winter solstice, the log house is bright with firelight and candlelight. The adults: friends, neighbors, parents, writers and musicians look on as their children, each holding a decorated candle lantern, file out the door. The little lights disperse to be hung on tree limbs: tiny beacons of hope on the longest night of the year.

The huge jet rose through the cloud and burst into the sunshine. I raised my glass. *Here's to you, Dad.*

This was a sweet period, yet it still wasn't "Happily Ever After." We'd have new and more onerous challenges. We would be brought low and rise again. That is the human condition.

The wheel keeps turning.

The Big Ones keep on coming.

You just have to ride them.

EPILOGUE

Woden's Day, 1002 AD*: Aboard a longship sailing west, somewhere off the coast of Newfoundland.*

"Your father was Erik the Red, but you can't be Leif the Red," the gray old man says. "You haven't got his red hair, or his fiery temper."

"I'm just Leif Eriksson," the blond young man at the steering oar says. "'Leif the Looney' they might call me after this ill-fated voyage. The great serpent, Jormungand, waits for us with open jaws."

"Don't lose hope, lad. I can smell land. Somewhere out there. Your father was lucky in Greenland, and his father I also knew in Iceland, Thorvald Olaffson."

"Grandpapa sailed with Leif Eyvindson, who was my father's mentor. I was named for him."

"And you got your mother's hair. Golden haired as Freya, she was."

"LAND!" The lookout at the bow shouted and pointed at the thin dark band on the horizon.

The old one claps Leif on the shoulder. "You lucky bastard. There is your new found land, Leif the Lucky."

Port Townsend, WA, 2014: One recent October I took my son Johnny to a creek a few miles from our house, where the chum were spawning. For a long time we watched the battered, exhausted salmon struggle upstream; they whipped their tails in fits and starts before stopping to rest in mere inches of water.

"Why do they need to go upstream so far?" Johnny asked.

"They need to find a place to lay their eggs, where the little fish will be able to find food and survive on their own. They remember where they were born and come back to have their children, or die trying," I said. Dead fish littered the banks, but many more still thrashed their way forward against the current. No matter what, they would return to where they were born, as their ancestors had.

But I was no fish. I wasn't blindly following some ancestral tradition, living their same life in their same way. I chose my own path.

Didn't I?

I looked at Johnny, who by now had picked out favorites and climbed atop a log to cheer them on. I thought about the long journey I made to get here. Not just the Big One, but everything that came before to make the Big One possible, and then all that followed like dominoes in a line: the move, the house, the job, the marriage; all to make possible the small being before me; this better version of myself.

Will he one day outgrow this "paradise" his parents dreamed about, labored to find, sweated and sacrificed to get to; this podunk little Northwest town that seemed to have everything they wanted? Will he pack his bags on that day and go live somewhere far away?

Of course he will. He comes from a long line of discontented wanderers.

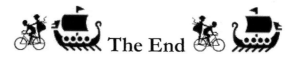 **The End**

ACKNOWLEDGMENTS

When you finally set off on that Big One you find you're never alone. For the actual ride, legions unnumbered smoothed the hills, conjured up tailwinds, lightened our load, and pushed us further down the road and they are named in the story.

For the writing of this book, I stood on the shoulders of some literary giants. On the west coast: JC and Sherry Husfelt, who helped me to know myself in countless ways; Anna Quinn, who started me writing and lighted my path; Christine Hemp, who forbade me to stop writing; Mark Clemens, Capt'n Bob Febos, Le Hornbeck, Kim Hinton, and Russ Morgan who all provided invaluable editorial feedback, guidance, and the occasional metaphorical butt-kicking that shaped the adolescence of this work. On the east coast, more busy hands and quick minds materialized to polish up the finished product: Susanna Baird and the Salem "long-form" writing group, early readers Daniel Lord, Rick Keesler and Suzy Dillon, my son John E. Owens (who laughed in all the right places), and of course Jane Justice, my stoker, soulmate, true love and driving force through this life and beyond. A final acknowledgement goes out to my parents and all my ancestors, for living such interesting lives and for making the choice to continue their line.

To all of you, my heartfelt thanks and eternal gratitude.

Made in the USA
Monee, IL
21 January 2020